William E. Schenck

Children in Heaven

The infant dead redeemed by the blood of Jesus

William E. Schenck

Children in Heaven
The infant dead redeemed by the blood of Jesus

ISBN/EAN: 9783337389895

Printed in Europe, USA, Canada, Australia, Japan

Cover: Foto ©Andreas Hilbeck / pixelio.de

More available books at **www.hansebooks.com**

CHILDREN IN HEAVEN

OR

The Infant Dead Redeemed by the Blood of Jesus.

WITH

WORDS OF CONSOLATION TO BEREAVED PARENTS

BY

WILLIAM E. SCHENCK, D. D.

" Suffer little children, and forbid them not, to come unto me ; for of such is the kingdom of heaven."—MATT. xix. 14.

" It is not the will of your Father which is in heaven, that one of these little ones should perish."—MATT. xviii. 14.

PHILADELPHIA:
PRESBYTERIAN BOARD OF PUBLICATION,
No. 1334 CHESTNUT STREET.

CONTENTS.

CONTENTS.

CONTENTS.

PREFACE.

THIS volume has been compiled to meet what was plainly a want in our religious literature. Many inquiries after such a work have, from time to time, been addressed to the writer, and no book could be found which precisely answered the description of the one desired.

In this compilation two principal objects have been aimed at. The first was, to exhibit fully and fairly the views of the great body of evangelical Christians, more especially of those embracing the system of doctrines commonly called Calvinistic, upon the interesting subject of Infant Salvation. Great numbers of professing Christians who believed that children dying in infancy were saved, have not distinctly understood the grounds on which that belief was entertained, or how naturally and logically it might be deduced from the precious doctrines of divine sovereignty and abounding grace through our Redeemer, Christ. It is important that the foundations and relations of this belief should be intelligently examined and comprehended. Moreover, there have been unceasing attacks made upon the doctrines of predestination, election, regeneration, and faith in Christ, by those who looked with an unfriendly eye upon those doctrines as set forth in the standards of the Calvinistic churches, on the ground that they unavoidably consigned dying infants for ever to the pit of woe. Few Calvinistic ministers have escaped these assaults, often made with much ingenuity and pertinacity. The following pages will show every candid reader that all such assaults are not only utterly groundless, but that the very doctrines assailed, afford the only firm foundation on which we can place the eternal safety of the early dead.

The second object was, to furnish consolation to those sorrowing parents who had been bereaved by the removal of their little ones. How numerous a class these form among God's dear children, will scarcely be suspected by the unthinking and uninquiring.

> "There is no flock, however watched and tended,
>   But one dead lamb is there;
> There is no fireside, howsoe'er defended,
>   But has one vacant chair."

Millions of such mourners live, carrying about in their bosoms sorrows, the existence of which the world knows nothing of. The world is full of Rachels weeping for their children. We were once listening to a discourse of the venerable Dr. Archibald Alexander, upon the text, "In my Father's house are many mansions." The audience was carried along with the preacher as he glowingly described the heavenly home of the believer. At a certain point in his sermon he unexpectedly remarked, "Those mansions contain numerous apartments, suited to their various occupants—there are among others, ample and delightful accommodations provided for the countless hosts of little children who will be gathered there." The effect was electric. As he went on to describe the bliss of these hosts of little ones in heaven, we could not help noticing how many a parent's head was drooped, and how many an eye was moistened with tears. My own thoughts turned to a row of little graves where five infant brothers and a sister lay, and I rejoiced to feel that they were sharing the happiness of the "Father's house." We earnestly hope that God may bless this book, in some humble measure, to the comforting of his bereaved children.

It will be seen that the sources whence the materials for this volume have been drawn, are numerous and widely diversified. These materials were ample enough to have made many such volumes. Indeed a strong testimony to the great importance and unspeakable interest of the subject may be found in the fact, that nearly every divine or poet of note has written something upon this theme. Does not this show how general is the yearning of the human heart for light and consolation in reference to those blossoms of humanity which have faded at the chill touch of death?

W. E. S.

Philadelphia, 1865.

EPITAPH ON AN INFANT.

Bold Infidelity, turn pale and die!
Under this stone an Infant's ashes lie:
    Say, Is it lost, or saved?
If death's by sin, it sinned, for it lies here;
If heaven's by works, in heaven it can't appear.
    Ah, reason! how depraved!
Revere the bible's sacred page—the knot's untied,
It died through Adam's sin:—it lives, for Jesus died.

13

AN INFANT'S SPIRIT.

An infant's soul—the sweetest thing on earth,
To which endowments beautiful are given,
As might befit a more than mortal birth—
What shall it be. when, 'midst its winning mirth,
And love, and trustfulness, 'tis borne to heaven?
Will it grow into might above the skies?
A spirit of high wisdom, glory, power—
A cherub guard of the Eternal Tower,
With knowledge filled of its vast mysteries?
Or will perpetual childhood be its dower;
To sport for ever, a bright, joyous thing,
Amid the wonders of the shining thrones,
Yielding its praise in glad, but feeble tones,
A tender dove beneath the Almighty's wing?

CHILDREN IN HEAVEN.

A. D. F. RANDOLPH.

I.

I HEAR a shout of merriment,
A laughing boy I see;
Two little feet the carpet press,
And bring the child to me.

Two little arms are round my neck,
Two feet upon my knee:
How fall the kisses on my cheek;
How sweet they are to me!

II.

That merry shout no more I hear,
No laughing child I see;
No little arms are round my neck,
Nor feet upon my knee!

No kisses drop upon my cheek;
Those lips are sealed to me.
Dear Lord, how could I give him up
To any but to Thee!

Opinions on Infant Salvation.

THOMAS SMYTH, D.D.*

AMONG the Jews, the hope of salvation seems to have been confined to themselves, and to their children who had received circumcision. ·"They imagined that the law of Moses made the very infants of the Gentiles be treated as sinners and hateful to God, because they were uncircumcised, and descended from uncircumcised parents. They of course imagined that all their own children were saved, and that all those of the Gentiles perished. It is partly on this account that the apostle, after mentioning the universal reign of death from Adam to Moses, distinctly adds, that it came upon infants, as well as upon adults, without distinction of Jew and Gentile; and then shows that infants, whether they descend from Gentiles or Jews, are treated as sinners, not by virtue of the law of Moses, but in consequence of the sin of Adam, the common father of the human race."

A corresponding faith was early developed in the Christian church. Erroneous views of baptism, as in itself communicative of regeneration, led to the belief of its absolute necessity in order to salvation. Of course, those who failed to enjoy the benefits of this ordinance were believed to be excluded from

* Extracted from "Solace for Bereaved Parents, or Infants Die to live."

16

all participation in the benefits of that gospel, with which it was so essentially connected. And hence it was supposed that the children even of Christian parents who were not baptized, as well as all others in the same unfortunate condition, were cast, with unbelievers, into hell for ever; or, at least excluded from the divine presence, and the blessedness of heaven.

This opinion prevailed *generally* in the church until after the Reformation. It was the opinion of Augustine, of Gregory, Ariminiensis, Driedd, Luther, Melanchthon, Tilmanus, Heshusius, " who have all fallen into the worst of St. Austin's opinion, and sentence poor infants to the flames of hell for original sin, if they die before baptism."* " The Catholic faith," says Augustine, " resting on divine authority, believes the first place to be the kingdom of heaven, WHENCE THE UNBAPTIZED ARE EXCLUDED; and the second hell, where every apostate and alien from the faith of Christ will experience eternal punishments. A third place we are wholly ignorant of, nor shall we find it in the Scriptures."† The decree of the council of Trent, by which it is determined that " whosoever shall affirm that baptism is indifferent, that is, not NECESSARY TO SALVATION, let him be accursed," is still binding on the Roman Catholic Church: for their catechism also teaches that children, " be their parents Christians or infidels, UNLESS REGENERATED BY THE GRACE OF BAPTISM, ARE BORN TO ETERNAL MISERY AND EVERLASTING DESTRUCTION."‡ " Nothing," says the Council of Trent, " can

---

* See Jer. Taylor's Works, vol. 9, p. 129.

† August. Hypostgnost. Contra Pelag. lib. v. tom. iii. Col. 1405. C. Basil, 1569.

‡ See Cramp's Hist. of Council of Trent, p. 129, and the works quoted.

3

be apparently more necessary, than that the faithful should be taught, that the law of baptism was ordained by the Lord for all men ; so that *unless they be regenerated by God, through the grace of baptism, they are begotten by their parents, be they believers, or unbelievers, to everlasting misery and perdition.*"* "*No other means of salvation,*" adds the Catechism, "*is supplied to infants, except baptism be administered to them.*"† "There is a third place for infants," says Bellarmine, "who *die without baptism. This Limbus Puerorum is for the eternal punishment of loss only :*" that is, "the loss of the presence of God."‡ "Since, then," adds this defender of the Papacy, "infants are without reason, so that they cannot imitate the sins of their fathers, and are nevertheless punished with the most severe of all punishments, that is to say, *death temporal and eternal ;* it necessarily follows that they have some other sin, for which they are justly punished; and this is what we call *original sin.* It cannot, therefore, be doubted that infants (for whom it is shown from the word of Christ and apostolical tradition that *Baptism is necessary,*) have sin, which they bring with them from their mother's womb."§ This belief passed down to the Reformed Churches, and was at first very generally held. The Church of England placed the unbaptized on the same footing with the suicide and the excommunicated, and denied to them the office of burial.‖ And this

* Concil. Trid. Sess. vii. can. v. p. 51.   Romæ, 1564.

† Catechismus ad Parochos, pp. 189, 191.   Lugduni, 1579.

‡ Bellarm. de Purgat lib. ii. chap. vi. tom. ii. p. 410.   A. Coloniæ, 1628.

§ Bellarm. de Amiss. Gratiæ et Statu Peccati. lib. iv. c. 7. tóm. iv. p. 61. G. 62. B.

‖ See Burns' Eccles. Law, vol. i. p. 266, and Wheatley on the Book of Prayer, p. 477.

still continues to be the doctrine of the church, and of all high-church prelatists who agree on this subject with the Romanists. " Without baptism," say the Oxford Tracts, " none can enter the kingdom of heaven."* " And so momentous is this dogma in their judgment, that one leading object," says Mr. Bridges, himself an Episcopalian, " of their great movement confessedly was to bring it more fully before the church."† The question of the future condition of infants became thus involved with that of baptism, and was not considered upon its own merits. Ecclesiastics, who were secluded from all personal interest in domestic life, were of course insensible to the happiness connected with the enjoyment of children, or to the distress consequent upon their loss. The fate of children awakened, therefore, but a relative interest, as it affected other truths considered of more importance.

The horror naturally associated with this fearful doctrine was nevertheless very early felt, and at different times manifested. Various theories were adopted to throw over it a veil of charity, and to render it more tolerable to the wounded spirit of mourn-

---

* Vol. i. p. 260. See also Dr. Pusey's work on Baptism, *passim*, Bethel on Baptismal Regeneration, pp. 7, 8, 9, &c.

† See his Sacramental Instruction, p. 46, 47, where he quotes a host of authorities, including Perceval, Keble, Dr. Pusey, Sewell, Bishop Mant, &c. It would even appear that some evangelical Episcopalians of our present day are unwilling to say anything about the future condition of *unbaptized* children who die in infancy. See the Churchman's Monthly Rev. May 1843, p. 372. This doctrine of the *absolute* necessity of baptism to salvation was established in the Western church by papal authority, and was retained in the English church after the Reformation, until the year 1604, when it was declared to be necessary " where it may be had." See Hallow on the Order of Baptism, &c., and Ogelby on Lay Baptism, p. 159, 160, &c.

ing parents.   In the time of Augustine, Vincentius, Victor, and some others, believed that infants dying without baptism might, notwithstanding, be saved.*   This opinion was favoured by some of the School Divines, in reference to cases where baptism could not be had, inasmuch as it was the will of the parents that it should be enjoyed.†   Bernard, Biel, Cajetan, and some others, adopted this charitable supposition.‡   And so also did Peter Martyr, Wickliffe, the Hussites, and the Lollards, who adopted, preached, and suffered for, ALL those doctrines which are *now* denominated Calvinistic.   But this opinion has been considered as involving unconquerable difficulties.   Jeremy Taylor says, "What will be the condition of unbaptized infants, so dying, I do not profess to know or teach, because God hath kept it as a secret."§   Baxter, with all his charity, and perhaps too liberal views of Christian doctrine, could only go so far on this subject as to say, "I think that no man can *prove* that all unbaptized infants are damned or denied heaven.   Nay, I think I can prove a promise to the contrary."   Beyond "penitent believers and their seed," he says, "what God may do for others unknown to us, we have nothing to do with, but his covenant hath made no other promise that I can find."‖   Similar were the sentiments of Bishop Hopkins : "Not only infants baptized," says he, "but all infants of *believing* parents, though they should *unavoidably* die before baptism, are in the same safe and blessed

* See Jer. Taylor's Works, vol. ix. p. 90.

† See list of, in Hooker's Works, vol. ii. p. 219.

‡ Jer. Taylor's Works, vol. ix. p. 91 and 93.

§ Jeremy Taylor's Works, p. 92.

‖ See Works, vol. v. p. 326 and 323.

condition." This, however, is the extent to which he could apply his hopes.*

To this charitable view of the matter, which Calvinists, and Calvinistic churches generally adopted, the Pelagians could not fully assent.† They excluded infants when unbaptized from the kingdom of heaven, but promised to them an eternal and a natural beatitude. This opinion was embraced by Ambrosius Catharinus, Albertus Pighius, and Hieronymus Savanarola, Gregory Nazianzen, Athanasius, Ambrose, Pope Innocent III., and others.‡ Hence arose the present doctrine of the Romish Church, which teaches that there is a *limbus patrum*, or place on the borders of hell, for those who had believed in Christ before his advent; and a *limbus infantum*, for children who die unbaptized.

When the mists, however, which had gathered round the ordinance of baptism were gradually dispersed, this subject was examined on more impartial grounds. The natural feelings of the heart were permitted to declare their interest in the decision of the question. The hope expressed by Wickliffe in reference to unbaptized children was eagerly embraced by his followers, who were all Calvinists, and who all regarded baptism in its truly simple and scriptural character. Zuinglius was perhaps the first who proclaimed hope for the salvation of ALL INFANTS, WHETHER CHRISTIAN OR HEATHEN, who died in their infancy, and before they became chargeable with the guilt of actual transgres-

* See Works, vol. ii. p. 429.

† See the Articles of the Synod of Dort, with Scott's Notes. Works of Scott vol. viii. p. 576.

‡ See Jer. Taylor, vol. ix. p. 90.

sion.   He maintained, that in consequence of the atonement of
Christ offered for all, " original sin does not even damn the
children of the heathen."   For this conclusion concerning children generally, Zuinglius quotes Romans v.; though he admits
that we have but little light upon the subject.   He rejects the
idea that baptism washes away original sin and condemnation.
The blessing, he says, is not tied to signs and symbols; baptism
recognizes and *attests* the privilege rather than *confers* it.
" What scriptural authority," he asks, " is there for ascribing
such an effect to baptism?"   " The words of Mark xvi. 16,"
says he, " relate to those only to whom the gospel was sent.
They that hear the gospel and believe it were blessed; they
who hear it, and believe it not, are accursed.   But this is no
prejudice to election, for both they who come to Christ are
drawn to him by the Father, which is election: and they
who come to the Father are chosen by him; but so that they
may at length come to him by Christ.   The (infant) children
of Christians are the children of God by virtue of the covenant.
Concerning the children of heathens, we decide nothing: though
I confess that I incline to the sentiment which considers the
death of Christ as available to the salvation of all who are free
from actual sin."*   For this doctrine Bossuet charges Zuinglius
with being a Pelagian, and pronounces this a " strange decision."†
This opinion of Zuinglius excited considerable controversy.‡

---

* See Epist. fo. 17, 18. Zuingl. Op. 1. 382. and Scott's Contin. of Milner, vol. iii.
p. 143, 144, 146.

† See Hist. Var., vol. i. p. 66.

‡ See an account of, in De Moor's Comment., vol. ii. p. 104, &c.

Eckard says, "*perhaps* Zuinglius pronounced too liberally when he included the children of the heathen." The same doctrine was, however, maintained by Cornelius Wigger, and by John Iac-Schultens, who embraced in the decree of predestination to eternal life those who die in infancy, whether born of Gentile or infidel parents. This was the declared sentiment of Arminius,[*] Triglandius, Walders, Heidanus, Curcelleus, Maresius.[†] Maresius says, "The question is, whether the decree of election and reprobation affects infants. There is not the smallest ground from Scripture to think it does. Let parents then be comforted for departed children. These words of Christ, ('of such is the kingdom of heaven,') why are they so general, but that they seem to include the children not only of believers but of unbelievers also."[‡]

The Remonstrants believed that such infants as were not entitled to heaven by their relation to the covenanted mercies of God, would be consigned only to the punishment of loss, their bodies not being raised, and their souls not being annihilated, yet being eternally separated from the beatific vision of God.[§]

Many, however, regarded the decision of this question as presumptuous. They left the whole matter in the hands of God, determining nothing one way or another, but quieting themselves with the assurance, that as far as God's purpose of salvation extended it would be secured; and that infants, as far as included in it, would be assuredly ransomed. Infants were, however, universally regarded as involved in all the guilt of original sin,

---

[*] See an account of, in De Moor's Comment., vol. ii. p. 104, &c.

[†] See ditto.   [‡] See ditto, p. 105.   [§] See ditto, p. 104.

and as requiring for their salvation the exercise of the same mercy, and the bestowment of the same grace, as adults. They were described by some as, "*damnabilibus et forte quibus dum etiam damnandis.*" But even when infants were included by any in the decree of reprobation, their punishment was believed to consist, not in the positive infliction of misery, but only in the deprivation of heavenly rewards.*

Calvin clearly recognized the fact that all infants are involved in the guilt of Adam's sin, and therefore *liable* to the misery in which it has involved our race. But at the same time he encourages the belief that they are redeemed from these evils by Christ, are capable of regeneration, and are, when taken away in infancy, "redeemed by the blood of the Lamb." He argues against those who, like the Anabaptists, asserted that regeneration cannot take place in early infancy. For says he, "if they must be left among the children of Adam, they are left in death, for in Adam we can only die. On the contrary, Christ commands them to be brought to him. Why? because he is life. To give them life therefore he makes them partakers of himself, while these men, by driving them away from him, adjudged them to death."† He then goes on to prove, by incontestable arguments, that infants both have been, and can be, regenerated by God. And in his Commentary on the words of our Saviour, "Of such, &c.," without any limitation of his meaning, he unequivocally declares, that "God adopts infants and washes them

---

* See Stapfer, vol. iv. p. 518. On the ground of their condemnation, see Buddeus Theol. Dogm. p. 591.

† See Institutes, B. iv. ch. xvi.

in the blood of his Son," and that "they are regarded by Christ as among his flock." "In this passage," he adds, "Christ is not speaking of the general guilt in which all the descendants of Adam are involved, but only threatening the despisers of the gospel who proudly and obstinately reject the grace that is offered them; and this has nothing to do with infants. I likewise oppose a contrary argument: all those whom Christ blesses are exempted from the curse of Adam and the wrath of God; and as it is known that infants were blessed by him, it follows that they are exempted from death."*

Certain it is, that Calvinists were foremost in overthrowing the dogma that baptism was essentially connected with salvation, and in establishing the truth, that want of it does not militate against their future safety.† It is well known that the former opinion is still extensively held by those who are opposed to Calvinistic sentiments. On this subject Scott, in answer to Bp. Tomline, remarks, "a *few* presumptuous, extravagant Calvinists have spoken shocking things of the damnation of infants: but to consign the innumerable multitudes of those all over the world, and in every age, who die before they commit actual sin, and die unbaptized, to eternal damnation, is far more shocking. Even *such* Calvinists may suppose *some* of these children to be elected and saved: but the sentiment that none dying

---

* Institutes, book iv. chap. 16, sec. 31, vol. ii. p. 460. See also pp. 461, 456, 436, 435.

† See Cartwright's reply to Hooker on this subject, in Hanbury's Hooker, vol. ii. p. 221. See also, Bp. Hopkins' Works, vol. ii. p. 429; Davenant on Col., vol. ii. p. 448; Heywood's Works, vol. iv. p. 447; Pictet's Theology, p. 399.

4

when infants, except such as have been baptized, are saved, excludes them all."* "The most unfeeling supra-lapsarian never ventured on so dire an opinion as to consign *all* the unbaptized infants, in every age and nation, to eternal misery."† This is the language of a Calvinist addressed to that large body of his own church who oppose Calvinism, and take occasion to impeach its charity. Some Calvinists, it is true, have in former times avoided the decision of this question, leaving dying infants in the hands of a merciful God. But, "why," asks the same writer, " might not these Calvinists have as favourable a hope of all infants dying before actual sin as Anti-Calvinists can have?"‡ What doctrine of the most rigid Calvinism is there, with which such a hope can possibly militate? Is it the doctrine of God's sovereignty, whereby is attributed to him all power and right of dominion over his creatures, to dispose of them, and to extend or withhold favour, as seemeth to him good—but why may it not please God, in the exercise of this sovereignty, to extend his favour to all dying infants? Is it the doctrine of election, whereby God, out of his mere love, for the praise of his glorious grace, to be manifested in due time, hath, in Christ, chosen some men to eternal life and the means thereof—but why may not dying infants be among these chosen ones? Is it the doctrine of the divine decrees, whereby, for his own glory, God hath fore-ordained whatsoever comes to pass, especially concerning angels and men—but why may not the salvation of all dying infants have been thus decreed? Is it the doctrine of

* See Works, vol. vii. p. 502.

† See Works, vol. x. p. 407.   ‡ Do. vol. viii. p. 573.

God's free and rich grace, whereby the holiness, obedience, and righteousness of Christ are imputed to us for justification; and inherent grace is wrought in the heart by the Spirit of God, in regeneration;—but why may not this grace be imparted to all dying infants? If God gives us hope for such in his blessed word, then is it not manifest that their salvation, instead of being thrown upon the contingency of human will; or being made dependent upon human effort; or connected with the moral character or personal agency of infants themselves; or left at hazard, through the indifference or neglect of men;—is based by these doctrines upon the unchangeable purpose, and the all-sufficient grace of God; and is therefore rendered GLORIOUSLY CERTAIN to the bereaved and mourning spirit of the disconsolate parent? If however, rejecting these doctrines (which Calvinists love because doctrines of the Bible) we make election to rest on the foreknowledge of good works;—or moral character to depend on moral conduct;—and salvation to be limited, in its flow, to the channel of Christian ordinances;—then what hope can be entertained for those who have been taken away while as yet they could not discern good from evil;—while without any moral character, and thus wholly unfit for enjoyment or reward;—and while, as "nameless things," they have never passed through the "purifying entrance" to the kingdom of heaven? We answer— none that is reasonable or satisfactory.

But on the ground of Calvinism this hope is all that can be desired, and arises most naturally from its principles. "In perfect consistency," says Dr. Harris, in his Essay on this subject, "with their theological creed, have some Calvinists entertained the *opinion* advocated in the preceding pages; while others, expressing a hope of its truth *to the full extent*, have discovered the wished-for *evidence*, in favour of the children of pious persons only; but none of any consideration are known to have maintained, or even allowed, that the inference in question (*i. e.* the damnation of *any* infants) is an evident and necessary deduction from Calvinistic doctrines. In direct opposition to what must, therefore, be considered an unfounded aspersion, it would require but little labour to prove, that the great peculiarities of this system supply the MOST TENABLE AND SATISFACTORY GROUNDS OF HOPE FOR THE SALVATION OF ALL WHO DEPART THIS LIFE ANTECEDENT TO PERSONAL TRANSGRESSION."

I would here quote the language of one of our oldest and most thoroughly Calvinistic divines, the celebrated William Perkins, a Puritan: "Infants have no works whereby they may be judged, seeing they do neither good nor evil, as the Scripture speaketh of Jacob and Esau, Rom. ix. 11. Therefore all shall not be judged according to works. Ans. These phrases of Scripture, *as a man sows, so shall he reap: every one shall receive according to his works, &c.*, are not to be extended to all, but must be restrained to such as have works, and knowledge to discern betwixt good and evil, which infants have not. For besides that they are destitute of works, they also want the use of reason; and therefore they shall not be judged by the book of conscience, but by the book of life. For to say as *Hugo de S. Vict.* doth upon the Romanes, *quæst.* 59, that they shall be condemned for the sins which their parents committed in their conception and nativity, as though they themselves had actually committed them, is contrary to that, *Ezek.* xviii. 20, The son shall not bear the iniquity of the Father.

"Again, some may say, if children do not apprehend Christ's benefits by their parent's faith; how then is Christ's righteousness made theirs and they saved? Ans. By the inward working of the Holy Ghost, who is the principal applier of all graces, whereas faith is but the instrument. As for the places of Scripture that mention justification and salvation by faith, they are to be restrained to men of years: whereas infants dying in their infancy, and therefore wanting actual faith, which none can have without actual knowledge of God's will and word, are no doubt saved by some other special working of God's Holy Spirit, not known to us." "Infants," he adds, "already elected, albeit they, in the womb of their mother before they were born, or presently after, depart this life, they, I say, being after a secret and unspeakable manner, by God's Spirit engrafted into Christ, obtain eternal life." 1 Cor. xii. 13: Luke i. 35, 41, 44: and Jer. i. 5.*

And equally strong speaks the great Coryphæus of Calvinism, who carried out its principles to their extremest limits, I mean the celebrated Toplady. In his vindication of the Church of England from Arminianism, he had asserted his belief in the salvation of all infants dying in infancy. This opinion his opponents interpreted as involving the doctrine of general redemption. "As if," says Toplady, "all died in infancy." "I testify my firm belief, that the souls of all departed infants are with God in glory: that, in the decree of predestination to life,

* Works, fol. vol. iii. p. 386. Vol. ii. p. 127, and vol. i. p. 77.

God hath included all whom he intended to take away in infancy; and that the decree of reprobation hath nothing to do with them."*

"In the mean while (says he) I should be obliged if he would, with the help of Mr. Wesley's irradiation, show me what becomes of departed infants, upon the Arminian plan of conditional salvation, and election of good works foreseen."

Dr. Gill, who resembled Toplady in carrying out the principles of Calvinism to their extremest limit, also resembled him in holding this comfortable view of the doctrine of election. In his *Complete Body of Practical and Doctrinal Divinity,* he makes the following remark on the case of infants dying in infancy: "Now such a number as they are, can never be thought to be brought into being in vain, God is and will be glorified in them; now though their election is a secret to us, and unrevealed, it may be reasonably supposed, yea in a judgment of charity it may rather be concluded, that they are all chosen, than that none are. But the election of them cannot be owing to their faith, holiness, obedience, good works, and perseverance, or to the foresight of these things, which do not appear in them."

I may *refer* also to the sentiments of Tyndale, the translator of the New Testament into English;† of Pictet, the learned Professor of Geneva;‡ to the touching letter of Whitefield on the death of his infant son;§ of Watts to a lady bereaved of

---

* Works. fol. vol. i. p. 207.

† See Works, vol. ii. p. 516.

‡ See his Theol. b. xi. chap iv. pp. 194, 495, and p. 444, 445.

§ See Life of. by Philip.

several infant children ; and of the pious Rutherford to a lady on the loss of a daughter;* of Addington,† and of Robert Hall;‡ of Howe,§ and of Cotton Mather,‖ Buchanan,¶ and these are all Calvinists.

It may be well, however, to add a few more quotations from Calvinistic writers. Dr. Williams, in his " Defence of Modern Calvinism" against the attacks and misrepresentations of Bishop Tomline, at p. 75, says : " That they [infants] are capable of regeneration indeed, is admitted, as well as of remission, justification, holiness of nature, and heavenly blessedness ; and we reflect with pleasure, that the Holy Scriptures afford many encouraging intimations relative to the salvation of dying infants— whether baptized or not. Though *they* have no hope, *we* have hope concerning them." The same view is also presented in that noble defence of Calvinistic doctrine, the Lime Street Lectures, where it is said, "an elect infant is as capable of being effectually called, or renewed by grace, of being freely justified, and for ever glorified, as a grown person."** Again at another place, the subject is more fully discussed—" As for infants, we take it for granted, in the present argument, that they are conceived in sin, and shapen in iniquity ; that that which is born of

* See Letters, part 2, letter iii.

† Work on Baptism, p. 62–64, 67, 76.

‡ Works, vol. i. p. 88, 89.

§ Works of John Howe, vol. iv. p. 4, 5, and vol. vii. p. 544–5.

‖ See quoted afterwards.

¶ Rev. James Buchanan of Edinburgh, in his Office and Work of the Holy Spirit, Part 1, ch. viii. on the Regeneration of Infants.

** P. 279, 280, Eng. ed.

the flesh, is flesh; that they are, by reason of the disobedience of the first man, sinners, and so unworthy of, and unmeet for, the heavenly glory, and must be excluded from it, unless washed in the blood of Jesus and sanctified by the Holy Spirit. To suppose them all, or indeed any of them, to perish IS TO BE CRUELLY WISE ABOVE WHAT IS WRITTEN: and to imagine they are so holy, as to need no cleansing, or that any thing defiled can enter into heaven, is directly flying in the face of Scripture: so that, though we are not told positively what is their portion; yet WE MAY SAFELY DETERMINE THAT THEY ARE MADE MEET, IF IN HEAVEN, FOR THAT INHERITANCE WHICH IS INCORRUPTIBLE AND UNDEFILED."

I will only add to these authorities the following remarkable quotation from the National Covenant adopted in Scotland in the year 1581, again in 1590, 1638, 1639, 1640, 1650 and 1651. " But," says this venerable document, in detailing the enormous errors of the Roman Antichrist, " in special we detest and refuse his cruel judgment against infants departing without the Sacrament, and his absolute necessity of baptism," &c.*

Dr. George Junkin, also, of the Presbyterian Church in this country, and one of the strongest defenders of strict old-fashioned Calvinism, in his late work on the doctrine of Justification, heads his 10th chapter thus: " Original Sin—proved from the salvation of those that die in infancy." " It is not inconsistent," says he, " with any doctrine of the Bible, that the souls of deceased infants go to heaven." " As to the opinion that ALL who die in infancy, BOTH CHILDREN OF BELIEVERS AND UNBELIEV-

* See Irving's Confessions, p. 135.

ERS, CHRISTIANS AND PAGANS, go to happiness and heaven, it may be harmlessly entertained ; it may however operate an evil influence upon the minds of wicked and unbelieving parents." " While therefore I have no objection to the opinion that *all* who die in infancy go to happiness, yet I must think that in reference to the infants of *unbelievers*, it is mere opinion, although it is in all probability an opinion according to truth."*

The Rev. Thomas Scott, the author of the Commentary, and another of the boldest defenders of the Calvinistic doctrines, says, " I do not propose it as an article of faith; for it is not expressly revealed (though it appears to be favoured in scripture) that as infants, without actual transgression, are involved in the ruin of our race by the first Adam, so infants, as such, dying before actual transgression, before they are capable of knowing right from wrong, are, without personal repentance and faith, but not without regeneration, made partakers of the salvation of the second Adam. I do not say, ' It is so ;' but, ' probably it may be so.' And, when we consider what a large proportion of the human race, in every age and nation, die in infancy, it appears to me a cheering thought."

Thus, also, speaks Newton : " I hope you are both well reconciled to the death of your child. Indeed, I cannot be sorry for the death of *infants*. How many storms do they escape ! Nor can I doubt, in my private judgment, that they are included in the election of grace. Perhaps those who die in infancy are the exceeding great multitudes of all people, nations, and languages mentioned (Rev. vii. 9,) in distinction from the visible body of

* P. 141, 143.

5

professing believers, who were marked in their foreheads, and openly known to be the Lord's."

But these quotations it is unnecessary to multiply. In the Presbyterian and other Calvinistic churches, including the Congregational, which embrace the doctrinal portions of the Westminster Confession of Faith, there is, it is true, no *canonical* determination on this subject. This Confession says: "Elect infants, dying in infancy, are regenerated and saved by Christ through the Spirit."* It teaches, therefore, THE CERTAINTY OF THE SALVATION OF ALL INFANTS, WHO ARE ELECT. It also teaches that baptism is not necessarily connected with grace and salvation, and that exclusion from it does not exclude from regeneration.† It teaches further that infants, though incapable of exhibiting their faith, may be regenerated.‡ It leaves every one therefore from an examination of the Scriptures to decide how far the electing love of God extends. At this time it is, I suppose, universally believed by Presbyterians, and those who hold to the doctrine of election, that all dying infants are included among the elect, are made heirs of grace, and become members of the kingdom of heaven. I, at least, am not acquainted with any who hold an opposite sentiment. Possibly, when the doctrine is extended to the infants of heathen parents, some might not be prepared *fully* to concur in it; but that there is ground from Scripture to believe that even *they* are included in the promises of Divine mercy, and are, as Mr. Toplady confi-

---

* Ch. 10, sec. 3. † Ch. 28, sec. 5.

‡ See note 3, and see Larachi Op. tom. ii. p. 47. Dick's Theol. vol. iv. p. 75, and Calvin's Instit. 13, 4.

dently says, "all undoubtedly saved," is, I have no doubt, an opinion to which Presbyterians will, *generally,* subscribe. The opposite opinion, which has been maintained by *some* Calvinists, in common with many Arminians *of former days,* and which *is* held by the Roman Catholic Church *at the present time,* may be most certainly regarded, as a recent writer has said, as "an excrescence, and not an essential feature, of the system of Calvinism."

The assertion, however, is still frequently and most slanderously published, that Calvinists believe that children, dying in infancy, are damned ; that this is the doctrine of our Confession of Faith ; and that Calvin expressly taught that there are infants in hell only a span long. Nothing, however, can be more untrue. As to the opinion of Calvinists, we have shown that it is now universally in favour of the hope that all children dying in infancy are saved through the merits of Christ's death, applied by the Holy Ghost. Calvin, also, as has been shown, was among the very first of the reformers to overthrow the unchristian and most horrible doctrine of the Romish and High church divines, that no unbaptized infant can be saved; to maintain the possibility of their regeneration by the Spirit without baptism; and to' encourage the hope of their general salvation. And as to the passage in the Westminster Confession of Faith, which is supposed to teach the damnation of infants, it is contained in ch. x. sec. 3, and is as follows:

"Elect infants, dying in infancy, are regenerated and saved by Christ through the Spirit, who worketh when, and where, and how he pleaseth. So also are all other elect persons, who are incapable of being outwardly called by the ministry of the word."

The subject of this chapter is "effectual calling," by which, it is believed, that "all those whom God hath predestinated unto life he is pleased, in his appointed time, effectually to call out of that state of sin and death in which they are, by nature, to grace and salvation by Jesus Christ," &c. (See sect. 1.)—The Confession proceeds in sect. 2d, to say: "This effectual call is of God's free and special grace alone, not from anything at all foreseen in man, who is altogether passive therein, until, being quickened and renewed by the Holy Spirit, he is thereby enabled to answer this call, and to embrace the grace offered and conveyed in it."

Now the objection which would naturally arise in the mind against this doctrine, would be this—If this is so, then does not this doctrine apparently exclude infants from any participation in this salvation, since they clearly are not capable of obeying this call, and of embracing this offered grace. The Confession, therefore, proceeds to obviate this objection, by showing that, as this calling in itself considered, and the power and the disposition to answer this call, and embrace the grace conveyed in it, is a different thing from that answer and embrace—there is no more difficulty in bestowing this quickening and renewing influence of the Holy Spirit upon infants than upon adults. Infants as well as adults may be thus effectually called and regenerated, though adults only are in a state fitting them to act upon this call by the exercise of their renewed powers and sanctified will. Regenerated infants are equally, with adults, endued with a renewed and holy disposition, which will develope itself, when the subject is capable, in holy acts.   Our Confession, therefore, wisely, charitably, and scripturally concludes, that this grace is co-extensive with God's electing love and mercy, and is bestowed upon the objects of that love, whether they are removed from this world in a state of infancy, or of maturity.   It overthrows the doctrine of Romanists, High Church Episcopalians, and others, who teach that this grace of salvation, by the renewing of the Holy Ghost, is tied down and limited—*first*, by what they most vainly and arrogantly call the only true Church, to wit, the Romanist or Episcopal Churches; and *secondly*, by the ordinances of baptism as administered in these churches; and what the passage does decide, is, as Calvinists now universally agree in believing, THAT THERE IS EVERY REASONABLE GROUND TO HOPE THAT ALL INFANTS DYING IN INFANCY ARE INCLUDED IN THE DECREE OF ELECTION AND ARE MADE PARTAKERS OF EVERLASTING LIFE.* This, then, is the view of Calvinists; and while it favours the most unbounded charity and hope, it rests that hope, not upon any thing in the infant itself, nor upon any thing done for it by any church, but upon the sure purpose of a merciful God, and the comfortable promises and declarations of his word.

Among all evangelical denominations this opinion is now received. We have given the names of evangelical Episcopalians. Gil-

---

lard, whose treatise I have mentioned, was, I presume, both a
Baptist and a Calvinist.   Dr. Gill's sentiments have been alluded
to, and they are quoted with approbation in the Baptist Confession of Faith.   The Rev. Robert Robinson, who has written the
History of Baptism, thus expresses himself: " Various opinions
concerning the future state of infants have been adopted.   The
most probable opinion seems to be, that they are *all* saved
through the merit of the Mediator, with an everlasting salvation.
This hath nothing in it contrary to the perfections of God, or to
any declarations of the holy Scriptures ; and it is highly agree-
able to all those passages, which affirm, *where sin hath abounded,
grace hath much more abounded.*   On these principles, the death
of Christ saves more than the fall of Adam lost."

Wesley does not appear to have determined this question at
all.   The salvation of all dying in infancy is, however, the prevalent belief among his followers.   The Rev. Richard Watson,
who is deservedly regarded as the ablest writer, and a stand-
ard authority, among the Methodists, very powerfully advocates
this opinion.*

This is also the established belief of the Lutheran Church,†
as it is of the Quaker denomination.‡

But whence, we ask, arose this community of opinion?   It
originated, as has been shown, among the Calvinists.   The battle
for liberty and charity of opinion against the dogmas of the

* See his Institutes, vol. ii. p. 228, and vol. iii. p. 72.

† See Schmucker's Theology, p. 128, and p. 220.   Storr & Flatt's Theology, sec. 68,
p. 394.   Mosheim wrote a treatise, which we have not seen, on this subject.

‡ See Barclay's Apology.

church was fought by them. Even when light had not irradiated the subject, and it was still shrouded in the darkness of prejudice, many Calvinists, rather than yield to the gloom of the generally entertained opinion that all unbaptized infants perish, groped about for any possible theory that might relieve them of their distress. Some, as I have shown, threw a veil of impenetrable darkness over the whole subject, and regarded an entrance upon its examination as presumption.* Others were induced to believe that the souls of all such children would be annihilated.† Others, that their souls remained in a state of insensibility either to good or evil.‡ All advocated the *possibility* of their salvation—the *practicability* of their regeneration—and all denied the absolute necessity of baptism to either. And can any one deny that the present clear and settled views on this subject have been introduced by Calvinists? Let him only remember that every one of the works and discourses on the subject to which I have alluded, were written by Calvinists ; that almost all the selections I have been enabled to collect are from writers holding the same views ; and that much even of the finest of our Poetical Selections are from authors whose muse was guided by Calvinistic views. Our work, in fact, may be regarded as a noble testimony to the truly scriptural and CHARITABLE nature of those much abused, because misunderstood, doctrines which most evangelical churches agree in adopting. And surely it may be expected, that these facts will give joy and con-

---

* See De Moor, Stapfer, Doddridge, (sec. 168,) Baxter.

† This was Dr. Watts's laboured hypothesis. See Works.

‡ Dr. Ridgley advocated this opinion. See his Divinity.

solation to those Christians whose ideas of Calvinism have been such as to lead them to cherish the prejudices that are so commonly and so ignorantly entertained, and enable them to cherish more kind and liberal feelings towards Calvinistic churches.

And that the reader may still more clearly perceive how much bereaved parents are indebted to Calvinism for the present comfortable and established hopes for dying infants, let me call his attention to the conflicting opinions which once prevailed on this much controverted subject, as they are given by Baxter:

"Some think that all infants (baptized or not) are saved from hell, and positive punishment, but are not brought to heaven, as being not capable of such joys.

"Some think that all infants (dying such) are saved as others are, by actual felicity in heaven, though in a lower degree. Both these sorts suppose that Christ's death saveth all that reject it not, and that infants reject it not.

"Some think that all unbaptized infants do suffer the 'pœnam damni,' and are shut out of heaven and happiness, but not sensibly punished or cast into hell. For this Jansenius hath wrote a treatise; and many other Papists think so.

"Some think that all the children of sincere believers dying in infancy are saved, (that is, glorified,) whether baptized or not; and no others.

"Some think that God hath not at all revealed what he will do with any infants.

"Some think that all the adopted and bought children of true Christians, as well as the natural, are saved (if baptized, say some; or if not, say others.)

" Some think that elect infants are saved, and no other.

" Some think that all that the pastor dedicateth to God are saved.

" Some think that this is to be limited to all that have right to baptism 'coram Deo;' which some think the church's reception giveth them.

" And some think it is to be limited to those that have right 'coram ecclesia,' or are rightfully baptized."

Bereaved Parent! what would be the aggravation of your distress if still plunged in this vortex of conflicting opinions? and how much, therefore, should it add to your patient resignation to the will of God in the removal of your children, when you find that *all branches of the protestant evangelical church, have now come to a common and united belief, that there is every reason to hope, that, in so doing, God has secured their salvation, and would also lead to your spiritual and everlasting good.*

6

Shade and Sunshine.

MARGARET JUNKIN.

EARTH is the home of sorrow! life,
  Though joyful it appears,
Is given, continued, and sustained,
  And borne away in tears.
The sentient throngs of earth and air
  Join Nature's voice to keep
Existence festive,—man alone
  Is privileged to weep.

Sweet as the "music of the spheres"
  Creation's hymn should be,
Yet evermore the human voice
  Is wailing mournfully;
And 'mid the still majestic strain
  Of praise and pæan high,
Are mingled death's despairing shriek,
  And hopeless misery's cry.

The earliest beams of every morn
  Fall on some mourner's head,

And flit in mockery across
  The dying and the dead;
The light of every parting sun
  Finds sorrowful repose
On new-made graves, whose turf was still
  Unbroken when he rose.

The trembling stars look nightly down
  On brows that, 'mid the glare
Of day, when all were smiling round,
  Seemed glad as any there:
But in the darkened solitude
  The mask aside is thrown,
And the crushed spirit speaks its woe
  Before its God alone.

And yet it is not ceaseless wail
  That earthly voices raise;
For some have learned the symphony,
  And joined the song of praise.
Ah, tear-dimmed eyes must long have closed,
  Had not a hand of love
Upheld the faltering step, and turned
  The wandering gaze above!

Then, with divinely lighted eye,
  They read their sufferings o'er,
And find a meaning in their grief
  They failed to find before:

A beauty touches all the past,
  And from the future fled
Is every fear,—and stars of hope
  Are shining overhead.

Who then can call this glorious world,
  With such a radiance, dim
And desolate, since on its sky
  Is stamped the seal of Him,
Who, in His rich magnificence,
  Has lavished all abroad
A splendour that could only spring
  Beneath the hand of God!

No, Earth has something more than gloom,
  And pain, and sickening fear,
For holy Peace has often come,
  And made its dwelling here;
Nor ever will it quite depart,
  Until our closing eyes
Are turned from Earth, to find in Heaven
  A fadeless paradise!

The Good Shepherd.

BICKERSTETH.

WITH thankful hearts our songs we raise,
To celebrate our Saviour's praise;
Yet who but saints in heaven above,
Can tell the riches of his love?

His love, with gentle accents, sheds
A blessing on our infants' heads;
Bids us for infants seek his face,
And ask for them renewing grace.

He, the good Shepherd, kindly leads
The wanderer, and the hungry feeds;
Deigns in his arms the lambs to bear,
And makes them his peculiar care.

Jesus, to thy protecting wing
Our helpless little ones we bring;
O grant them grace and strength, that they
May find and keep the heavenward way.

"Of such is the Kingdom."

MRS. MARY S. B. DANA.

I DEARLY love a little child,
And Jesus loved young children too;
He ever sweetly on them smiled,
And placed them with his chosen few.
When, cradled on its mother's breast,
A babe was brought to Jesus' feet,
He laid his hand upon its head,
And blessed it with a promise sweet.

"Forbid them not!" the Saviour said,
"Oh! suffer them to come to me!
Of such my heavenly kingdom is—
Like them may all my followers be!"
Young children are the gems of earth,
The brightest jewels mothers have;
They sparkle on the throbbing breast,
But brighter shine beyond the grave.

The Angels of Grief.

J. G. WHITTIER.

WITH silence only as their benediction,
  God's angels come,
Where in the shadow of a great affliction,
  The soul sits dumb.

Yet would we say, what every heart approveth,
  Our Father's will,
Calling to him the dear ones whom he loveth,
  Is mercy still.

Not upon us or ours the solemn angel
  Hath evil wrought;
The funeral anthem is a glad evangel,
  The good die not!

God calls our loved ones, but we lose not wholly
  What he has given;
They live on earth in thought and deed as truly
  As in his heaven.

On a Fair Infant.

JOHN MILTON.

O FAIREST flower, no sooner shown than blasted,
 Soft, silken primrose, fading timelessly,
Summer's chief honour, if thou hadst outlasted
 Bleak Winter's force that made thy blossom dry;
 For he, being amorous on that lovely dye
That did thy cheek envermeil, thought to kiss,
But killed, alas! and then bewailed his fatal bliss.

Yet can I not persuade me thou art dead,
 Or that thy corse corrupts in earth's dark womb,
Or that thy beauties lie in wormy bed,
 Hid from the world in a low delved tomb,
 Could Heaven, for pity, thee so strictly doom?
Oh, no! for something in thy face did shine
Above mortality, that showed thou wast divine.

Ah! wert thou of the golden-winged host,
 Who, having clad thyself in human weed,
To earth from thy prefixed seat didst post,
 And after short abode fly back with speed,
 As if to show what creatures heaven doth breed;

48

Thereby to set the hearts of men on fire,
To scorn the sordid world, and unto heaven aspire.

But, oh! why didst thou not stay here below?
  To bless us with thy heaven-loved innocence,
To slake his wrath whom sin hath made our foe,
  To turn swift-rushing, black Perdition hence,
  Or drive away the slaughtering Pestilence,
To stand 'twixt us and our deserved smart?
But thou canst best perform that office where thou art.

Then thou, the mother of so sweet a child,
  Her false-imagined loss cease to lament,
And wisely think to curb thy sorrows wild;
  Think what a present thou to God hast sent,
  And render him with patience what he lent;
This, if thou do, he will an offspring give,
That, till the world's last end, shall make thy name to live.
   7

Early Lost, Early Saved.

GEORGE W. BETHUNE, D.D.

WITHIN her downy cradle there lay a little child,
And a group of hovering angels unseen upon her smiled;
A strife arose among them, a loving, holy strife,
Which should shed the richest blessing o'er the new-born
    life.

One breathed upon her features, and the babe in beauty grew,
With a cheek like morning's blushes, and an eye of azure
    hue;
Till every one who saw her, was thankful for the sight
Of a face so sweet and radiant with ever fresh delight.

Another gave her accents, and a voice as musical
As a spring bird's joyous carol, or a rippling streamlet's fall;
Till all who heard her laughing, or her words of childish
    grace,
Loved as much to listen to her, as to look upon her face.

Another brought from heaven a clear and gentle mind,
And within the lovely casket the precious gem enshrined;
Till all who knew her wondered, that God should be so good,
As to bless with such a spirit our desert world and rude.

Thus did she grow in beauty, in melody and truth,
The budding of her childhood just opening into youth;
And to our hearts yet dearer, every moment than before,
She became, though we thought fondly, heart could not love
    her more.

Then out-spake another angel, nobler, brighter than the rest,
As with strong arm, but tender, he caught her to his breast;
" Ye have made her all too lovely for a child of mortal race,
But no shade of human sorrow shall darken o'er her face.

"Ye have tuned to gladness only the accents of her tongue,
And no wail of human anguish shall from her lips be wrung;
Nor shall the soul that shineth so purely from within
Her form of earth-born frailty, ever know the taint of sin.

"Lulled in my faithful bosom, I will bear her far away,
Where there is no sin, nor anguish, nor sorrow, nor decay;
And mine a boon more glorious than all your gifts shall be—
Lo! I crown her happy spirit with immortality!"
Then on his heart our darling yielded up her gentle breath,
For the stronger, brighter angel, who loved her best, was
    DEATH!

Little Ones Going Home.

"Suffer little children to come unto me, and forbid them not; for of such is the kingdom of heaven."

They are going—only going—
  Jesus called them long ago;
All the wintry time they're passing
  Softly as the falling snow.
When the violets in the spring-time
  Catch the azure of the sky,
They are carried out to slumber
  Sweetly where the violets lie.

They are going—only going—
  When with summer earth is dressed,
In their cold hands holding roses
  Folded to each silent breast;
When the autumn hangs red banners
  Out above the harvest sheaves,
They are going—ever going—
  Thick and fast, like falling leaves.

All along the mighty ages,
  All adown the solemn time,

They have taken up their homeward
  March to that serener clime,
Where the watching, waiting angels
  Lead them from the shadow dim,
To the brightness of His presence
  Who has called them unto him.

They are going—only going—
  Out of pain and into bliss—
Out of sad and sinful weakness
  Into perfect holiness.
Snowy brows—no care shall shade them;
  Bright eyes—tears shall never dim;
Rosy lips—no time shall fade them:
  Jesus called them unto him.

Hearts to be for ever stainless—
  Hands to be as pure as they—
Little feet by angels guided
  Never in forbidden way!
They are going—ever going!
  Leaving many a lonely spot;
But 'tis Jesus who has called them—
  Suffer, and forbid them not.

Are Infants Saved?[*]

DAVID M'CONOUGHY, D.D.

"It is not the will of your Father which is in heaven, that one of these little ones should perish."—Matt. xviii. 14.

THE birth of human beings is a momentous event, nor are they less interesting in actual possession and enjoyment. He who perfectly knows the human heart, recognizes it as most rare and unnatural that "a mother should forget her sucking child, and cease to have compassion on the son of her womb." How tenderly are they caressed! what yearnings of affection move a mother's heart! what surpassing endearment and anxious concern are felt! Care expended augments interest. Dangers apprehended increase affectionate estimation. Watchfulness and toils only give greater vehemence to ardent and solicitous concern for the object beloved. Nor is the father's heart without its devotion and attachment, though its emotions may not be so vivid, or its tenderness so deep and constraining. Even relatives and friends share the sympathy and interest: and they are strangers to the promptings of nature who can regard with indifference the tender and endearing claims of infancy. Its smiles, and even its tears, its comparative innocence and helpless dependence,

[*] Tract No. 132, Presbyterian Board of Publication.

its germs of intellect and affection, what it is, and what it may yet be, elicit deep solicitude and present claims to the sympathy of every benevolent heart.   I add that they are objects of very special interest *prospectively*.   Their character as intelligent, moral and immortal beings gives to them importance beyond all the present and immediate interest felt.   They may now present many reasons of affectionate regard; but the developments which their progressive years may exhibit are of paramount concern and importance.   We admire the flower so sweet and beauteous, but on its future fruits depends its chief importance.   Its eminence of interest results not from what it now is, but from what it will be in its maturity.   It is not only a living creature, but one which is destined to responsibility.   It is to form a character which is to last for ever, sustain a place among men— if it live—be a benefactor or a curse to the world, and receive in eternity the retribution which an unerring Judge will award.   What unutterable interest results from these facts!   To every considerate mind what deep solemnity is in the question—what is this child to be?   If life be prolonged, and its bodily, mental, and moral powers be developed and brought into operation, what will be its character and influence? will it bring joy to its parents, or anguish?—will it be to the world useful, or useless and noxious? will it be honoured, or despised? will it be happy, or wretched?

There is another anxious question—will their lives be prolonged, or will they die in infancy? will they live to mature years, or be cut down as a flower?   How often is this matter of painful apprehension!—how often of sad reality, of most poignant grief, of hopes blasted, and of fondly cherished expectations utterly disappointed!

And there is still another most tender and serious question. If they thus early die, what will be their future allotment and condition? As to the future condition of those who die in infancy, there have been much conjecture and many conflicting opinions. I will not enumerate nor examine them. One opinion only can be true. What God teaches must be true. Christ, the faithful and true witness, as the expounder of his Father's will, affirms—"It is not the will of your Father who is in heaven that one of these little ones should perish."

In attempting to present a correct view of this most interesting case, I make the following remarks:—

1st. Infants in their original character and condition are liable to perish. There are no testimonies of Scripture, nor are there any facts in their actual condition and character, which warrant the opinion that they are exempt from "original guilt and depravity." In Adam all descending from him by ordinary generation, die. They inherit depravity, and are liable to death and other penal evils. That they are the subjects of sufferings and death is a matter of notorious and indisputable fact; and the first and continuous developments of their moral character are no less proofs of connate depravity, and that every imagination of the thoughts of their heart "from their youth is only evil, continually." The whole human race, infants not excepted, are "by nature children of wrath." "There is none righteous: no; not one." If they remain in this condition they must inevitably perish. Death, already, has dominion over them. In, or by themselves, from this ruin there is no possibility of escape; and no created power can effect their redemption. By the righteous judgment of God this ruin has befallen them, and nothing less than his own gracious purpose and power can avert the disastrous result. But if he so wills, "not one of these little ones will perish," but they will be "saved to the praise of the glory of his grace."

I remark, 2dly, That infants, just like all other human beings, if saved, are saved only through the mediation of Christ. "There is none other name under heaven given among men whereby we must be saved, neither is there salvation in any other." Of the righteousness of that dispensation by which the whole race was lost in Adam it would be impious to doubt. It is a fact. To its full vindication we may be incompetent; but the all-wise God had good and sufficient reasons for ordering it thus; and in this as ever, he is "righteous in all his ways and holy in all his works." So the issue will certainly and clearly show; and grace will reign through righteousness in all who are saved. If the condemnation and ruin of all in Adam be righteous,—and who in defiance of facts and the testimony of Scripture will deny it?—the moral government of God must have its full vindication when that condemnation and ruin are averted. He must be just when he saves sinners; and if, as some allege, infants and all men were restored by Christ to a salvable state or opportunity of salvation, they must antecedently have been guilty and perishing. Christ did not die to save those who were in no danger, or whose perdition could not have been just. If Christ died to save men, without his death they had perished, and that justly. God did not require of him a ransom price for what had not been justly forfeited and lost. His death for sinners justice indispensably required, or for them he had never died. Redemption through Christ is a distinct recognition of the righteousness of the Adamic dispensation. The interposition of Christ was a sovereign and gracious dispensation in behalf of those who might have justly been left to perish. Scripture and facts prove that infants need salvation. In Christ there is salvation, but not in any other. If saved it must be through his mediation, and in him there is all that salvation which their case requires. Such as die in infancy have no actual sins to be pardoned, but they need a removal of original guilt, or that liability to penal evils under which they are. They need a righteousness which will entitle them to the glory and felicity of heaven, which can be conferred only on account of the righteousness of Christ reckoned to them as their meritorious title to eternal life. And no less do they necessarily require the " washing of regeneration, and the renewing of the Holy Ghost." Without the removal of their depravity and the positive impartation of a holy character, they cannot be admitted to heaven, or enjoy happiness there. This needful salvation Christ alone bestows. He can bestow it, and if he does, infants thus become " fit for the inheritance of the saints in light." They are thus prepared to be inhabitants of that kingdom of heaven where God, their Saviour, and all his redeemed, are in the possession of " fulness of joy and pleasures for evermore."

I remark, 3dly, That redemption by Christ, as respects moral government, in this case, has removed all hinderances to their salvation. By his holy life, his perfect obedience to the law under which man is, and by his full endurance of the penalty as incurred by man's transgression, he has brought in a righteousness which will fully avail for salvation to all to whom God graciously reckons it. In the case of infants their personal acceptance and appropriation of Christ for their salvation is impossible; but if God so wills, the benefit in all its fulness may be bestowed on them. The everlasting righteousness is brought in and the whole law is magnified and made honourable. According to my understanding of the Scripture, Christ, as the second Adam, assumed the responsibility which rested on man as to the law which he had violated, which responsibility and obligation were, to render the perfect obedience which fallen man could not now render, and endure its penalty, which would have consigned the whole race to utter and endless ruin. To this obligation he fully responded. The justice of God by his obedience unto death is fully satisfied, and the honour and requirements of the law, as they respect man, are vindicated in full measure. God can now be just in bestowing salvation on all, or as many as may accord with his infinite wisdom and sovereign good pleasure. The demands of the divine law and justice interpose no impediment to the salvation of infants.

I remark, 4thly, That the salvation of infants is a case which wholly depends on the will of God. Whatever opinions may be entertained as to the ability of man, when adult, to " work out his own salvation," or whatever concurrence he may be supposed to exert with divine grace, this case wholly excludes them all. Infants are not moral agents, in such measure, as to be car

of any efficiency, voluntary agency, or co-operation. If they be
saved, it must be entirely by the sovereign mercy and positive
operation of God. If it be his will that not one of them should
perish, they will be certainly saved. No other will can here interpose. Salvation is of God only; will he not save them?

In this connexion I add, that, in so far as I am aware, actual
sin, or the rejection of offered mercy, is always, in Scripture,
assigned as the reason why any perish. I have asserted the
liability of infants to perish, unless grace through the mediation
of Christ interpose; but I allege that Scripture always recognizes
voluntary agency, and the consequent responsibility, as reasons
of condemnation;—that they who perish knew their duty and
did it not. On perdition for original guilt and depravity, without actual sin, the Scriptures are silent. We of course have no
authority to affirm it: but may not this silence encourage the
opinion that infants are of those who are saved by the grace of
God abounding through his Son? Erskine, in his "Gospel
Sonnets," representing the redeemed of every class as alleging
their special and pre-eminent reasons to give glory to God for his
saving grace, concludes—

> Babes thither caught from womb and breast,
> Claim right to sing above the rest;
> Because they found the happy shore,
> They neither saw nor sought before.

All redeemed sinners owe their salvation to sovereign grace,
and have reason for holy wonder and for everlasting praise; but
the salvation of infants is with peculiar circumstances of favour.
They are exempted from the tedious, toilsome, dangerous journey

of life, which is the allotment of those whose years are prolonged. Without a knowledge of their fall and ruin, they are rescued from danger and from sin. Without repentance, faith, hope, or effort, they inherit "fulness of joy and pleasures for evermore." Like tender plants, the natives of bleak and chilling climes, they are transplanted to grow and bloom, and produce their precious fruits, under the genial warmth and propitious influences of the heavenly paradise. The process of their eradication may be with violence and momentary injury, but that will be fully compensated by the more favoured condition in which they will attain their beauty and maturity, where no adverse causes will ever interpose.

There is another consideration which is worthy of notice. I refer to the manner in which the sacred record speaks of the death of infants. It never suggests the notion of their death being accompanied with the wrath of God against them specially and individually. Their death is sometimes mentioned as constituting a part of the calamity where guilty cities or nations are visited by the signal judgments of God. They are cut off by death in common with their parents who had provoked the Divine displeasure, and as an aggravation of the general calamity. Elsewhere, they die as trials of the faith and resignation of their parents; sometimes as the chastisement of their unfaithfulness, or as a judgment for their sins. But they were not the actual offenders, nor are they recognized as the direct objects of the Divine displeasure thus manifested. The death of wicked and unbelieving men is represented as wrathful and utterly ruinous. "They are driven away in their wickedness"—"they die in their sins "—" their hopes perish "—" they are cast into hell where their worm dieth not." No such wrathful declarations are connected with the death of infants; but wherever anything seems to be implied as to their future state, it is peaceful and soothing. Such I judge to be the fact always. I will refer to a few cases which now occur to me, as of special import in this respect.

The first is the death of the first child of David, king of Israel, by Bathsheba. During the child's illness he fasted and wept;—on its death he ceased from his grief and said, "Now he is dead, wherefore should I fast? Can I bring him back again? I shall go to him, but he shall not return to me." Did he mean, merely, that he would at his death follow him to the tomb? That presented no ground of consolation. It might be understood as a recognition of his own mortality, and of his humble acquiescence in the bereavement which he had experienced, but not of sustaining faith, fond anticipation and soothing hope. That would imply the expectation of a reunion with him in that better world, in which he himself hoped to dwell after he had completed his pilgrimage and finished the work which was assigned him, of serving his generation according to the will of God. He sorrowed not as those who have no hope, but cherished cheerful anticipation as well as peaceful submission to the will of God.

Another case is that of the pious Shunammite, recorded in 2 Kings, ch. iv. When her son had suddenly died, she hastened to visit the prophet Elisha. On her near approach, the prophet sent his servant to meet her, and to ask, "Is it well with thee?

is it well with thy husband? is it well with the child?" And she answered, "It is well." How could she so answer in relation to her child who was dead, and for aught she knew, irrecoverably? If no future existence nor future bliss awaited the recently living object of her fond affections, how was it well with it? Such a fact might claim humble acquiescence, but presented no consolation, no fond anticipation nor soothing hope; but with good reason she might say, "It is well," if she believed that her departed son was removed to heaven, and was then an heir of immortal life. Parental affection cannot find the needful consolation in the waste, the dreariness and the silence of the grave. It looks and longs and hopes for the continued conscious existence and happier condition of those whom they had so fondly caressed and so dearly loved. Is not this desire, so natural, an earnest of what is the will and purpose of God? Over the death of infants the sacred record casts no appalling gloom, but rather irradiates it with promises of peace and earnests of immortality.

The unnatural and horrid crime of the people of Israel in sacrificing their children to Moloch, is thus denounced by the prophet Jeremiah: "And in thy skirts is found the blood of the souls of the innocents." This phrase, "the innocents," is twice used by the prophet to denote the death of infants. This is not designed to affirm their innocence in the sight of God but to denote the cruelty of this conduct as the act of man; and that their death was not the infliction of the wrath of God, but a murderous deed of vile idolatry which God abhorred and condemned. Their age and condition render them comparatively innocent. They have not the guilt of actual transgressors, and their death is never represented with those circumstances of Divine displeasure and vengeance which are associated with the death of wilful and actual sinners.

5th. The declarations of Christ in relation to infants or little children imply that they will be heirs of everlasting life. Condescension and kindness characterized all his intercourse with men. Obscurity of rank or humility of condition he did not overlook. "To the poor the gospel was preached;" and the afflicted, and such as worldly pride disdained, were the objects of his special notice and kindness. Little children he treated with distinguishing favour and peculiar regard. This fact is full of tenderness, and has much instructive meaning. His language and actions are most explicit and affectionate. On different occasions children are incidentally noticed; but one case deserves distinct consideration. It is minutely and almost in the same words recorded by three evangelists, Matthew, Mark, and Luke. —Matthew thus records it, xix. 15: "Then were there brought unto him little children, that he should put his hands on them and pray; and the disciples rebuked them. But Jesus said, Suffer little children, and forbid them not, to come unto me; for of such is the kingdom of heaven." What is the meaning of this express declaration? On this phrase, George Campbell, an eminent critic, remarks: "It is often rightly translated 'the kingdom of heaven,' as it is, manifestly, often applied to the state of perfect felicity to be enjoyed in the world to come." If we so understand it here,—and I know of no reason which forbids,—it is an explicit affirmation, by him who not only knows what will be, but himself "holds the keys of death, and of the unseen world," that of them, and of those who by renewing grace are made like to them, will the inhabitants of the heavenly world consist. Henry on this case remarks, "Little children are welcome to Christ as respects themselves, for whom he has upon all occasions expressed a concern; and who having participated of the malignant influences of the first Adam's sin, must needs share in the riches of the second Adam's grace; else, what would come of the apostle's parallel in 1 Cor. xv. 22, and in Rom. v. 14, 15, &c.?" Doddridge says, "Let parents view this sight with pleasure and thankfulness; let it encourage them to bring their children to Christ by faith, and to commit them to him in baptism and by prayer; and if he who 'has the keys of death and of the unseen world' see fit to remove those dear creatures from us in their early days, let the remembrance of this story comfort us, and teach us to hope that he who so graciously received these children has not forgotten ours; but that they are sweetly fallen asleep in him, and will be the everlasting objects of his care and love; 'for of such is the kingdom of heaven.'" On this affirmation, Dr. Scott remarks, "Indeed, the expression may also intimate that the kingdom of heavenly glory is greatly constituted of such as die in infancy. Infants are as capable of regeneration as grown persons; and there is abundant ground to conclude that all those who have not lived to commit actual transgressions, though they share in the effects of the first Adam's offence, will also share in the blessings of the second Adam's gracious covenant, without their personal faith and obedience, but not without the regenerating influence of the Spirit of Christ.'

9

By "the kingdom of heaven" and "the kingdom of God," in Scripture language, is sometimes meant the gospel church; and it may be alleged that the import of Christ's declaration is that children may be recognized as members of the church. That believers as members of the church are entitled to claim the same privilege for their children, is a fact under both the Jewish and Christian dispensations. This, as respects the visible church, entitles them to its watchful care, prayers, and means of religious education and training; and when they arrive at years of reason and moral responsibility, it is their duty and privilege to assume for themselves the obligations and privileges of believing men and women. If they refuse, and live in disobedience and unbelief, they forfeit the blessings and hopes of the believing and obedient; and these can be regained only by repentance toward God and faith in the Lord Jesus. But the question here is respecting those who die in infancy. Does not their recognition as members of Christ's church on earth imply that they will be recognized as such in heaven? It is on Christ's authority that they are now acknowledged as the lambs of his flock —will he not own them as such when, being yet little children, they are in his providence called to the world of spirits? Men may mistake as to those who are entitled to the privileges of divine grace: Christ cannot. Will he exclude from the company of the redeemed those to whom he had assigned a place among his people here? Called away by death before they had reached a condition of moral agency, will they not be transferred from the church on earth to the church in heaven? The church in heaven is only the highest department of the same gracious system. All who, in truth and in the judgment of God, are members of the church on earth, will be admitted to the church in heaven.

As to the relation of the children of believers to the visible church, what is the import and matter of fact? That relation in itself does not imply, as a matter of certainty, their actual salvation. Many baptized children, and even the children of pious parents, live and die impenitent and unbelieving. In how far this may follow from the want of faith and faithfulness on the part of the parents, I undertake not to decide. As respects those who die in infancy, pious parents can never suppose that their salvation is the reward of their parents' faith and holiness. They are therefore saved wholly by grace; and by the same sovereign grace alone can their children be saved. But if their children live to years of discretion or maturity, to them, as moral and accountable beings, it is of the utmost importance to have the means of religious knowledge and a pious education. And by pious parents it must be regarded as a precious privilege to have the means of training up their children for God, and holiness and heaven. The influence of the church and the gospel dispensation is designed to have its effect specially, in forming men to wisdom and holiness by a process of education assigned by God and made effectual by his blessing. Of its saving effect in any other way I am not aware. Human beings who do not live here to become moral agents are under a different dispensation.

6th. The consideration of the benevolence of God favours the belief that children dying in infancy will be saved and be heirs of heaven. I am aware that we may entertain unwarranted and presumptuous expectations from the Divine benevolence. Unbelieving and even profligate sinners often do. They overlook the fact that God is just, and holy, and true, as well as merciful. All we know of his mercy is from his own revelation, which asserts his perfect righteousness no less strongly and clearly than his mercy. He is always represented as a just God, even when he is a Saviour. Divine revelation does not any where give intimations of mercy to fallen man unless through mediation and atonement. In this way grace and mercy abound. "God so loved the world, that he gave his only begotten Son, that whosoever believeth on him may not perish, but have everlasting life." "In this was manifested the love of God, that he gave his only begotten Son, that we might live through him." "God is love." I take it as a fact, that Divine benevolence does not in any case inflict penal evil upon any intelligent creature, nor withhold from them appropriate happiness, unless where the penalty has been incurred and the forfeiture made by sin ;—in that case Divine law and justice must be vindicated. In the case of infants, the vindication has been made, and through Christ they may be saved. That believers may and will be saved is absolutely certain. Infants cannot believe ; but will they for that reason perish ? May not—will not Divine benevolence impart to them the prepared salvation which they need, but which through natural incompetency they cannot seek and accept ? Under the moral government of God it is a recognized fact, that responsibility is always proportional to the opportunities and means which he has given to men to know and do his will. "The servant who knew his master's will and did it not, shall be beaten with many stripes; but he who knew not his master's will and committed things worthy of stripes, shall be beaten with few." Absolute and invincible ignorance of duty can involve no responsibility;—as many as have sinned without the revealed law will be dealt with accordingly; and they who sin under and with a knowledge of the law will be judged by the law. The heathen will not be condemned for not believing the gospel which they had never heard, and of which they had no knowledge. No more will be required of them, nor of any, than a faithful improvement of the means of knowledge and obedience which they had. It is their unfaithfulness to what they knew, or might and ought to have known, that leaves them guilty and without excuse. Will infants perish because of their non-acceptance of a Saviour, although their natural imbecility renders such acceptance an absolute impossibility? I admit and believe that they "are by nature children of wrath;" but, as they do not live to years of moral agency to resist and reject either natural or revealed religion, will they not be saved by grace? Will they not be the objects of the benevolence and mercy of Him who has sworn that he has no pleasure even in the death of those who defy his authority, reject his grace, and die in their sins? God's vindictive displeasure is exercised against wilful sinners only. Where there is no crime, he delights in showing favour and conferring happiness. This is true as to holy angels and all other upright and intelligent creatures; and even on fallen man he delights to bestow happiness where his justice is recognized and his mercy sought, and the grace which reigns through righteousness unto eternal life, by Jesus Christ our Lord, does not will that one of these little ones should perish.

My remarks on this very tender and interesting case imply that all children dying in infancy are heirs of salvation. I know of nothing in the teachings of the Scriptures, or in the circumstances of this case, which requires a different opinion. They all are involved in the same ruin by the operation of the same causes. "In Adam all die." The mediation of Christ has, as respects the law and government of God, made provision for the exercise of mercy to them, in common with all the race. "By the righteousness of one (Christ, the second Adam) the free gift came upon all men to justification of life." Their salvation depends entirely on the pleasure of God. They cannot have any agency in the case. No other creature can. God alone has the right or power to save. If he wills it, it cannot fail of accomplishment. Their case and condition as respects themselves, severally and individually, is the same, be they the offspring of Christians or heathen. God, as a sovereign, may justly make a difference; but there is no evidence that, in this case, he will. The punishment of wilful rebels and unbelievers is indisputably just. The salvation of the penitent and believing is certain in the way which God has assigned. They who die in infancy are in circumstances different from both; they are all in the same undistinguished ruin, and may all be the objects of the same indiscriminating and abounding grace. Their parentage, in so far as they are concerned, makes them neither better nor worse.

Presbyterians are charged with entertaining veiy harsh opinions on this subject, and with pronouncing a sentence of perdition at least on a part of those who die in infancy. I can truly say that, in all my intercourse with ministers and intelligent private Christians of our denomination, I never heard an avowal of such a belief. If not clear in affirming the salvation of all such, they left them at the disposal of Him who gave them existence, and who can inflict no cruelty or injustice on any of his creatures; and who as moral governor of the world can do only what is wise and right. Our Confession of Faith, which we recognize as a faithful and scriptural summary of Bible doctrines, refers but once explicitly to this subject, where it says—" Elect infants, dying in infancy, are regenerated and saved by Christ, through the Spirit who worketh when and where and how he pleaseth. So also are all other elect persons who are incapable of being outwardly called by the ministry of the word." In accordance with Scripture, and with the very nature and reason of the case, we believe that all men are not saved; and that they who are saved are saved according to the purpose and by the grace of God;—that fallen man would not and could not devise and effect his own salvation, and that God alone can. This every truly converted and saved sinner feels, and believes, and confesses. This is the sum and substance of what we mean by election. Though a full and free salvation be provided and offered; yet such is the indifference, pride, and wickedness of man, that not one would embrace this salvation if God did not enlighten, dispose, and enable them to accept of the offered mercy. He must be ignorant of himself, and still in ruinous delusion and error, who arrogates to himself the purpose, wisdom, and efficiency by which he is saved. By grace men are saved, through faith; and that not of themselves: it is the gift of God. The disposition and moral power to return to God by repentance and faith no sinful man has, until the Spirit of God awakens him to see his danger, and believe in Christ as the only and all-sufficient Saviour. All the race, without exception, are lost, and would be for ever lost, unless God in mercy quickens them from their death in trespasses and sins. The phrase "elect in-fants" does not necessarily suppose and imply that some are lost. They may all be included among the saved, as a part of the ruined race, together with the exceeding great multitude whom God will raise to life, and holiness, and heaven. And no doubt it is true that, "It is not the will of your Father who is in heaven, that one of these little ones should perish."

Admitting as true and scriptural the doctrine now advanced, it follows,

1st. That the redeemed infants and little children will consti-tute a large number. What proportion that number may bear, more or less, to the number of adults who will be saved, is known to God only; and all is wise and right. The Judge of all the earth ever does that which is right—and "his tender mercies are over all his works." The past history of our race, even of those who enjoyed a divine revelation, presents, indeed, a sad-dening array of facts. But we remember the desponding com-plaint of Elias in the case of Israel, and find some consolation. The prophet judged the apostasy to be universal, himself excepted; but what saith the answer of God unto him? "I have reserved to myself seven thousand men who have not bowed the knee unto the image of Baal!" Even so then at this present time also there is a remnant according to the election of grace. If *then*, no doubt at all other times there have been many partakers of divine grace and mercy known to God, though disowned by the imperfect knowledge and unkind judgment of man. Besides, we anticipate millennial times of glory for the church, when Christ,—not by a personal reign on earth, but in the power of his Spirit,—shall subdue the nations to the obedience of faith, and send from all kindreds and people very many to augment "the assembly and church of the first-born in heaven." We are sad in thinking of the comparatively few accessions to the world of glory from the generations that are gone; but have hope and consolation in the prospect of the exceeding great multitude which will throng heaven when all ends of the earth shall hear of and accept the salvation of God. To this joy immense interest is given, by the consideration of the myriads of infant spirits which from all countries and generations have entered on the light, and love, and joy of a glorious immortality.

2d. This doctrine of the salvation of all who die in infancy presents no reason against the baptism and religious education of children.

What may be the wise and sovereign pleasure of God as to the disposal of their lives is known to him alone. Parents cannot foresee whether they will die early, or live for many years. In either result the way of duty and of privilege is one and the same. If it should be the will of God that their children die in infancy or in childhood, in the revelation of Divine mercy through Christ, pious parents will find the best preparation for acquiescence in the will of God, and for enjoying the most available consolations. This is the only hope for themselves or for their children. To commit them in believing prayer to his wise and merciful disposal is privilege and duty : and as he has instituted the ordinance of baptism as emblematical and significant of the needful salvation, the use and observance of it will be considered a precious privilege. Parents thus recognize the necessity of salvation, and make express reference to the manner in which it is obtained, while at the same time they manifest their humble desire and hope that their children may be thus saved, to the praise of the glory of God's grace. With such a hope, the dedication of their children to God in baptism is a reasonable service, an act of faith, and a means of peaceful trust and intelligent consolation.

If it should be the good pleasure of God to prolong the lives of their children to years of accountability and of participation in the duties of life, that early consecration of them is a matter of special privilege and of sacred obligation. And all that is fairly implied in their baptism is no less privilege and duty. It is a privilege and duty to commend them to the grace of God in confiding, fervent prayer; to secure for them in God's assigned way the benefit of divine ordinances ; and to employ their own prayers and faithful efforts to make them wise, holy and happy. As said before, " The church or gospel dispensation is designed and adapted to have its special effect in forming men to wisdom and holiness, by a process of education assigned by God and made effectual by his blessing;" and by pious parents it must be re-garded as a precious privilege to have divinely-appointed means of training up their children for God, and holiness, and heaven. In the faithful use of those means there is great and special rea-son to hope for that all-important result. In the neglect of those means there is no warrant to hope. So God teaches:— "Train up a child in the way he should go, and when he is old he will not depart from it." The contrary is no less true, that "a child left to himself" will probably become the grief and shame of his parents, and do little good, if not much harm, to himself and to the world. This the nature of the case forebodes, and facts generally furnish the sad illustration and proof. Intel-ligent and moral beings, that they may act virtuously, must have a knowledge of their duty and appropriate motives to fulfil it. These they can have only by religious instruction and training. In the want of these there will be ignorance, folly and sin.

3d. Baptism, though a duty and a privilege, where the Divine appointment is known, is not essential to salvation; nor does it, in itself, insure salvation.

Abraham was in a state of justification and acceptance with God before he was circumcised. Simon, the sorcerer, though baptized, was in the "gall of bitterness and bond of iniquity;" and so it is with all ungodly and unbelieving men. Baptism is not, nor does it necessarily, or even by Divine appointment, in-volve in it spiritual regeneration. It would then be essentially necessary; because, "except a man be born again, or spiritually regenerated, he cannot see the kingdom of God." If it were regeneration, it would always be followed by evidences of spiritual life, which is very far from being matter of fact. Many baptized persons are infidels, and impious and profligate men. If it were real regeneration, it would be imperisnable. The spiritual life which God communicates he will never permit to die: having begun a good work he will perfect it until the day of Jesus Christ. Baptism is merely emblematical of that gracious change which is effected by the Holy Spirit in the application of the redemption purchased by Christ. This gracious change may be, and no doubt is often effected without the external ordinance. The salvation of those who die in infancy cannot depend on the faithfulness or unfaithfulness of their parents; it depends wholly on the gracious will and sovereign pleasure of God. Their being baptized or not, is a matter in which they can have no choice nor agency, and consequently neither praise nor blame. In this case, parents have a responsibility which infants cannot have. It is one of those external means which pertain to the visible church, ordained by God to encourage the faith of pious parents in hoping for the salvation of their children, and to be the means of expressing their trust in the mercy of God, and recognizing their obligations to bring them up in the nurture and admonition of the Lord, if life be prolonged.

4th. The fact that so great a number of the human race die in infancy or early childhood, is one of the dispensations of Providence which is involved in no little obscurity. All the reasons of it we pretend not to explain or assign. That it is proof of their connate guilt and depravity the Scriptures assert. But there are questions which the case seems to suggest, which, perhaps, it may not be presumptuous in us to ask and humbly seek for some solution. As they live not to years of moral agency, nor to act a part in the scenes of life, why are they born or brought into life? It is manifest that this was indispensable to their being of the human race. They make a part of that number of human beings which God purposed to create. Had they not been thus born, they would not have been in fact of that particular order of creatures. Their non-existence would have left the predestined number incomplete, and if called into life in any other way they had not been of the race of man. That their continuance on earth is so short, is according to the Divine purpose and pleasure. But may He not, in his sovereign good pleasure, design to exempt them from the cares, dangers, and ills of the present world, and favour them with an early entrance on an immortal existence to be the heirs of an interminable but progressive knowledge and happiness? The life bestowed and begun he would not annihilate, nor would he perpetuate in endless woe. "It is not his will that they should perish." They belong to "the kingdom of heaven." They constitute a part of "the travail of the Redeemer's soul"—"the exceeding great multitude of his redeemed which no man can number." In order to their being of the human race they must derive their existence in the ordinary way. That they may be partakers with Adam in his fall, they must be his natural descendants. If not the children of wrath they could not be the objects of mercy. If not of the human race they could not partake in the redemption through Christ. He came to save men only;—"He took not upon him the nature of angels, but the seed of Abraham." Those who die in infancy are a numerous portion of the generations of men. As to all the rest of men, they are fallen and perishing. They need salvation and may be the trophies of a Redeemer's gracious power, and " the travail of his soul." For such purposes of wisdom and sovereign benevolence, and such manifestations of the power and grace of Christ, may they not well exist? And if these be some of the facts and reasons, do they not shed some light upon those obscure dispensations of the all-wise and righteous God ? What appears to us a premature departure from life, in the case of infants, is not more unsearchable and strange than many other cases, in which God's way is in the sea and his footsteps in the deep waters. How many are cut off in the morning of life and in all the vigour and hopes of youth! —how many are wisely, yet to us mysteriously, called away from places of usefulness, and from promises and prospects of accomplishing great good !—" What we know not now we will know hereafter." In the administration of the world by God there is no error. " He is wise in counsel as well as mighty in working." Nothing comes too soon—nothing occurs too late. He who notices the fall of a sparrow, orders well the issues of man's life ; —by him the days of our life are numbered no less than the hairs of our head.

The Reaper and the Flowers.

LONGFELLOW.

THERE is a Reaper whose name is Death,
 And with his sickle keen,
He reaps the bearded grain at a breath,
 And the flowers that grow between.

"Shall I have naught that is fair?" said he,
 "Have naught but the bearded grain?
Though the breath of these flowers is sweet to me,
 I will give them all back again."

He gazed at the flowers with tearful eyes;
 He kissed their drooping leaves;
It was for the Lord of paradise
 He bound them in his sheaves.

"My Lord hath need of these flowerets gay,"
 The reaper said, and smiled;
"Dear tokens of the earth are they,
 Where *he* was once a child.

"They shall all bloom in fields of light,
 Transplanted by my care,

And saints upon their garments white,
  These sacred blossoms wear."

And the mother gave in tears and pain
  The flowers she most did love;
She knew she should find them all again
  In the fields of light above.

Oh, not in cruelty, not in wrath,
  The reaper came that day;
'Twas an angel visited the green earth,
  And took the flowers away!

Our Little Sister.

ADA.

She came and went.
This life to her was as a passing dream,
So short, so fleeting. And yet she gained
A place within our hearts.
As most we love those tender flowers
Which bloom but for a day,
So loved we her, and mourned when she departed.
But wherefore should we mourn?
Oh went she not from a dark world
Of sorrow, pain, and tears,
To a more blessed home, a place
Of holiness, of happiness, and peace?
Then may we dry our tears;
For now more blest, and happier far,
Than any here below,
She sings with e'en her infant voice
Sweet praises to her Saviour, who declared,
That of such babes, heaven's kingdom is composed.

Passing Under the Rod.

MRS. MARY S. B. DANA.

I SAW the young mother in tenderness bend
  O'er the couch of her slumbering boy,
And she kissed the soft lips as they murmured her name,
  While the dreamer lay smiling in joy.
O sweet as the rose-bud encircled with dew,
  When its fragrance is flung on the air,
So fresh and so bright to that mother he seemed,
  As he lay in his innocence there.
But I saw when she gazed on the same lovely form,
  Pale as marble, and silent, and cold,
But paler and colder her beautiful boy,
  And the tale of her sorrow was told!
But the Healer was there who had stricken her heart,
  And taken her treasure away;
To allure her to heaven he has placed it on high,
  And the mourner will sweetly obey:
There had whispered a voice—'twas the voice of her God,
  "I love thee—I love thee—*pass under the rod!*"

Over the River.

MISS N. A. W. PRIEST.

OVER the river they beckon to me—
  Loved ones who've crossed to the further side;
The gleam of their snowy robes I see,
  But their voices are drowned in the rushing tide
There's one with ringlets of sunny gold,
  And eyes the reflection of heaven's own blue;
He crossed in the twilight, gray and cold,
  And the pale mist hid him from mortal view.
We saw not the angels who met him there;
  The gates of the city we could not see;
Over the river, over the river,
  My brother stands waiting to welcome me!

Over the river, the boatman pale
  Carried another—the household pet:
Her brown curls waved in the gentle gale—
  Darling Minnie! I see her yet.
She crossed on her bosom her dimpled hands,
  And fearlessly entered the phantom bark;
We watched it glide from the silver sands,
  And all our sunshine grew strangely dark.

We know she is safe on the further side
  Where all the ransomed and angels be;
Over the river, the mystic river,
  My childhood's idol is waiting for me.

For none return from those quiet shores,
  Who cross with the boatman cold and pale;
We hear the dip of the golden oars,
  And catch the gleam of the snowy sail,—
And lo! they have passed from our yearning heart;
  They cross the stream, and are gone for aye;
We may not sunder the veil apart,
  That hides from our vision the gates of day.
We only know that their barks no more
  May sail with us o'er life's stormy sea:
Yet somewhere, I know, on the unseen shore,
  They watch, and beckon, and wait for me.

And I sit and think, when the sunset's gold,
  Is flushing river, and hill, and shore,
I shall one day stand by the water cold,
  And list for the sound of the boatman's oar;
I shall watch for a gleam of the flapping sail;
  I shall hear the boat as it gains the strand;
I shall pass from sight, with the boatman pale,
  To the better shore of the spirit land;
I shall know the loved who have gone before,—
  And joyfully sweet will the meeting be,
When over the river, the peaceful river,
  The angel of Death shall carry me.

The Cheerful Giver.

MRS. L. H. SIGOURNEY.

"What shall I render Thee! Father Supreme,
For thy rich gifts, and *this* the best of all?"
Said a young mother, as she fondly watched
Her sleeping babe.
        There was an answering voice
That night in dreams.
        "Thou hast a little bud
Wrapt in thy breast, and fed with dews
Of love; give me that bud, 'twill be
A flower in heaven."
But there was silence, yea, a hush so deep,
Breathless and terror-stricken,
                That the lip
Blanched in its trance—
                "Thou hast a little harp
How sweetly would it swell the
Angels' songs! Give me that harp."
There burst a shuddering sob
As if the bosom, by some hidden sword,
Was cleft in twain.

Morn came, a blight had found
The crimson velvet of the unfolding bud;
The harp-string rang a thrilling strain,
And broke,
  And that young mother lay upon
The earth in childless agony.
      Again the voice
  That stirred her vision—
     "He who asked of thee
Loveth a cheerful giver."
      So she raised
Her gushing eye, and ere the tear-drop
Dried upon its fringes, smiled—
      Doubt not that smile,
  Like Abraham's faith,
     "Was counted righteousness."

The Meeting-place.

HORATIUS BONAR, D.D.

WHERE the faded flower shall freshen,—
  Freshen never more to fade;
Where the shaded sky shall brighten,—
  Brighten never more to shade:
Where the sun-blaze never scorches;
  Where the star-beams cease to chill;
Where no tempest stirs the echoes
  Of the wood, or wave, or hill:
Where the morn shall wake in gladness,
  And the moon the joy prolong,
Where the daylight dies in fragrance,
  'Mid the burst of holy song:
      Brother, we shall meet and rest
      'Mid the holy and the blest!

Where no shadow shall bewilder,
  Where life's vain parade is o'er,
Where the sleep of sin is broken,
  And the dreamer dreams no more:
Where the bond is never severed;—
  Partings, claspings, sob and moan,

Midnight waking, twilight weeping,
  Heavy noontide, all are done:
Where the child has found its mother,
  Where the mother finds the child,
Where dear families are gathered,
  That were scattered on the wild:
     Brother, we shall meet and rest
     'Mid the holy and the blest!

Where the hidden wound is healed,
  Where the blighted light re-blooms,
Where the smitten heart the freshness
  Of its buoyant youth resumes:
Where the love that here we lavish
  On the withering leaves of time,
Shall have fadeless flowers to fix on
  In an ever spring-bright clime:
Where we find the joy of loving,
  As we never loved before,—
Loving on unchilled, unhindered,
  Loving once and evermore:
     Brother, we shall meet and rest,
     'Mid the holy and the blest!

Where a blasted world shall brighten
  Underneath a bluer sphere,
And a softer, gentler sunshine
  Shed its healing splendor here:

Where earth's barren vales shall blossom,
  Putting on their robe of green,
And a purer, fairer Eden
  Be where only wastes have been:
Where a king in kingly glory,
  Such as earth has never known,
Shall assume the righteous sceptre,
  Claim and wear the holy crown:
      Brother, we shall meet and rest,
      'Mid the holy and the blest.

12

The Singing of Children.

Who shall sing, if not the children?
    Did not Jesus die for them?
May they not, with other jewels,
    Sparkle in his diadem?
Why to them were voices given—
    Bird-like voices, sweet and clear?
Why, unless the song of heaven
    They begin to practise here?

There's a choir of infant songsters,
    White-robed, round the Saviour's throne;
Angels to their music listen.
    Oh! 'tis sweeter than their own!
Faith can hear the rapturous choral,
    When her ear is upward turned;
Is not this the same, perfected,
    Which upon the earth they learned?

Jesus, when on earth sojourning,
    Loved them with a wondrous love;

And will he to heaven returning,
  Faithless to his blessing prove?
Oh! they cannot sing too early;
  Fathers, stand not in their way!
Birds sing while the day is breaking—
  Tell me, then, why should not they?

The Little Sleeper.

RICHARD C. TRENCH.

No mother's eye beside thee wakes to-night,
  No taper burns beside thy lonely bed,
Darkling thou liest, hidden out of sight,
  And none are near thee but the silent dead.

How cheerless glows this hearth, yet glows in vain,
  For we uncheered beside it sit alone,
And listen to the wild and beating rain
  In angry gusts against our casement blown.

And though we nothing speak, yet well I know
  That both our hearts are there, where thou dost keep
Within thy narrow chamber far below,
  For the first time unwatched, thy lonely sleep.

Oh no! not thou!—and we our faith deny,
  This thought allowing: thou, removed from harms,
In Abraham's bosom dost securely lie,
  Oh! not in Abraham's, in a Saviour's arms—

In that dear Lord's, who in thy worst distress,
  Thy bitterest anguish, gave thee, dearest child,

Still to abide in perfect gentleness,
   And like an angel to be meek and mild.

Sweet corn of wheat, committed to the ground
   To die, and live, and bear more precious ear,
While in the heart of earth the Saviour found
   His place of rest, for thee we will not fear.

Sleep softly, till that blessed rain and dew,
   Down lighting upon earth such change shall bring
That all its fields of death shall laugh anew—
   Yea, with a living harvest laugh and sing.

On the Death of a Son.

PAUL GERHARDT.

THOU'RT mine, yes, still thou art mine own!
  Who tells me thou art not?
But yet thou art not mine alone,
  I own that He who crossed
My hopes hath greatest right in thee;
Yea, though He ask and take from me
Thee, O my son, my heart's delight,
My wish, my thought, by day and night.

Ah might I wish, ah might I choose,
  Then thou, my star, should'st live,
And gladly for thy sake I'd lose
  All else that life can give.
Oh fain I'd say: Abide with me,
The sunshine of my house to be,
No other joy but this I crave,—
To love thee, darling, to my grave!

Thus saith my heart, and means it well,
  God meaneth better still;

My love is more than words can tell,
  His love is greater still;
I am a father, He the Head
And Crown of fathers, whence is shed
The life and love from which have sprung
All blessed ties in old and young.

I long for thee, my son, my own!
  And He who once hath given,
Will have thee now beside His throne,
  To live with him in Heaven.
I cry, alas! my light, my child!
But God hath welcome on him smiled,
And said, "*My* child, I keep thee near,
For there is naught but gladness here."

Oh blessed word, oh deep decree,
  More holy than we think!
With God no grief or woe can be,
  No bitter cup to drink,
No sickening hopes, no want or care,
No hurt can ever reach him there.
Yes, in that Father's sheltered home
I know that sorrow cannot come.

We pass our nights in wakeful thought
  For our dear children's sake;
All day our anxious toil hath sought
  How best for them to make

A future safe from care or need,
Yet seldom do our schemes succeed;
How seldom does their future prove
What we had planned for those we love!

How many a child of promise fair
  Ere now hath gone astray,
By ill example taught to dare
  Forsake Christ's holy way.
Oh fearful the reward is then,
The wrath of God, the scorn of men!
The bitterest tears that e'er are shed
Are his who mourns a child misled.

But now I need not fear for thee,
  Where thou art, all is well;
For where thy Father's face doth see,
  With Jesus thou dost dwell!
Yes, cloudless joys around him shine,
His heart shall never ache like mine;
He sees the radiant armies glow
That keep and guide us here below.

He hears their singing evermore,
  His little voice too sings,
He drinks of wisdom's deepest lore,
  He speaks of secret things
That we can never see or know,
Howe'er we seek or strive below,

While yet amid the mists we stand
That veil this dark and tearful land.

Oh that I could but watch afar,
  And hearken but a while
To that sweet song that hath no jar,
  And see his heavenly smile,
As he doth praise the holy God,
Who made him pure for that abode!
In tears of joy full well I know
This burdened heart would overflow.

And I should say: Stay here, my son,
  My wild laments are o'er,
Oh well for thee that thou hast won,
  I call thee back no more;
But come, thou fiery chariot, come,
And bear me swiftly to that home,
Where he with many a loved one dwells,
And evermore of gladness tells!

Then be it as my Father wills,
  I will not weep for thee;
Thou livest, joy thy spirit fills,
  Pure sunshine thou dost see,
The sunshine of eternal rest;
Abide, my child, where thou art blest;
I with my friends will onward fare,
And, when God will, shall find me there.

13

My Child.

JOHN PIERPONT.

I CANNOT make him dead!
His fair sunshiny head
Is ever bounding round my study chair;
    Yet, when my eyes, now dim
    With tears, I turn to him,
The vision vanishes—he is not there!

    I walk my parlour floor,
    And, through the open door,
I hear a foot-fall on the chamber-stair;
    I'm stepping toward the hall,
    To give the boy a call,
And then bethink me that—he is not there!

    I tread the crowded street;
    A satcheled lad I meet,
With the same beaming eyes and coloured hair;
    And as he's running by,
    Follow him with my eye,
Scarcely believing that—he is not there!

I know his face is hid
Under the coffin-lid:
Closed are his eyes, cold is his forehead fair;
My hand that marble felt;
O'er it in prayer I knelt;
Yet my heart whispers that—he is not there!

I cannot make him dead!
When passing by the bed
So long watched over with parental care,
My spirit and my eye
Seek it inquiringly,
Before the thought comes that—he is not there!

When at the cool gray break
Of day, from sleep I wake,
With my first breathing of the morning air,
My soul goes up with joy,
To Him who gave my boy,
Then comes the sad thought that—he is not there!

When at the day's calm close,
Before we seek repose,
I'm with his mother offering up our prayer,
Or evening anthems tuning,
In spirit I'm communing
With our boy's spirit, though—he is not there!

Not there!—Where, then, is he?
The form I used to see

Was but the raiment that he used to wear!
　　The grave, that now doth press
　　Upon that cast-off dress,
Is but his wardrobe locked: he is not there!

　　He lives!—in all the past
　　He lives; nor, to the last,
Of seeing him again will I despair.
　　In dreams I see him now,
　　And, on his angel-brow,
I see it written: "Thou shalt see me there!"

　　Yes, we all live to God!
　　Father, thy chastening rod
So help us, thine afflicted ones, to bear,
　　That in the spirit-land,
　　Meeting at thy right hand,
'Twill be our heaven to find that—Thou art there!

Are Infants Elected?

ASHBEL G. FAIRCHILD, D.D.*

IT is objected, that Election involves the doctrine of "infant damnation."

On the contrary it furnishes the only ground on which the salvation of infants can be consistently maintained; for if those who die in infancy are chosen to eternal life, then we have the strongest possible assurance of their final happiness. On the other hand, if, as some Anti-Calvinists argue, infants are not elect to salvation, they cannot be of that happy number which Christ will finally gather to his heavenly kingdom. Matt. xxiv. 31. These brethren, however, in their lively concern for our *orthodoxy*, complain of a passage in our Confession, ch. 10, sec 3, which says, "Elect infants dying in infancy are regenerated and saved by Christ, through the Spirit." From this they argue "that if some who die in infancy are elect, others who die in infancy are reprobate." But this is a gross error, founded upon a misapprehension of the scriptural application of the term "elect." This term, when used with reference to salvation, does not signify chosen out of a particular *age* or *class*, but out of

* From "*The Great Supper.*" Published by the Presbyterian Board of Publication.

the general mass of mankind. Thus, when John, addressing the
"elect lady," speaks of her "*elect sister,*" (2 John 13,) we are
not to conclude with our good brethren, that she must have had
also a *reprobate* sister, but that the sister was one of those who
were elect out of the fallen family of Adam. Also, when the
phrase " elect children of God" occurs in sermons or writings,
we do not understand it as implying that there are also *reprobate*
children of God. Accordingly, our Confession of Faith uni-
formly uses the word " elect" in its true scriptural sense, to
signify chosen out of the whole race of fallen men. When it
speaks of infants dying in infancy as *elect,* its obvious meaning
is, that they are elected out of the whole mass of human beings;
and this is perfectly consistent with the opinion that *all* who die
in infancy are chosen to salvation.

Let us now inquire whether the public standards of other denominations are more *orthodox* on this point than ours. The
Methodist Discipline, under the head of " ministration of
baptism to infants," directs the minister to pray that the infant
to be baptized, " may ever remain in the number of thy faithful
and elect children." Ch. 3, sec. 2. Of course if the infant be
in the number of the elect, it must itself be elect—an *elect infant.*
Here then is the doctrine of " infant election" in all its length
and breadth. I will add, what is not perhaps generally known to
the world, that the great founder of Methodism in his treatise on
Infant Baptism, published by the General Conference, boldly
avows the sentiment that infants cannot ordinarily be saved
without baptism. " If," says he, " infants are guilty of original
sin, then they are proper subjects of baptism; seeing, in the

ordinary way, they cannot be saved, unless this be washed away by baptism. It has already been proved," he adds, "that this original stain cleaves to every child of man; and that hereby they are children of wrath and liable to eternal damnation." *Doct. Tracts*, p. 251. Still further on, in summing up his argument, Mr. Wesley urges that "outward baptism is generally, in an ordinary way, necessary to salvation," and that "infants may be saved, as well as adults." He adds, "Nor ought we to neglect any means of saving them." P. 259. From this reasoning the inference is unavoidable that infants dying without baptism, *ordinarily* at least, suffer eternal damnation. The very thought of this is enough to make any one shudder! But it is not so much my object to convict our Methodist brethren of holding "infant damnation," as to show with what an ill grace charges of that kind are preferred against others, by members of their communion.

Our Cumberland brethren in their Confession of Faith, chap. 10, sec. 3, admit the salvation of infants; and yet in section 1, of the same chapter, limit the blessings of eternal life to "those whom God calls, and who obey the call, and *those only;*" from which number infants are necessarily excluded.* Nor do they recognize the election of infants; but on the contrary affirm that none are elect "in a saving sense," but those who are "enlightened in the knowledge of God," and have "spiritual wisdom to

* Old Arminian divines, as Episcopius, Curcellæus, and others, contended that infants in a future world, though saved from the pains of hell, would always remain in an infantine state, and thus be incapable of enjoying the blessedness of heaven. See Ridgely, vol. 2, pp. 139, 140.

discern and detect deceivers." *Confession of Faith*, ch. 3, *note*. May I not suggest, that as their own public standards leave this subject so much in the dark, they should be somewhat cautious in charging others with excluding infants from the blessedness of heaven?

Let me now ask the opponents of infant election, what they will do with those who die in infancy, if they are not the "elect of God?" Will they people the realms of glory with the *reprobate?* Will they have it that the Lord Jesus will gather the *non-elect* to his heavenly kingdom? Ah! this doctrine of infant election is a serious annoyance to our brethren. They can neither deny nor admit its truth, without involving themselves in inextricable difficulties. If they admit that they are chosen to salvation, then they must at once admit the doctrine of gratuitous, unconditional election, with all its tremendous consequences. For if infants are elect unto salvation, it cannot be pretended that they were elected on account of foreseen faith or works, or any other good thing in the creature. I say, if God has chosen them to life and glory, he must have chosen them " according to the counsel of his own will," and prompted by his own spontaneous mercy. Here, then, is a part of mankind, comprising at least one fourth of the species, dying in infancy, and all subjects of free, sovereign, gratuitous election ! Let us ask these brethren, Why does God take one infant to heaven, while as yet it is unstained with actual sin, and leave another to grow up in impenitence, to become polluted with crime, and sink at last under his fearful displeasure? What is this but sovereign, discriminating mercy, exerted to the utmost extent ever contended for by the most rigid Calvinist?   Let me repeat the question ; Why is one taken to glory in infancy, and another, born on the same day, spared to old age only to treasure up wrath against a day of wrath?   Truly our Anti-Calvinist brethren cannot admit this doctrine of the election of infants, without involving their whole scheme in absolute ruin.

Again : these brethren are compelled to admit that infants cannot be saved without regeneration.   But look for a moment at the consequences of such admission by Anti-Calvinists.   Ask them the question, What if an infant should die before regeneration?   "Oh," they will reply, "infants cannot die before they are regenerated."   Why, then, it follows that the unregenerated part of our species are immortal while in a state of infancy!   Let no one start at this, for it is the only ground on which these brethren can resist the damnation of infants,—the immortality of the unregenerate while they are infants!   The Calvinist easily avoids this appalling difficulty, since he holds that God has fore-ordained the salvation of infants, and consequently has ordained all the means necessary to its accomplishment.   Thus their election secures their regeneration.

I am aware that some individuals have long been labouring to produce the impression that our church teaches the doctrine of "infant damnation."   I say, *some individuals,* for I will not suppose that the great body of any Christian denomination are willing to countenance so wicked a slander.   It has often been proved, and is well understood by the intelligent part of the community, that the Presbyterians do not now and never did maintain that doctrine.   Nor, indeed, has there ever existed a

14

Calvinistic body who maintained it.*   Yet in opposition to the clearest evidence, these individuals either secretly or openly, by cowardly insinuation, or by confident assertion, labour to fix this stigma upon the members of our communion. No means are left untried to effect their object. So systematically and extensively has this sort of calumny been practised, in some parts of our country, that not a single Calvinistic minister can escape it by the most public and explicit disavowals. Certain individuals can be found who are willing to say they have heard him preach, "that there are infants in hell not a span long." Now, my friends, we must regard all this as an evidence of a persecuting spirit. As these men cannot wield the civil power against us, they will do what they can to punish us for holding doctrines which they cannot overthrow by fair and manly argument. God only knows the extent to which we might have to suffer for our religion, were it not for the protection of the laws! For if men will propagate the most wilful and deliberate untruths against us, as they certainly do, for no other offence than an honest difference of religious belief, what would they not do, if their power were equal to their wickedness? Presbyterians, however, can look beyond the agency of evil men, to the Supreme Disposer of all events, and say with David, when Shimei cursed and cast stones at him, "Let them alone, for the Lord hath bidden them."

* More than two centuries ago, when the Calvinists were accused by their Arminian opponents of holding "that infants are torn away from the breasts of their mothers, and tyrannically precipitated into hell," the charge was indignantly repelled by the Synod of Dort. See the conclusion of their *Articles.*

The Election of Infants.[*]

CUTHBERT.

It is alleged that God, in delivering fallen men from sin and condemnation, proceeds on the principle of selection—that, irrespective of character, or desert, or external circumstances, he chooses some and passes by others—that his choice is represented as embracing, not all without exception comprehended in any particular class, but individuals belonging to every class—and, that those who die in infancy, being a distinct and immensely numerous section of the human family, God deals with them as he does with the different communities and nations of the earth : " he has mercy on whom he will have mercy."

Admitting that God does proceed on the principle of selection, in framing and carrying into effect the scheme of redemption, those who die in infancy cannot, in the proper sense of the term, be considered a distinct class. They are taken from the entire human race, and belong to " every kindred, and tongue, and people, and nation." And I should imagine that Divine sovereignty is as really exercised in fixing upon the families, and the individual or individuals, in each of these families, who are to be removed from this world by death, and conveyed to the

* From " Light on Little Graves."

mansions of glory in early childhood, as it is in calling to the faith and hope of the gospel those who are ordained to eternal life, from the mighty mass of accountable agents dead in trespasses and sins. The principle of selection is not less strikingly apparent in the one case than it is in the other. And since that principle is neither infringed nor set aside, why not rather suppose—especially, as the spirit of the mediatorial economy, and the rule which will be acted upon by the Supreme Judge at the last day, in determining the state of the subjects of his moral government, alike point to the conclusion—that children, who die in infancy, are comprehended in "the election of grace;" and that they are, without exception, included in God's eternal purpose to save?

This view of the subject, whilst it is in perfect harmony with all that we know of the Divine character, and the principles of the Divine government, commends itself to our hearts. It is fitted to produce, in our minds, elevated conceptions of the worth of the Saviour's sacrifice, and adoring wonder at the results which flow from it. It invests, with thrilling interest, the statements of Scripture, relating to the number of the redeemed from among men, and imparts to them peculiar significancy and force. And whilst each one in the vast multitude before the celestial throne gratefully recounts his obligations to sovereign grace, and celebrates the glories of redeeming love, none, perhaps, express their rapturous emotions in louder strains than those who find themselves amid the felicities of heaven, almost immediately after they are ushered into being.

Glorified Children.

Sure, to the mansions of the blest
    When infant innocence ascends,
Some angel, brighter than the rest,
    The spotless spirit's flight attends.
On wings of ecstasy they rise,
    Beyond where worlds material roll,
Till some fair sister of the skies
    Receives the unpolluted soul.

That inextinguishable beam,
    With dust united at our birth,
Sheds a more dim, discoloured gleam,
    The more it lingers upon earth.
Closed in this dark abode of clay,
    The stream of glory faintly burns :—
Not unobserved, the lucid ray
    To its own native fount returns.

But when the Lord of mortal breath
    Decrees his bounty to resume,
And points the silent shaft of death
    Which speeds an infant to the tomb—

No passion fierce, nor low desire,
   Has quenched the radiance of the flame;
Back to its GOD the living fire
   Reverts, unclouded as it came.

Fond mourner! be that solace thine!
   Let Hope her healing charm impart,
And soothe, with melodies divine,
   The anguish of a mother's heart.
Oh, think! the darlings of thy love,
   Divested of this earthly clod,
Amid unnumbered saints above
   Bask in the bosom of their GOD.

Of their short pilgrimage on earth
   Still tender images remain:
Still, still they bless thee for their birth,
   Still filial gratitude retain.
Each anxious care, each rending sigh,
   That wrung for them the parent's breast,
Dwells on remembrance in the sky,
   Amid the raptures of the blest.

O'er thee, with looks of love, they bend;
   For thee the LORD of life implore:
And oft from sainted bliss descend,
   Thy wounded quiet to restore.
Oft in the stillness of the night,
   They smooth the pillow of thy bed,

Oft till the morn's returning light
   Still watchful hover o'er thy head.

Hark! in such strains as saints employ,
   They whisper to thy bosom peace;
Calm the perturbed heart to joy,
   And bid the streaming sorrow cease.
Then dry, henceforth, the bitter tear:
   Their part and thine inverted see,
Thou wert their guardian angel here,
   They guardian angels now to thee!

Weep not for the Dead.

MARY E. BROOKS.

Oh, weep not for the dead!
Rather, oh rather give the tear
To those that darkly linger here,
   When all besides are fled.
Weep for the spirit withering
In its cold cheerless sorrowing,
Weep for the young and lovely one
That ruin darkly revels on;
      But never be a tear-drop shed
      For them, the pure enfranchised dead.

      Oh, weep not for the dead!
No more for them the blighting chill,
The thousand shades of earthly ill,
   The thousand thorns we tread;
Weep for the life-charm early flown,
The spirit broken, bleeding lone;
Weep for the death-pangs of the heart,
Ere being from the bosom part;
      But never be a tear-drop given
      To those that rest in yon blue heaven.

Happy are They.

JAMES MONTGOMERY.*

" HAPPY, thrice happy were they thus to die,
Rather than grow into such men and women,
—Such fiends incarnate as that felon-sire,
Who dug its grave before his child was born;
Such miserable wretches as that mother,
Whose tender mercies were so deadly cruel!

I saw their infant's spirit rise to heaven,
Caught from its birth up to the throne of God;
There, thousands and ten thousands, I beheld,
Of innocents like this, that died untimely,
By violence of their unnatural kin,
Or by the mercy of that gracious power,
Who gave them being, taking what he gave
Ere they could sin or suffer like their parents.
I saw them in white raiment crowned with flowers,
On the fair banks of that resplendent river,
Whose streams make glad the city of our God;
—Water of life, as clear as crystal swelling

* From " Pelican Island," canto vii., where he describes a heathen parent sacrificing her child.

Forth from the throne itself, and visiting
Fields of a Paradise that ne'er was lost;
Where yet the tree of life immortal grows,
And bears its monthly fruits, twelve kinds of fruit,
Each in its season, food of saints and angels;
Whose leaves are for the healing of the nations.
Beneath the shadow of its blessed boughs,
I marked those rescued infants, in their schools,
By spirits of just men made perfect, taught
The glorious lessons of Almighty Love,
Which brought them thither in the readiest path
From the world's wilderness of dire temptations
Securing thus their everlasting weal.

Yea, in the rapture of that hour, though songs
Of cherubim to golden lyres and trumpets,
And the redeemed upon the sea of glass,
With voices like the sound of many waters
Came on mine ear, whose secret cells were opened
To entertain celestial harmonies,
—The small sweet accents of those little children,
Pouring out all the gladness of their souls
In love, joy, gratitude, and praises to Him,
—Him, who had loved and washed them in his blood;
These were to me the most transporting strains,
Amidst the hallelujahs of all heaven.—
Though lost a while in that amazing chorus
Around the throne,—at happy intervals,

The shrill hosannas of the infant choir,
Singing in that eternal temple, brought
Tears to mine eye, whilst seraphs had been glad
To weep, could they have felt the sympathy
That melted all my soul, when I beheld
How condescending Deity thus designed,
Out of the mouths of babes and sucklings here,
To perfect his high praises;—the harp of heaven
Had lacked its least but not its meanest string,
Had children not been taught to play upon it,
And sing, from feelings all their own, what men
Nor angels can conceive of creatures, born
Under the curse, yet from the curse redeemed,
And placed at once beyond the power to fall,
—Safety which men nor angels ever knew,
Till ranks of these, and all of those had fallen.

The Death of an Infant.

In heart divided, and in spirit rent,
Who could forbid a mother to lament?
Death! thou dread looser of the dearest tie,
Was there no aged and no sick one nigh?
No languid wretch who longed, but longed in vain,
For thy cold hand to cool his fiery pain?
And was the only victim thou couldst find,
An infant on its mother's arms reclined?
But 'tis thy way to pass the ripest by,
And cause the flowers and buds of life to die;
Full many a flower is scattered by the breeze,
And many a blossom shaken from the trees,
And many a morning beam in tempest flies,
And many a dew-drop shines a while and dies:
But oftener far, the dream that fancy weaves,
Of future joy and happiness, deceives.
And thou pale mourner, o'er an infant's bier,
Brighten thy cheek, and dry the trickling tear;
This came, though veiled in darkness, from above,
A dispensation of eternal love!

He who perceived the dangerous control,
The heart-twined spell was gaining on thy soul,
Snatched from thine arms the treacherous decoy,
To give thee brighter hope and purer joy.
Oh! see how soon the flowers of life decay,
How soon terrestrial pleasures fade away.
This star of comfort, for a moment given,
Just rose on earth, then set to rise in heaven.
Yet mourn not, as of hope bereft, its doom,
Nor water with thy tears its early tomb;
Redeemed by God from sin, released from pain,
Its life were punishment, its death were gain.
Turn back thine eye along the path of life,
View thine own grief, and weariness and strife:
And say, if that which tempts thee to repine,
Be not a happier lot by far than thine.
If death in infancy had laid thee low,
Thou hadst escaped from pain, and sin, and woe;
The years thy soul the path of sorrow trod,
Had all been spent in converse with thy God;
And thou hadst shone in yonder cloudless sphere,
A seraph there, and not a pilgrim here.
O! it is sweet to die,—to part from earth,—
And win all heaven for things of little worth;
Then sure thou wouldst not, though thou couldst awake .
The little slumberer, for its mother's sake.
It is when those we love, in death depart,
That earth has slightest hold upon the heart.

Hath not bereavement higher wishes taught,
And purified from earth, thine earth-born thought?
I know it hath. Hope then appears more dear,
And heaven's bright realms shine brightest through a tear.
Though it be hard to bid thy heart divide,
And lay the gem of all thy love aside—
Faith tells thee, and it tells thee not in vain,
That thou shalt meet thine infant yet again.
On seraph wings the new-born spirit flies
To brighter regions and serener skies;
And, ere thou art aware, the day may be
When to those skies thy babe shall welcome thee.

While yet on earth, thine ever-circling arms
Held it securest from surrounding harms;
Yet even there, disease could aim her dart,
Chill the warm cheek, and stop the fluttering heart.
And many a fruitless tear-drop thou hast paid,
To view the sickness that thou couldst not aid.
No ill can reach it now, it rests above,
Safe in the bosom of celestial love:
Its short but yet tempestuous way is o'er,
And tears shall trickle down its cheek no more.
Then far be grief! Faith looks beyond the tomb,
And heaven's bright portals sparkle through the gloom.
If bitter thoughts and tears in heaven could be,
It is thine infant that should weep for thee.

On the Death of my Son.*

RICHARD HUIE, M.D.

My little one, my fair one, are then thy troubles o'er,
And has thy slight and feeble bark arrived at Canaan's shore?
Hast thou at length a haven reached, where thou canst anchor
    fast,
And heed no more the pelting storm, the billow or the blast?

My little one, my fair one, though brief thy course has been,
Few days of sunshine cheered thee on, few smiling coasts were
    seen;
It seemed as o'er thy shallop frail the raven flapped his wing,
And scared the bright and halcyon tribes, which might thine
    advent sing.

My little one, my fair one, thy couch is empty now,
Where oft I wiped the dews away, which gathered on thy brow;
No more amidst the sleepless night I smooth thy pillow fair,
'Tis smooth indeed, but rest no more thy small pale features
    there.

My little one, my fair one, thy tiny carriage waits,
But waits in vain to bear thy form through yon inviting
    gates;

* From "Sacred Lyrics."

Where bloom the flowers as erst they did, when thou couldst
    cull their sweets,
But roams in vain thy father's eye, no answering glance it
    meets.

My little one, my fair one, thy lips were early trained
To lisp that gracious Saviour's name, who all thy guilt sus-
    tained:
Nor would I weep because my Lord has snatched my gourd
    away,
To blossom bright, and ripen fair, in realms of endless day.

My little one, my fair one, thou canst not come to me,
But nearer draws the numbered hour, when I shall go to thee,
And thou, perchance, with seraph smile, and golden harp in
    hand,
May'st come the first to welcome me, to our Emmanuel's land!

The Infant's Miniature.

Yes! thou art here, my sainted babe!
  Thy lustrous eyes of blue—
The long dark fringe which o'er them sleep,
  As silken curtains drew—
The full red lip, the dimpled cheek,
  The polished lofty brow—
The matchless smile that lighted all—
  They're here before me now.

Yet years, long years, have passed away,
  Since I, a mother blest,
And thou, a babe too fair for earth,
  Didst nestle to this breast.
Thy rosy dreams were not more sweet
  Than were the moments then;
But all their joys are numbered now
  With pleasures that *have been*.

The most that I retain of thee
  Is one small sunny curl;
A treasure I would not exchange
  For ocean's rarest pearl;
Though this bright picture, true to life,
  Recalls thy infant charms

So vividly, I seem again
  To clasp thee in my arms.

'Tis beautiful to look upon—
  But only doth portray
The casket, which a jewel held
  That God hath borne away;
For shining in his dazzling crown,
  Is many an infant gem,
And he required this precious one
  To deck that diadem.

And oh! to paint a cherub SOUL,
  In vain the artist tries!
For *this*, his pencil must be dipped
  In azure of the skies;
Borrow the rainbow's hue, and make
  The glittering stars its own;
For angel beauty never yet
  In earthly colours shone.

So let me think of thee, my babe!
  As when thou wert of earth;
And, like this picture, radiant with
  The smiles of infant mirth,
Forget the dismal hour when God
  Recalled what he had given,
And hope to see thee as thou art,
  And claim thee still in heaven!

A Child's Death.

R. B. SHERIDAN.

In some rude spot where vulgar herbage grows,
  If chance a violet rear its purple head,
The careful gardener moves it ere it blows,
  To thrive and flourish in a nobler bed;
    Such was thy fate, dear child,
      Thy opening such!
Pre-eminence in early bloom was shown;
  For earth, too good, perhaps;
    And loved too much—
Heaven saw, and early marked thee for its own.

Death of an Infant.

MRS. L. H. SIGOURNEY.

DEATH found strange beauty on that polished brow,
And dashed it out.—

         There was a tint of rose
On cheek and lip.—He touched the veins with ice,
And the rose faded.—

         Forth from those blue eyes
There spake a wishful tenderness, a doubt
Whether to grieve or sleep, which innocence
Alone may wear. With ruthless haste he bound
The silken fringes of those curtaining lids
For ever.—

         There had been a murmuring sound,
With which the babe would claim its mother's ear,
Charming her even to tears. The spoiler set
His seal of silence.—

         But there beamed a smile
So fixed, so holy, from that cherub brow,
Death gazed—and left it there.

         He dared not steal
The signet ring of Heaven.

Baby's Shoes.

WM. C. BENNETT.

OH! those little, those little blue shoes!
Those shoes that no little feet use;
    Oh! the price were high
    That those shoes would buy,
Those little blue unused shoes!

For they hold the small shape of feet
That no more their mother's eyes meet;
    That by God's good will,
    Years since grew still,
And ceased from their totter so sweet.

And oh! since that baby slept,
So hushed, how the mother has kept,
    With a tearful pleasure,
    That little dear treasure,
And over them thought and wept!

For they mind her for evermore
Of a patter along the floor;

And blue eyes she sees
Look up from her knees,
With the look that in life they wore.

As they lie before her there,
There babbles from chair to chair
A little sweet face
That's a gleam in the place,
With its little gold curls of hair.

Then, oh! wonder not that her heart
From all else would rather part
Than those tiny blue shoes
That no little feet use,
And whose sight makes such fond tears start.

Low she Lies.

MRS. NORTON.

Low she lies, who blest our eyes
   Through many a sunny day;
She may not smile, she will not rise,—
   The life has past away!
Yet there is a world of light beyond,
   Where we neither die nor sleep;
She is there, of whom our souls were fond,
   Then, wherefore do we weep?

The heart is cold, whose thoughts were told
   In each glance of her glad bright eye;
And she lies pale, who was so bright,
   She scarce seemed made to die.
Yet we know that her soul is happy now,
   Where the saints their calm watch keep;
That angels are crowning that fair young brow,
   Then, wherefore do we weep?

Her laughing voice made all rejoice,
   Who caught the happy sound;

There was gladness in her very step,
　As it lightly touched the ground.
The echoes of voice and step are gone,
　There is silence still and deep;
Yet we know that she sings by God's bright throne,
　Then, wherefore do we weep?

The cheek's pale tinge, the lid's dark fringe,
　That lies like a shadow there,
Were beautiful in the eyes of all,
　And her glossy golden hair!
But though that lid may never wake
　From its dark and dreamless sleep;
She is gone where young hearts do not break,
　Then, wherefore do we weep?

That world of light with joy is bright,
　This is a world of woe;
Shall we grieve that her soul has taken flight
　Because we dwell below?
We will bury her under the mossy sod,
　And one long bright tress we'll keep;
We have only given her back to God,
　Then, wherefore do we weep?

Favour of God in Christ to Little Children.[*]

GEORGE W. BETHUNE, D.D.

THE great truth of the Gospel is, that God delights to save, of which he has given the strongest possible assurance in the mission of his only begotten Son (John iii. 16.) He has commanded his gospel to be preached throughout the world, and so worded his invitations as to show, that whosoever will, may come and take of the waters of life freely (Rev. xxii. 17.) Therefore, though he had given no tokens of regard for those, who, because of their tender age, cannot come unto him, nor put forth their hands to receive his grace ; the silence itself, connected with the gracious spirit of what he has revealed, would warrant us in believing that not one of the little ones should perish. But he is not silent respecting them, nor has he refused them tokens of his special regard, as may be shown abundantly from his Holy Scriptures.

The favour of God in Christ toward little children, confirms this doctrine.

This favour appears in the very first promise of mercy, for it

---

[*] From "Early Lost, Early Saved," an excellent little volume published by the Board of Publication of the Reformed Dutch Church, New York.

was by the seed of the woman that God declared the head of the
serpent should be bruised (Gen. iii. 15.)   When, therefore, our
first mother embraced her first-born, she saw proof of the coming
salvation in her babe, and exclaimed: " I have gotten a man
from the Lord " (Gen. iv. 1.)   So, throughout subsequent ages,
believers under the Old Testament looked upon their offspring
as peculiarly precious, because proofs of Divine faithfulness.
Farther to consecrate and encourage this sentiment, God appointed
in the family of Abraham the rite of circumcision, by which the
parent manifested his faith that God was the God of his child.
It was not possible for them to believe the promise of a future
Redeemer, without seeing that their babes were included by its
blessings.   The child, if he lived to grow up, might cut himself
off from the covenant by his own sin (Ex. xii. 15 ; xxxi. 14 ;)
the first-born of woman became the murder-cursed Cain ; but
the babe, as a babe, was from his birth an object of the Divine
favour and compassion.

Nor was this regard confined to the children of God's believing people; though, for obvious reasons, their privileges were
greater.   Among the grounds of condemnation, which, by his
prophet, he denounces against the worshippers of Baal, not the
least is, that they had shed the blood of many " innocents " (Jer.
xix. 4 ;)* alluding, doubtless, as the fifth verse shows, to the cruel
custom of sacrificing young children in honour of the demon.
It was an aggravation of the crime that these children were
descendants of the covenanted fathers, from whose faith their

---

* Compare Ezekiel xvi. 17, "*my* children."

more immediate parents had apostatized; yet the prophet does not speak of them in that character, but as "innocents," and, therefore, because of their helpless innocency, peculiarly objects of the Divine care.*

Another remarkable passage, often cited by advocates of our doctrine, occurs in the book of Jonah (iv. 10, 11,) where God, answering with rebuke the unmerciful complaint of the disappointed prophet, says: "Should I not spare Nineveh, that great city, wherein are more than six-score thousand persons that cannot discern between their right hand and their left?" by which is meant infants. What we are particularly to remark, in these two citations, is the reason which God assigns for his tender concern respecting " little ones ;" their personal innocence, their incapacity of actual moral wrong. Their adult fathers were guilty on their own account, and he might with justice have destroyed them ; but the little ones who " could not discern between their right hand and their left," the " innocent," were regarded by him with affectionate compassion.

Now, asks an excellent writer, commenting on the 19th of Jeremiah : " Can it be supposed that he, who undertook, in such tremendous language, to avenge their temporal injuries, was at the same time intending to destroy them for ever ; that he left those murdered babes an eternal prey to devils, in whose obscure and sanguinary orgies. their innocent blood had been

---

* The author here adopts the opinion of some very able commentators; but he is aware that others refer the " innocent blood" also to the martyrdom of prophets and other just persons. Still, the sacrificed children are included, and the inference is strengthened by the babes being put in the same category with holy men.

shed ?"*   And again he says, in the 4th of Jonah, "Of the six-score thousand Ninevite children, about sixty thousand were probably removed from life while they knew not their right hand from their left.   It seems incredible, that after these expressions of regard, such infants, dying without having forfeited this tender concern by personal transgression, should be excluded from the presence of God for ever."

Some may think that the force of these passages is neutralized by others, where God commanded little ones to be slain with their idolatrous parents, as in the case of the Midianites (Numbers xxxi. 17 ;) but we have nowhere denied (what, indeed, every hour's observation should convince us of,) that children may be involved by the temporal consequences of their parents' crimes, as those of Nineveh would have been if the repentance of the city had not turned away the Divine vengeance, and as the little ones of idolatrous Israel were when sacrificed unto Baal.   God in ancient times, as now, punished national sins with national calamities ; and, when his decree went forth to destroy a nation by the sword, the children were not spared any more than they are from a pestilence or earthquake.   Besides, his providence towards Israel was peculiar.   His design was, for wise reasons, to keep them in the land of Canaan as a separate people, their Abrahamic lineage pure, and their Divine religion uncorrupt. Therefore, he cleared the land of those idolatrous nations which had possessed it, and provoked him to anger.   Had any number, particularly of the males, been permitted to survive, there must

* Rev. Dr. Harris' "Grounds of Hope for the Salvation of all Dying in Infancy." London, 1821.

have been constant insurrections, a depravation of their blood, and a tendency to idolatry. Severe as the measure was, and far from justifying imitation by men, it was as necessary to the conservation of Israel as it was deserved by the Canaanite tribes. It is, however, by no means a proof that God pursued the little ones of his enemies with vengeance in another world. They passed from under the sword of Moses, punishing their nation for the capital crime of idolatry, before that judgment-seat where every soul is tried by its own acts. If our doctrine be true, we see the light of saving mercy shed over the darkest and bloodiest pages of temporal providence.

With the fulness of time, the light of hope for the dying infant, which before was glimmering, became clear and bright.

Among the characteristics of Christianity, not the least remarkable and beautiful, is its tender favour towards little children.

The great Forerunner of our Lord came not in the strength of a full-grown man. The first intimation, that the kingdom of God was nigh at hand, was given in the promise of a little child: " Fear not, Zacharias, for thy prayer is heard ; and thy wife Elizabeth shall bear thee a son, and thou shalt call his name John. And thou shalt have joy and gladness, and many shall rejoice at his *birth*. And he shall be great in the sight of the Lord, and shall drink neither wine nor strong drink; and he shall be filled with the Holy Ghost, *even from his mother's womb*" (Luke i. 13, 14, 15.) So, when the promise was fulfilled, and the happy father held his son in his arms, he prophesied over him with gladness, and said, " Thou, *child*, shalt be called the prophet of the Highest!" (Luke i. 67–80.) The Harbinger of the gospel was *a sanctified little child.*

Then, when to the humble shepherds in the fields, keeping watch over their flock by night, the angel of the Lord came, and the glory of the Lord shone round about them, what was his announcement of good tidings of great joy, which should be to all people? "Unto you *is born* this day, in the city of David, *a Saviour*, which is Christ the Lord. And this shall be a sign unto you, Ye shall find THE BABE wrapped in swaddling clothes, lying in a manger" (Luke ii. 8, 12.) They ran with haste unto Bethlehem, and there they found the blessed Virgin Mother gazing upon her mysterious CHILD, already named by the Holy Ghost, JESUS, the Saviour; EMMANUEL, God with us.

Wise men from the east, moved by traditions of ancient prophecy, the appearance of the star of which Balaam had spoken (Num. xxiv. 17,) and, doubtless, by inspiration from on high, came with princely gifts to worship Him that was *born King of the Jews;* and lo! the star which they had seen in the east went before them till it came and stood near where THE YOUNG CHILD lay; and when they saw the star they rejoiced with exceeding great joy. And when they were come into the house, they saw THE YOUNG CHILD, with Mary, his mother, and fell down and *worshipped* HIM (Matt. ii. 1–11.)

Can any one read these passages, without perceiving that our Divine Lord was a Saviour worthy of all adoration and trust from his very birth? It was, indeed, necessary for him to be born of a woman, that he might be truly man; and having been born, to pass through the years which intervene before the full age, when, agreeably to Jewish rule, he might assume his office publicly. We see, also, in his feeble beginning, a parable of his cause, which, though apparently weak and of little worldly account at first, is destined to attain the highest glory. These, however, were not all the reasons why he came as a little child, yet a Saviour, passed through all the weaknesses, sorrows, and trials of infancy, being tried in all points as little ones are; and rewarded the care of his pious mother with child-like, affectionate observance. It was to teach us that he is the Saviour of little children, who bear his likeness more closely than the best disciple of mature years ever can, as well as of the adults who believe in his name. It was to claim the whole world of infancy as his own, however men might reject his grace. It was to assure the anxious mother bending over his image in her child, that

> " She may trust her sweet babe through the hour of danger,
> To the mercy of Him, who was laid in a manger."

Nor did the " HOLY CHILD JESUS " wait long for an opportunity of saving his little fellows. The cruel Herod, fearful of losing his throne because the true King of the Jews was born, " sent forth and slew all the children that were in Bethlehem, and in all the coasts thereof, from two years old and under" (Matt. ii. 16 ;) and, though the one he sought was carried beyond his malice, hundreds (or as some think, thousands) of babes and sucklings yielded their young lives to a persecution of the infant Saviour. On earth, " in Rama was there a voice heard, lamentation and weeping, and a great mourning; Rachel weeping for her children and refusing to be comforted, because they were not" (Luke ii. 18 ;) but in heaven there was great joy, as tne happy angels bore on rejoicing wings to their Father's house the young redeemed, a numerous proof that Jesus had entered his kingdom and claimed little children for his own. The rage o1 Herod against the infant King, but sent the little ones to shout, among the blessed, His praises,

> " Who brought them there,
> Without a wish, without a care."

Dear Matthew Henry, here sweetly though quaintly says: "A passive testimony was given hereby to the Lord Jesus, as when he was in the womb he was witnessed to by· a little child leaping in the womb for joy at his approach ; so now, at two years old, he had contemporary witnesses to him of the same age. They shed their blood for him, who afterwards shed his blood for them. These were the *infantry* of the noble army of martyrs. If these infants were thus baptized with blood, though it were their own, into the church triumphant, it could not be said but that, with what they got in heaven, they were abundantly recompensed for all they lost on earth. 'Out of the mouth of these babes and sucklings God did perfect praise, otherwise it is not good to the Almighty that he should thus afflict.'" Good Jeremy Taylor speaks to the same import: "Jesus, when himself was safe, might have secured these poor babes of Bethlehem, with thousands of diversions or avocations of Herod's purposes, or by discovering in some safe manner, not unknown to the Divine wisdom, his own escape; but it did not so please God. He is Lord of his own creatures, and hath an absolute dominion over our lives, and he had an end to serve upon these babes, and an end of justice upon Herod; and to the children he made such compensation, that they had no reason to complain that they were so soon made stars, when they shone in their little orbs and participations of eternity; for so the sense of the church has been, that they having died the death of martyrs, though incapable of making the choice, God supplied the defects of their will by his own entertainment of the thing."*

These auguries and promises of favour to little children, in our blessed Lord's birth and nursing age, are most sweetly and richly confirmed by many passages and occasions of his riper ministry. Our beloved Master took peculiar pleasure in manifesting his tender love for little ones, and showed peculiar displeasure at those who doubted his willingness to receive them.

There are two remarkable instances of this preserved by the Evangelists; the one by Matthew xviii. 1–14, by Mark ix. 35–37, by Luke ix. 46–48; the other by Matthew xix. 13, 14, by Mark x. 14, and by Luke xviii. 15–17. We shall examine this last first, as the former presents us with additional matter for consideration.

Matt. xix. 13, 14. "Then were brought unto him little children, that he should put his hands on them and pray (that he should touch them, Mark and Luke.) And the disciples rebuked them (those that brought them, Mark,) and when Jesus saw it, he was much displeased. But Jesus said, Suffer (the) little children (to come unto me, Mark and Luke,) and forbid them not to

* "They were too young to fight, but not too young to be crowned with victory."
—*Cyprian.*

18

come unto me, for of such is the kingdom of heaven (*God*, Mark, and Luke.) (Verily, I say unto you, whosoever shall not receive the kingdom of God as a little child, he shall not enter therein, Mark.) And he laid his hands on them (and he took them up in his arms, put his hands upon them, Mark) and blessed them."

Who they were, that brought these little ones to Jesus, we are not told; most likely it was their parents, perhaps, some benevolent lovers of children, who had faith in his blessing, yes, even in his touch. They were very little children, for Luke uses the same word, which is applied to the Babe in the manger. " Christ," says Matthew Henry in his Sermon on Mark x. 16, " came to teach, to heal, and to bless. These little children were not brought to him to be taught, for they were too young; nor to be healed, for we are not told that they were sick ; but to be blessed, as his laying on them his hands signified." Now mark not only the tenderness of Jesus, but the reason he assigns for it. He takes them up in his arms ; he lays their little heads in his holy bosom ; he blesses them with Divine authority. He does so the more emphatically, to rebuke those who would have kept them from him. The Master himself, the Head of the Church, the perfect Example of the Church, clasps little children gladly to his heart. For what reason ? Because of a tenderness, natural in so loving a spirit as his, toward helpless, smiling babes ? That might well be. Or, that he might recommend little children to the care of his disciples ? This was certainly true. But the main reason he gives himself: " Of such is the kingdom of God." What can this mean, for our Lord was not wont to speak ambiguously when instructing his disciples, but that which the words express plainly. "Of such is the kingdom of God," or, little children, as such, belong to God's kingdom by his gracious determination. If they should grow to years of personal responsibility, their circumstances would be different, and personal faith would be necessary for their salvation; because then they would be no longer, except they were regenerate, such as his kingdom is made up of. But, if such as were of his kingdom died before they sinned by rejecting his grace, could they be rejected by him, and sent away to the kingdom of Satan?

We are not to be turned from this ground, by the question, How can they, who are once of the kingdom of heaven, in after years lose their part of it? We take the words of our Lord as we find them, nor shall any theological dilemma stumble us into unbelief of them. God can reconcile difficulties which we cannot.

We, however, can see no difficulty here. The Master does not speak of any particular child or children, but of the character and state in which all infants are. While they remain in that state and retain that character, they are of the kingdom of God; when they pass from the one or lose the other, they are beyond the condition which is covered by the mercy of Christ. If any of those little ones live to bring condemnation on their souls by obstinate impenitence, it is clear that they never belonged to the elect of grace; but, if any die before such personal sin, it is equally clear that they are safe, because our Lord says, "Of such is the kingdom of God." He is speaking of them in the circumstances of little children, not as possible adults; just as

God, under the Old Testament, promised blessing to the children of circumcision, thousands of whom, in riper years, lost the advantage of the covenant; though we doubt not that every one of them dying as infants were admitted to glory. When God determines the salvation of a soul, he also determines the means of its preparation for heaven; and we know nothing of his particular purposes but by their results in personal character. The dying infant has the character to which heaven is promised.

It may be said in reply, that the Saviour is speaking of the character, which his disciples should cultivate, if they would enter the kingdom of heaven; not of the little children themselves. We admit the first; we deny the second. Little children are set before us as types, examples of that temper to which only the kingdom of God is promised; but what right has any one to say, that the Master did not mean the little children themselves, when he directly points to them? Besides, if it be true that all, who become as little children, are saved, is not the inference irresistible, that those, whom they become like, are saved also, when they go as little children before God? Why this painful logic to shut out from heaven those who die in the very arms of Christ? We should tremble to adopt it, lest we should come under the rebuke of those who would have forbidden his little ones to come unto him. We can understand caution in so rendering Scriptures, that we give no encouragement to those who wilfully are impenitent; but what mischief can result from a belief, that He, who when on earth blessed little children, blesses them eternally when as little children they go to him in heaven? Let us rather, my reader, rejoice in a faith which gives to the Almighty, just and most merciful Saviour, the glory of so vast a salvation.

The other passage of which we spoke, occurs in Matthew 18th, from the first to the end of the fourteenth verse: "At the same time came the disciples unto Jesus, saying, Who·is the greatest in the kingdom of heaven? And Jesus called a little child unto him, and set him in the midst of them; and said, Verily, I say unto you, Except ye be converted and become as little children, ye shall not enter into the kingdom of heaven. Whosoever, therefore, shall humble himself as this little child, the same is greatest in the kingdom of heaven. And whoso shall receive one such little child in my name, receiveth me. But whoso shall offend one of these little ones, which believe in me, it were better for him that a millstone were hanged about his neck, and that he were drowned in the depth of the sea. . . . . Take heed that ye despise not one of these little ones, for I say unto you, that in heaven their angels do alway behold the face of my Father which is in heaven. For the Son of man is come to seek and to save that which was lost. How think ye? If a man have an hundred sheep, and one of them be gone astray, doth he not leave the ninety and nine and goeth into the mountains, and seeketh that which is gone astray? And if so be that he find it, verily I say unto you, he rejoiceth more of that sheep than of the ninety and nine that went not astray. Even so it is not the will of your Father which is in heaven, that one of these little ones should perish." (Compare Mark ix. 33 to the end, and Luke ix. 46—48.)

Our Lord here answers the question of the Twelve, Who is

the greatest in the kingdom of heaven? by showing them the character of a true Christian disciple, and the great regard he has for all those who bear such a character. To do this, he takes for his text a little child ; not any particular child, but the one upon whom his eye chanced to fall. He " calls " the little one to him ; from which, and the term in the original, we may suppose that it was a " child" able to walk, though " little." He sets him in the midst of the listening circle, and says : " Verily I say unto you, Except ye be converted and become as little children, ye shall not enter into the kingdom of heaven. Whosoever, therefore, shall humble himself as this little child, the same is greatest in the kingdom of heaven." Childhood is the emblem of Christianity. Child-likeness is Christian character ; and he who is most like a little child is greatest in his kingdom, the most advanced and honoured disciple, because his " conversion" from a contrary spirit is the most thorough.

Having stated the character which he most approves, he goes on to show his extreme regard for all who possess it : " Whoso shall receive one such little child in my name receiveth me." This verse applies equally to little children and child-like disciples. In the next he speaks of faith, which shows that he is now referring more particularly to the true disciple : " Whosoever shall offend one of these little ones, *which believe in me*, it were better that a millstone were hanged about his neck, and that he were drowned in the depths of the sea." Yet his regard for those, to whom he compares the docile, teachable, meek-minded believer, cannot be less than for the believer himself. He takes the believer's part, because the believer is like a little child. He gives several arguments, why all such little children and child-like believers should receive from us this kind and considerate treatment.

(1.) They are identified with himself. "Whoso receiveth one such little child in my name, receiveth me." They are united to him; he sympathizes with them; they are his own.

(2.) They are under the care of his angels. "Take heed, how ye despise one of these little ones; for in heaven their angels do always behold the face of my Father which is in heaven." Christ is the Lord of angels, Jehovah of Hosts; and he brings all his glorious retinue to serve him in his office of Saviour; as the author of the Epistle to the Hebrews says of the angels: "Are they not all ministering spirits sent forth to minister for them who shall be heirs of salvation?" (Heb. i. 14). In the Old Testament, angels were declared to be guardians of God's people (Ps. xci. 11, 12). Here our blessed Master confirms the truth. His angels are his people's angels, standing ready before God to be sent upon any mission that concerns the welfare of his little ones: little children and child-like believers. Some find here the doctrine of particular guardian angels; whether that be true or not we are unprepared to say; but, certainly, all Christ's people are under the guardianship of Christ's angels. There is not one of all the radiant winged spirits who do God's will in providence, that is not ready to be a servant of those whom Jesus numbers among his little ones.

(3.) They are peculiarly dear to him, as Saviour of the lost (11–13); which he illustrates by an instance of a good shepherd seeking after a lost one from his flock, and bringing it back with joy. So does he love his "little ones" for the very pains it cost him to win them from ruin; and they are recommended to our love by the greatness of his love towards them and us.

(4.) The gracious will of our heavenly Father concerning them (14th verse): "Even so it is not the will of your Father which is in heaven, that one of these little ones should perish." The heavenly Father delights in the salvation of his little ones; and, therefore, they should be precious in our sight. Their Father is our Father; and he who is willing to save us is willing to save them.   That child-like believers are included by the term "little ones," may be cheerfully admitted; but the reference is most direct to little children; for it is not "*such* little ones," but "*these* little ones." The Master is not speaking *of* the Twelve, but *to* them.   He is answering their question; and they are encouraged to trust in their heavenly Father's care, only so far as they were converted to be like little children.   If it be our heavenly Father's will, that none who are like little children should perish; how can it be, that little children, who are set before them as emblems of simplicity and innocence, patterns for imitation, standards of character, should perish?   It is difficult to understand, how any sincere reader can hesitate about such a plain inference.   The words of our Lord do not render their salvation certain, if they should come to years of intelligence.   He is speaking of little children, and of those like little children in character.   If the former should pass beyond the condition of little children, without possessing a child-like character, they would then be beyond the ground covered by this gracious text; but if they died as little children, in either sense, it is not the will of our heavenly Father that they should perish. They are within the promise and safe. Those whom the ever-merciful Jesus unites with himself; whom he commends in his name to the tenderness of his people; whom he commits to the guardianship of holy angels; and of whom it is the will of his Father, our Father and their Father, that not one should perish; must, dying in a state so fenced in, and made holy by his Saviour-sympathy, go to be among the blessed in that heaven, to the kingdom of which he has declared they belong, even while on earth.

These inferences are confirmed by our blessed Lord's rebuke to the chief priests and scribes, when they were sore displeased at the hosannas of the children in the temple (Matt. xxi. 15, 16): "Jesus said unto them, Yea, have ye never read: Out of the mouth of babes and sucklings, thou hast perfected praise?" This Scripture is taken from the second verse of the eighth Psalm, where we read: "Out of the mouth of babes and sucklings, hast thou ordained strength, because of thine enemies; that thou mightest still the enemy and the avenger." Whatever other meaning or reference these words of prophecy may have, the use which our Master makes of them, demonstrates an intention on the part of God, to derive even from babes and sucklings, a praise magnifying his grace by Jesus Christ over all the power, and arts, and cavils of his and our enemies. Out of the mouth of such little ones he can ordain strength; his gracious influences can reach their young hearts, and throughout eternity, their hosannas, which were so welcome to him in the temple on earth, shall swell his triumphs in the temple above. Neither the little

19

one, nor the suckling babe, shall be left in the power of the enemy. The strength of him, who came as a "tender plant" (Is. liii. 2), (or, as the Septuagint translates, a tender or sucking child,*) will redeem out of the power of the avenger, the world of infancy; their souls shall be his trophies of victory, and their immortal hosannas celebrate his complete conquest over him that had the power of death (Heb. ii. 14).

No, thou gentle, compassionate Saviour, who wert once the Babe of Bethlehem, and now upon thy throne, art worshipped as the Holy Child Jesus (Acts iv. 27), it is not thy will that any little one shall perish! The arms which were open to them on earth, will receive them in heaven. They shall lie there in that holy bosom, to which they were clasped here. Death is thy ministering angel, to bear them up to thee. Sweet, excelling heaven's ordinary praise, to thy ear must be the voices of their countless multitudes, as they bless thee in the song of the redeemed, thee once a Babe like them, and now their Elder Brother!

Dry your tears, bereaved parents, or turn them into floods of joy. The Voice that called them away, was his who said: They belong to my kingdom. The hand that took them from you, was his, who once laid his benediction on the infant's head. He has set them in the midst of his admiring disciples above. They are now the darling little ones of their heavenly Father's house. The angels, who watched over their cradle beds, are now rejoicing over their immortal beauty, as lambs safely folded where

---

* See Joseph Mede's Sermon on Psalm viii. 2.

the spoiler can never come. Heed them not, who would bid you doubt; point them to the recorded censure of the Master, displeased at so unmerciful an unbelief. "Of such is the kingdom of heaven." "Out of the mouth of" your "babe," Christ's "praise" is "perfected" in the temple on high!

The Hindoo Mother.

MRS. M. ST. LEON LOUD.

"Weepest thou, pale Hindoo mother,
  By the Ganges bending low?
Canst thou not thy feelings smother?—
  Brightly doth the river flow,
Where thy children calmly sleep,
Buried in its waters deep;
And above, the smiling skies
Look upon thy sacrifice."

"Tell me not of bright waves flowing,
  They but mock my bosom's care;
Tell me not of sunlight glowing—
  All within is dark despair;
For I've heard of one whose eye
Frowns upon me from the sky.
Where can help be found for me—
Christian! whither shall I flee?"

"To the cross! behold, the Saviour
  Dies to save thee, calls thee home!

Listen to these words of favour—
   'Come, ye heavy-laden, come!'
Hindoo mother, weep no more!
Lo! to this benighted shore
Jesus' heralds gladly fly,
To proclaim salvation nigh."

"To your God my heart is given,
   He hath heard the Hindoo's prayer;
But my babes! in that bright heaven,
   Christian, shall I meet them there?"
"God's deep purpose who can know—
Faith and hope must soothe thy woe,
For upon that blissful shore
Mercy reigns for evermore."

The Idle Lyre.

MARGARET JUNKIN.

THERE was an idle lyre
  'Mid heaven's choral band,
A messenger was summoned
  To hear his Lord's command—
That from among earth's children
  Some favoured one he'd bring,
Who had a skilful finger
  To sweep the golden string.

Oh! high and holy honour!
  Whose shall the glory be,
To make a music fitting
  The ear of Deity?
What mighty minstrel laurelled
  With wreaths which fame has given,
Shall now be counted worthy
  To join the ranks of heaven?

No master-mind whose spirit
  Might lift itself to hymn

The praise of the Eternal
  With burning seraphim,—
Nor one whose life had lingered,
  Till age had quenched its fire,
Is from earth's myriads chosen
  To touch that silent lyre.

A little child was playing
  Beside his mother's knee,
Unconscious of the honour
  That was his destiny.
The angel bent above him,
  And breathed the low command,
And ere another morning
  The lyre was in his hand.

Ah! is the mother weeping
  Because her baby boy
Is tasting purer pleasure
  And feeling holier joy,
Than she could ever yield him
  With her most soothing tone,
While yet the darling's bosom
  Was pillowed on her own?

We know that she will miss him—
  Unworn his garments lie,
And every way she turneth
  There's something meets her eye

That marks his painful absence,
  And from his vacant bed,
Like Rachel in her sorrow,
  She turns uncomforted.

Mourns she that he is taken
  Where every pain is o'er?
Where not a human passion
  Shall mar his quiet more?
Oh! could she hear the sweetness
  Of his angelic strain,
Not life's best gifts would tempt her
  To call him back again!

Though transient was his visit
  To this bleak world of ours,
The pleasant buds of promise
  Gave pledge of early flowers,
Whose perfect bloom we only
  Can see when it is given
To join, as kindred spirits,
  The choristry of heaven!

Epitaph on an Infant.

CHARLES WESLEY.

WITHIN this tomb an infant lies,
  To earth whose body lent,
Hereafter shall more glorious rise,
  But not more innocent.

When the archangel's trump shall blow
  And souls to bodies join,
What crowds shall wish their lives below
  Had been as short as thine!

Children in Heaven.

Around the throne of God in heaven,
    Thousands of children stand;
Children, whose sins are all forgiven;
    A holy, happy band,
        Singing glory, glory, glory be to God on high.

In flowing robes of spotless white
    See every one arrayed:
Dwelling in everlasting light,
    And joys that never fade.
        Singing glory, glory, glory be to God on high.

What brought them to that world above?
    That heaven so bright and fair,
Where all is peace, and joy, and love;—
    How came those children there?
        Singing glory, &c.

Because the Saviour shed his blood,
    To wash away their sin;
Bathed in that pure and precious flood,
    Behold them white and clean!
        Singing glory, &c.

On earth they sought the Saviour's grace,
  On earth they loved his name;
So now they see his blessed face,
  And stand before the Lamb,
    Singing glory, &c.

The Mother and her Dying Boy.

BOY.

My mother, my mother, O let me depart!
Your tears and your pleadings are swords to my heart.
I hear gentle voices, that chide my delay;
I see lovely visions that woo me away.
My prison is broken, my trials are o'er!
O mother, my mother, detain me no more!

MOTHER.

And will you then leave us, my brightest, my best?
And will you run nestling no more to my breast?
The summer is coming to sky and to bower;
The tree that you planted will soon be in flower;
You loved the soft season of song and of bloom;
O, shall it return, and find you in the tomb?

BOY.

Yes, mother, I loved in the sunshine to play,
And talk with the birds and blossoms all day;

But sweeter the songs of the spirits on high,
And brighter the glories round God in the sky:
I see them! I hear them! they pull at my heart!
My mother, my mother, O let me depart!

MOTHER.

O do not desert us! Our hearts will be drear,
Our home will be lonely, when you are not here.
Your brother will sigh 'mid his playthings, and say,
I wonder dear William so long can delay:
That foot like the wild wind, that glance like a star,
O what will this world be, when they are afar?

BOY.

This world, dearest mother! O live not for this;
No, press on with me to the fulness of bliss!
And, trust me, whatever bright fields I may roam,
My heart will not wander from you and from home.
Believe me still near you on pinions of love;
Expect me to hail you when soaring above.

MOTHER.

Well, go, my beloved! The conflict is o'er;
My pleas are all selfish; I urge them no more.
Why chain your bright spirit down here to the clod,
So thirsting for freedom, so ripe for its God?
Farewell, then! farewell, till we meet at the Throne,
Where love fears no partings, and tears are unknown!

BOY.

O glory! O glory! what music! what light!
What wonders break in on my heart, on my sight!
I come, blessed spirits! I hear you from high;
O frail, faithless nature, can this be to die?
So near! what, so near *to* my Saviour and King?
O help me, ye angels, his glories to sing!

The Death of a Child.

CUNNINGHAM.

YES, thou art fled, and saints a welcome sing;
Thine infant spirit soars on angel wing;
Our dark affection might have hoped thy stay,—
The voice of God has called the child away.
Like Samuel early in the temple found—
Sweet rose of Sharon, plant of holy ground,
Oh more than Samuel blessed, to thee is given,
The God he served on earth to serve in heaven.

The Child's First Grief.

MRS. HEMANS.

"Oh! call my brother back to me,
  I cannot play alone,
The summer comes with flower and bee,—
  Where is my brother gone?

"The butterfly is glancing bright
  Across the sunbeam's track;
I care not now to chase its flight—
  Oh! call my brother back!

"The flowers run wild—the flowers we sowed
  Around our garden-tree;
Our vine is drooping with its load—
  Oh! call him back to me!"

"He would not hear thy voice, fair child!
  He may not come to thee;
The face that once like spring-time smiled,
  On earth no more thou'lt see.

"A rose's brief, bright light of joy,
  Such unto him was given;

Go! thou must play alone, my boy!
    Thy brother is in heaven."

"And has he left his birds and flowers?
    And must I call in vain?
And through the long, long summer hours,
    Will he not come again?

"And by the brook, and in the glade,
    Are all our wanderings o'er?—
Oh! while my brother with me played,
    Would I had loved him more!"

Infants in Heaven.

JAMES M. MACDONALD, D.D.[*]

INFANTS die to live. As stars, which glitter for a brief moment, through the darkness of the night, but when we look again are invisible; not because they have fallen from heaven, but because they have melted away into the light of a cloudless morning; so dying infants are taken to be planted in the diadem of the Sun of righteousness. In conversation with an eminent living divine,[†] the pleasing thought was suggested by him, that those who are taken to heaven in infancy may always remain children; not such weak, suffering, and dependent creatures, as they were on earth, but bright cherubs, perfect children;—perfect in beauty and in purity. The Scriptures speak expressly of the "small and great,"[‡] both appearing together in eternity, before God. It was to the small as well as to the great, that a voice came out of the throne, saying, "PRAISE OUR GOD;" and they responded when the voice of a great multitude was heard, "as the voice of many waters, and as the voice of mighty thunderings, saying, Alleluia: for the Lord God omnipotent reigneth." The hope is not altogether without warrant, therefore, that Christians who have lost infant

---

[*] From "My Father's House," a truly delightful and instructive book.
[†] Rev. Dr. Gardiner Spring.   [‡] Rev. xix. 5; xx. 12.

children shall never be without them—that their death was indeed a "kindly harshness, which blessed them into an eternal image of youth and beauty." What earthly home is not made happier by the presence of little children, with all their infirmities, the cares they impose, and the anxieties they awaken? Without them a home may be filled with much that is graceful and refined; like a garden it may have many fine walks and arbours, but it is a garden without flowers. What then will our "Father's House" in heaven be, filled with those who are infants, without weakness and without wants, and clothed upon with all the beauty and loveliness of angels; and who, like murmuring ripples, which serve to swell the voice of many waters, when they break upon the shore, shall bear their humble part in heaven's immortal song? As, of that great multitude, which no man can number, who already have gone from earth to heaven, they form the vast majority, it is obvious that we fail to do justice to the subject, if we ignore so important an element in the redeemed society.

The rule which an Apostle lays down* as that by which God will be governed in judging the heathen world, at the last day, which limits doom to such as actually have sinned, "ought to be considered," says Dr. Russel,† "in connexion with the reasoning in chap. v, which must be consistent with it in all its parts. And as the ground of condemnation now in question, cannot apply to infants, the reasoning in respect to it, so far from militating against the salvation of such, serves to establish it, because it supposes the abuse of at least a measure of light, and the

* Rom. ii. 12, 16.　　　　　　　† Essay on Infant Salvation, chap. 3.

imitation of the sin of Adam by actual transgression. If such, as is evident, be the declared ground of the condemnation of adults, and if not a word is said of any ground on which children dying in infancy shall be finally condemned, does it not follow that all of them are saved?

"It is obviously taught by the apostle, that the glory of the works of Christ is more illustriously displayed in overcoming the accumulated effects of the many personal offences of actual transgressors, than in simply overcoming those of the single offence of Adam, and this accounts for his passing from the latter display of glory to the former. He takes for granted the redemption of those who had 'not sinned after the similitude of Adam's transgression,' when reasoning on the transcendent grandeur of the plan of mercy, as embracing the remission of 'the many offences' of actual transgressors. On the full glory of the plan, as thus most impressively exhibited, he delighted to dwell, and what he says of the circumstances of infants, is introduced chiefly for the sake of illustrating this higher manifestation of 'the exceeding riches' of divine grace. In arguing for the greater, he takes for granted the less. He cannot but be considered as teaching us, that the scheme of redemption shields from the penal consequences of Adam's sin, separately viewed, or where they are not connected with actual sin and final impenitence, seeing he maintains that its object extends, not to this only, but much farther.

"When he reasons that if the forfeiture was incurred by one offence, we have *much more* reason to expect that the blessings of redemption will be communicated on the principle of representation, or through the work of Christ as a public head, and that those blessings shall far exceed the damage sustained by the fall of the first Adam, his reasoning proceeds on the principle that God delighteth in mercy, and is slow to anger, and reluctant to judgment. It also supposes that justice, in the infliction of punishment, is limited to desert, while grace, when not obstructed in its exercise by the claims of offended righteousness, can be imparted in the most unlimited abundance, according to the good pleasure of the Divine will. It seems, then, necessarily to follow, that, under the present dispensation, no exclusion occurs, where nothing additional to the sin of Adam has taken place, since all obstructions in the way of the honourable exercise of mercy and grace have been completely removed by the infinitely precious sacrifice of Christ. This conclusion is but the natural result of the foregoing premises, and it, of course, involves the salvation of all who have not been guilty of actual transgression.

" It may here be farther remarked, that the concern of infants in the sin of Adam is of a relative nature, and therefore cannot be divided among them, so as that one may have this share of it, and another that; as in the case, when a number have shared in the doing of a thing, for the whole of relative blame must be attached to every individual of the parties concerned in it. Now it will be granted that the guilt of this sin was expiated by Christ; for, otherwise, Adam could not have been saved, and not a *single infant* could have been delivered from its effects on his posterity; so that according to this principle, the universal perdition of infants must be maintained; a thing which none will admit as possible."

If without personal participation in the sin of Adam, all men are subject to death, may we not hope that without personal acceptance of the righteousness of Christ, all who die in infancy are saved?"* The doctrine of the imputation of Adam's sin to the whole of his posterity, does not mean that the moral turpitude of Adam's sin was transferred to his posterity; that his act in some mysterious manner was their act, or that his sin was personally that of all men; nor does it mean that there is a depravation of soul, or the infusion of any positive evil; it simply means that there is such a connection between Adam, as a natural and federal head, and his descendants, that his disobedience is the cause of their loss of original righteousness, whence arises an actual and universal tendency to sin, and is the ground of their subjection to penal evils. It is no part of the Scripture doctrine of imputation, that eternal death is ever the doom of any, merely on account of Adam's offence, without respect to their own depravity of heart, or actual transgressions of the law of God.† Men perish on account of their personal offences, and because they refuse to avail themselves of proffered deliverance from that state of corruption and condemnation, into which they are brought by the first Adam. Such, clearly, is the teaching of the great Apostle, in that memorable passage, contained in the fifth chapter of Romans, from the twelfth verse to the end. He is establishing the doctrine, in this passage, that sinners are justified by the righteousness of one, that is, Jesus Christ, just as they are condemned by the sin of one, that is, of Adam. He shows that such was the effect of Adam's sin, in

---

* Dr. Hodge on Rom. v. 12, 21. Rom. v.   † See Hodge. Idem. Doct. 2.

bringing death upon his posterity, that it reigns even over young infants that had not been guilty of actual transgression. Death reigns over them, not only because they are subject to mortality, but because every child is born in spiritual death, has a corrupt nature, brings into the world with him a native sinfulness of character, which, without regeneration, will belong to him for ever.

The Apostle farther teaches—and it is at this point that the gospel sheds so glorious a light, " discloses the fall slumbering under the sunbeams of the recovery, and the wrecks of sin presenting foretokens of the triumphs of grace, and, on the withered stem of humanity, revealing buds of approaching beauty, and . blossom and fruit,"*—the gospel, I say, teaches that the blessings purchased by the death of Christ far exceed the evils incurred by Adam's sin.   If Christ had done no more than to remove the sentence which was passed upon mankind because of Adam's sin, the gospel would open no door for the salvation of those who are guilty of actual transgressions ; but the door would be open wide, for the salvation of our dying infants; for not having sinned actually, the sentence passed upon the race on account of Adam's sin, is the only sentence that rests upon them. But the propitiation of Christ is sufficient to save actual transgressors—publicans, persecutors, and malefactors ; who then can doubt its efficacy to save those, our dying babes, who have not sinned "after the similitude of Adam's transgression," *i. e.* are incapable of sinning by actual personal transgression, as Adam did? We may rest assured, now, that Christ has died, and satisfied the

* Dr. Cumming's Infant Salvation : London, 1848, p. 34.

law not only for that breach of it by which death entered into the world, but has so satisfied it, that actual transgressors, even the vilest, may be saved, that all who die before they can possibly become actual transgressors, are admitted to heaven. All the obstacles in the way of their salvation have been effectually removed. As without their personal participation in the sin of Adam, they became subject to death, so by the imputation of Christ's righteousness, without their personal acceptance of it, they are made partakers of everlasting life.

Oh, it is a heart-consoling truth that Christ died for little children. If his blood was sufficient to cleanse a dying malefactor, it is sufficient to wash away the stains of original sin, in those who are innocent of personal offences. This world is full of the graves of little children. There is a grim reaper among the flowers, whose name is Death.

> " ' Shall I have naught that is fair,' saith he ;
> ' Have naught but the bearded grain ?'
> He reaps the bearded grain at a breath,
> And the flowers that grow between."*

Oh, it is a delightful thought, that the blood of Jesus Christ sets them free from the only sentence of condemnation that could be inflicted on them. Oh, it is an enrapturing thought, that HE who passed through several periods of human life, with our nature upon HIM, that HE might sanctify and save it, was once an infant, and that, when on the cross, HE saw of the travail of HIS soul, and was satisfied, HE beheld among the armies of his worshippers myriads of infant souls—an innumerable company

* Longfellow.

of those concerning whom, with matchless grace dropping from
HIS lips, HE had said, "Of such is the kingdom of heaven."

The salvation of infants is not in conflict with a single one
of the doctrines of the Reformation, or doctrines of grace. It
is not inconsistent with the doctrine of regeneration, and the
necessity of that change, in all who would enter into the heavenly kingdom. This change in infants, before they are yet fit subjects of instruction, must of course be effected without means, by
the immediate agency of the Holy Spirit. The same Being who
sanctified Jeremiah and John the Baptist from the womb is able,
in like manner, to sanctify others who are spared to a mature
age in this world, and all those young children, who are taken
out of it, before they have committed actual transgression.
"They are regenerated and saved by Christ, through the Spirit,
who worketh when, and where, and how HE pleaseth."* If we
reject the doctrine of infant regeneration, on the ground of its
mysteriousness, we may, on the same grounds, reject the regeneration of adults; for who can tell *how* the Spirit operates, in renewing the hearts of those who can understand the terms of the
gospel? The principle of real saving grace may exist in the
hearts of children who are, as yet, incapable of actively exercis-
ing that grace. "An adult cannot be regenerated, without his
new nature expressing itself in faith. But the Spirit comes to
infants as the dew on Hermon, and as HE works in the secret
parts of the earth, they may be regenerated, and be united to
Christ's body by the illapse of the quickening power from the
Divine head, though that life may slumber in them, as the living

* Westminster Confession, x. § 3.

principle slumbers in the unsown wheat."* There is nothing, then, incredible in the idea that God may commune with the spirit of a little child ;—rather is there something grateful in the thought that the Spirit who is so often grieved away from the worldly, perverse hearts of men and women, who comes to make them HIS temple, but finds them polluted with idols, may yet take up HIS residence in hearts which never yet have been defiled with evil thoughts, corrupt motives, impure desires, and unholy passions.

Nor is the doctrine of infant salvation irreconcilable with the sovereignty of divine grace. None will pretend that their salvation is left to accident, or that they are saved without a Divine purpose. But it cannot be pretended that they are chosen on account of foreseen faith and repentance, of which they are not capable. If God has chosen them, HE must have chosen them " according to the counsel of HIS own will." HE foreknew and predestinated them to be heirs of HIS glory. The doctrine of sovereign, unconditional salvation is, after all, one of the brightest revelations of heaven, because it secures the salvation of those millions of little beings who just alight on these mortal shores, then wing their way to mingle in the scenes of a brighter and happier world.

Such will be the triumphs of redeeming love. The whole tenor of the gospel makes it evident that all who die previous to the age of responsibility, are taken by the good Shepherd into HIS eternal fold. That gospel, which, while it affords the impenitent no hopes of safety, teaches that it is God's delight to

* Dr. Hodge in Bib. Repertory for April, 1855.

receive the returning prodigal, and declares that whosoever will, may come and take of the waters of life freely—that gospel I say, which bears so gracious an aspect towards rebellious offenders, opens wide the door of mercy to those who cannot be charged with impenitence and unbelief.

But the Scriptures are not wanting in passages which necessarily imply, or directly teach the consoling truth which is involved in its general system of doctrines. "Out of the mouth of babes and sucklings hast THOU ordained strength," or, "perfected praise."*

This is the passage which our Saviour quoted to confound the chief priests and scribes, who were greatly displeased, because the little children cried in the temple, "Hosanna to the Son of David!" If nothing more, it seems to teach that there is a peculiar excellence in the praise of children, who, by the Assembly of Divines, are said to come nearest to our lost estate of innocency. Out of their mouth praise may be more perfect, and, therefore, more acceptable to God, than from the lips of those who have defiled themselves by a long course of transgression. "It seems to me," says an intelligent American missionary, "we need infant choirs in heaven to make up full concert to the angelic symphony. Who will sing like unto them of the manger, and the swaddling clothes, and of the Lord of all, drawing nourishment from the bosom of mortal mothers! True, these are themes of infinite interest, and the delight and wonder of angels. But oh! they are too tender for the archangel's powerful

* Psalm viii. 2; Matt. xxi. 16.

trump—too tender for the thundering notes of cherubim and seraphim.   We must have infant choirs in heaven."*

> "The harp of heaven
> Had lacked its least, but not its meanest string,
> Had children not been taught to play upon it,
> And sing from feelings all their own, what men
> Nor angels can conceive of creatures born
> Under the curse, yet from the curse redeemed,
> And placed at once beyond the power to fall,—
> Safety which men nor angels ever knew,
> Till ranks of these, and all of those had fallen."

There are several passages in the New Testament which record the tender regard our Saviour had for little children, and seem expressly to teach that they are the heirs of salvation.   On a certain occasion, HIS disciples asked HIM this question, "Who is the greatest in the kingdom of heaven?"   HE answered it by taking a little child, and placing him in the midst of them, and telling them that unless they were converted, and became as little children, they could not enter the kingdom of heaven; and that in order to be greatest in that kingdom, they must humble themselves as that little child: and added, "Whoso shall receive one such little child in my name receiveth ME."†   He goes on to add, "Take heed that ye despise not one of these little ones; for I say unto you, that in heaven their angels do always behold the face of my Father which is in heaven.   For the Son of man is come to save that which is lost."   "Even so, it is not the will of your Father which is in heaven, that one of these little ones should perish."   How must the disciples have under-

* Rev. Dr. Shauffler.   † Matt. xviii. 5.

stood their Master, with the little child in their midst, and having just heard HIM say that they must be converted, and become as little children, or they could not enter heaven? They must have supposed, that by the "little ones," not one of whom it is God's will should perish, HE referred to little children. Those who are converted, and become like little children, are, doubtless, figuratively included ; it is not the will of our heavenly Father that they should perish :—how, then, can it be that those who are selected as the standards of comparison, patterns for imitation, should ever perish?

*" Of such is the kingdom of heaven."**

"I think it, at least, highly probable," says the Rev. John Newton, "that where our Lord says, 'Suffer little children to come unto ME, and forbid them not, for of such is the kingdom of heaven,' HE does not only intimate the necessity of our becoming like little children in simplicity, as a qualification, without which (as he expressly declares in other places) we cannot enter into his kingdom, but informs us of a fact, that the number of infants, who are effectually redeemed unto God by HIS blood, so greatly exceeds the aggregate of adult believers, that, comparatively speaking, HIS kingdom may be said to consist of little children." As if the full import of what HE had said to HIS disciples was, "Think not that little children are beneath my notice; think not that I am a stranger to little children ; suffer them to come to me, and forbid them not. I have often been in their society ; I love their society ; the world from which I came, and to which I go, is full of little children." Dr. Scott says that "the expression may intimate that the kingdom of heavenly glory is greatly constituted of such as die in their infancy." "The expression," says Dr. Russell, who has treated this subject with great ability, "means that, 'of such it is in a great measure made up,' because they will form a very great proportion of the redeemed family of heaven." The Saviour appears to have had the universal salvation of all them who die in infancy in his view. His reasoning is not " of persons resembling such in character is the kingdom made up," for this would not warrant the conclusion drawn, that children ought not to be hindered from being brought to him, in order to be blessed. When Christ says, "Suffer little children to come unto me," "nothing can be plainer," says John Calvin, "than that he intends those who are in a state of real infancy. And to prevent this from being thought unreasonable, he adds, ' Of such is the kingdom of heaven." And if infants be necessarily comprehended, it is beyond all doubt that the word 'such' designates both infants themselves and those who resemble them." " All those whom Christ blesses are exempted from the curse of Adam and the wrath of God; and as it is known that infants were blessed by him, it follows that they are exempted from death."* " When our blessed Lord," says Dr. Hodge, " uttered those dreadful words, ' He that believeth not shall be damned,' he did not mean to shut the doors of heaven in the face of the countless clouds of departed infants, the purchase of his blood, which flock as doves to the celestial gates, and of whom, as he himself says, his kingdom largely consists."† " Heaven has

---

* Institutes, iv. c. 16, §7 and 31.   † Bib. Repertory, April, 1855.

many joys, joys which no man has seen or could express; and all its joys must be from beholding the glory of the Lamb, as it sheds blessing, and beauty, and truth over all; but it were worth centuries of Christian service and trial here to reach, at last, the threshold of our ' Father's house,' and look in upon the happy family of his little children, growing in wisdom, and strength, and praise, under his delighted eye and perfect teaching."*

As it has pleased God to call so many from this world in their infancy, what multitudes have already gone up to the mansions of the blessed! If of the thousands of millions of our race who have gone down to the grave, one half died in infancy, and a considerable number of the remainder were prepared for death by repentance of their sins, and faith in the Lord Jesus, then does it appear that God is rapidly replenishing his kingdom with holy and happy subjects, that heaven has already become the most populous portion of his empire. Christ already sees of the "travail of his soul, and divides the spoil with the strong." For, mark, the doctrine is not that salvation is confined to the deceased infants of believing parents, but that the children of irreligious parents, of infidels, and of heathen who die before they are of sufficient age to incur personal guilt, are all saved. The thousands of infants that perished when the world was destroyed by a flood—those that were consumed when Sodom and Gomorrah were burned with fire and brimstone—those slain in the sack of towns and cities, in the bloody wars of ancient nations—those whose blood was spilt by Nebuzaradan, and by

* Dr. Bethune's " Early Lost Early Saved," p. 85.

Herod in Bethlehem and the adjacent villages, when a voice was heard, lamentation, and weeping, and great mourning—those that perished in the siege of Jerusalem—and those whose bodies have been offered up to heathen deities—went to heaven. God overrules the wars, the judgments, men's crime, and even the horrid custom of sacrificing infants, to the filling up of his kingdom. Thousands upon thousands, offered as victims upon pagan altars, have been borne by angels to heaven, who, if they had been permitted to live, would have become idolaters, and perhaps, in their turn, have sacrificed their offspring. Those ministering spirits are sent not only to Christian but to heathen shores, to bear the immortal spirit of the dying infant to the presence of that Saviour who said, "Suffer little children to come to me." And thus does he divide the spoil with the strong. "From the worst barbarities of the heathen, God's love and wisdom thus extract blessings." With all the numberless infants who have been thrust into the flaming arms of Moloch—who have been hurried from the womb to the grave by their Polynesian mothers—offered up in the groves of the Druids, or "left to perish in the Ganges, or to die in the streets of Pekin, it is well." They are a part of that multitude whom no man can number, of all nations, and kindreds, and people, and tongues, who stand before the throne and before the Lamb, with white robes, and palms in their hands.

It is true the death of infants and children often involves many circumstances of a very afflictive character. The smitten child, like the son of the poor widow of Zarephath, may be an only one; or, if not an only one, may be esteemed the flower of fairest promise, and have entwined its tendrils around the warmest affections of the heart. The object on which was centred many fondly-cherished hopes has been suddenly cut down, and a chasm produced in the domestic circle, and in the sympathies of the bosom, which no sublunary object can ever fill. A shadow is left by the hearth-stone which can never more depart. The parent takes his dear one from his bosom, and lays it down in the shroud, while his heart is pierced with the most poignant sorrow. Alas! how insecure are our choicest pleasures and our most valued blessings! Like the dew upon a flower, like the beauty of a full blown rose, how soon they vanish, and we see them no more.

Who but a bereaved parent can know the grief of those who are called to lay their children in the grave.

> "I've sat and watched by dying beauty's head,
> And burning tears of hopeless anguish shed;
> I've gazed upon the sweet, but pallid face,
> And vainly tried some comfort there to trace;
> I've listened to the short and struggling breath;
> I've seen the cherub eye grow dim in death."

But whilst the death of children involves many circumstances of a painful and distressing character, it is by Christianity rendered glorious, and even attractive. There is something lovely in the departure of an infant to be with Christ and his angels. We are fain to imagine that—

> "Some angel brighter than the rest"[*]

is sent to conduct the spirit to its mansion near the throne. We

* Pres. J. Q. Adams.

23

look upon the lifeless clay, beautiful in death. We can say, Better die young than incur a dishonoured name, at a riper age, and spend an old age of shame. Better that the opening flower, all moist with the dew of the morning, should be plucked by a gentle hand, to gladden, with its perfume and beauty, the choicest apartment of the house, than that the tempest, at night, should rudely shatter its stalk, and scatter its petals over the miry ground. We gaze upon features pale and cold, but which have never been disturbed by envy, malice, or revenge; never have been darkened by pining grief. And as we gaze there is no retrospect of reverses, of vicissitudes, of sorrows, and of sins. True, we behold the remains of one who was the offspring of degenerate parents; who was heir to a depraved nature, and could be saved only by the atoning merits of a crucified Saviour, and the renewing grace of the Holy Spirit; and who, if life had lasted, would have been exposed to temptation and sin. But how consolatory the reflection that the new-born soul, which so lately animated the now lifeless frame, adorns, like a starry gem, the crown of Immanuel, and vies with the angelic host in exalted songs to the Lamb that was slain.

* * * * * * *

Perhaps the eye of some irreligious parent, who has been bereaved of children, may fall on these pages. And are you, then, the parent of children "passed into the skies?" They cast their glittering diadems at the feet of that Saviour whose proffered mercy you are still neglecting. They praise and adore him to whom you neglect to pray. They are gone from you. Oh, are they lost for ever?

The Christian parent, when similarly bereaved, can say :

    " Gone, but not lost,
       A treasure but removed,
     A bright bird parted for a clearer day ;
      Mine still in heaven."*

Mine hereafter to meet—mine to love—mine with whom to rejoice in eternal hymns to a glorified Saviour.

Can you adopt this language ? Oh, will the period ever come when you shall again embrace those sweet cherubs—sweeter far than when they bore " the image of the earthy ?" Methinks they beckon to you from their thrones. Methinks they stand ready to welcome you to those blissful mansions.

* Mrs. Hemans.

Death of the First-born

WILLIS GAYLORD CLARK.

Young mother, he is gone!
His dimpled cheek no more will touch thy breast;
No more the music tone
Float from his lips, to thine all fondly pressed;
His smile and happy laugh are lost to thee;
Earth must his mother and his pillow be.

His was the morning hour,
And he hath passed in beauty from the day,
A bud, not yet a flower,
Torn, in its sweetness, from the parent's spray;
The death-wind swept him to his soft repose,
As frost, in spring-time, blights the early rose.

Never on earth again
Will his rich accents charm thy listening ear,
Like some Æolian strain,
Breathing at eventide serene and clear;
His voice is choked in dust, and on his eyes
The unbroken seal of peace and silence lies.

And from thy yearning heart,
Whose inmost core was warm with love for him,
    A gladness must depart,
And those kind eyes with many tears be dim;
While lonely memories, an unceasing train,
Will turn the raptures of the past to pain.

    Yet mourner, while the day
Rolls like the darkness of a funeral by,
    And hope forbids one ray
To stream athwart the grief-discoloured sky;
There breaks upon thy sorrow's evening gloom,
A trembling lustre from beyond the tomb.

    'Tis from the better land!
There, bathed in radiance that around them springs,
    Thy loved one's wings expand;
As with the choiring cherubim he sings,
And all the glory of that God can see,
Who said, on earth, to children, " Come to me."

    Mother, thy child is blessed;
And though his presence may be lost to thee,
    And vacant leave thy breast,
And missed a sweet load from thy parent knee;
Though tones familiar from thine ear have passed,
Thou'lt meet thy first-born with his Lord at last.

The Morning-glory.

MARIA WHITE LOWELL.

WE wreathed about our darling's head
  The morning-glory bright;
Her little face looked out beneath,
  So full of life and light,
So lit as with a sunrise,
  That we could only say,
"*She* is the morning-glory true,
  And her poor types are *they*."

So always from that happy time
  We called her by their name,
And very fitting did it seem;
  For sure as morning came,
Behind her cradle bars she smiled
  To catch the first faint ray,
As from the trellis smiles the flower
  And opens to the day.

But not so beautiful they rear
  Their airy cups of blue,

As turned her sweet eyes to the light,
  Brimmed with sleep's tender dew;
And not so close their tendrils fine
  Round their supports are thrown,
As those dear arms whose outstretched plea
  Clasped all hearts to her own.

We used to think how she had come,
  Even as comes the flower,
The last and perfect added gift
  To crown Love's morning hour:
And how in her was imaged forth
  The love we could not say,
As on the little dew-drops round
  Shines back the heart of day.

We never could have thought, O God,
  That she must wither up,
Almost before a day was flown,
  Like the morning-glory's cup;
We never thought to see her droop
  Her fair and noble head,
Till she lay stretched before our eyes,
  Wilted, and cold, and dead!

The morning-glory's blossoming,
  Will soon be coming round,
We see their rows of heart-shaped leaves
  Up-springing from the ground;

The tender things the winter killed
  Renew again their birth,
But the glory of our morning
  Has passed away from earth.

O earth! in vain our aching eyes
  Stretch over thy green plain!
Too harsh thy dews, too gross thine air,
  Her spirit to sustain:
But up in groves of Paradise
  Full surely we shall see
Our morning-glory beautiful
  Twine round our dear Lord's knee.

Little Bessie.

A. D. F. RANDOLPH.

Hug me closer, closer, mother,
  Put your arms around me tight,
I am cold and tired, mother,
  And I feel so strange to-night;
Something hurts me here, dear mother,
  Like a stone upon my breast;
Oh I wonder, wonder, mother,
  Why it is I cannot rest!

All the day while you were working,
  As I lay upon my bed,
I was trying to be patient,
  And to think of what you said;
How the kind and blessed Jesus
  Loves his lambs to watch and keep,
And I wish he'd come, and take me
  In his arms, that I might sleep.

Just before the lamp was lighted,
  Just before the children came;
While the room was very quiet,
  I heard some one call my name:

But I could not see the Saviour,
  Though I strained my eyes to see;
And I wondered if he saw me—
  Would he speak to such as me?
In a moment I was looking
  On a world so bright and fair,
Which was full of little children—
  And they seemed so happy there.

They were singing—oh! how sweetly!
  Sweeter songs I never heard!
They were singing sweeter, mother,
  Than the sweetest singing bird.
And while I my breath was holding,
  One so bright upon me smiled;
And I knew it must be Jesus,
  When he said, "Come here, my child."

"Come up here, my little Bessie,
  Come up here, and live with me,
Where the children never suffer,
  But are happier than you see!"
Then I thought of all you'd told me,
  Of that bright and happy land;
I was going when you called me,
  When you came and kissed my hand.

And at first I felt so sorry
  You had called me; I would go,—

Oh! to sleep and never suffer!—
　Mother, don't be crying so!
Hug me closer, closer, mother,
　Put your arms about me tight;
Oh! how much I love you, mother,
　But I feel so strange to-night!

*　　*　　*　　*　　*

And the mother pressed her closer
　To her over-burdened breast,
On the heart so near to breaking
　Lay the heart so near its rest.
At the solemn hour of midnight,
　In the darkness, calm, and deep,
Lying on her mother's bosom,
　Little Bessie fell asleep.

Resignation.

LONGFELLOW.

THERE is no flock, however watched or tended,
  But one dead lamb is there!
There is no fireside, howsoe'er defended,
  But has one vacant chair!

The air is full of farewells to the dying,
  And mournings for the dead;
The heart of Rachel, for her children crying,
  Will not be comforted!

Let us be patient! These severe afflictions
  Not from the ground arise;
But oftentimes celestial benedictions
  Assume this dark disguise.

We see but dimly through the mists and vapours;
  Amid these earthly damps,
What seem to us but sad funereal tapers
  May be heaven's distant lamps.

There is no death! What seems so is transition;
  This life of mortal breath

Is but the suburb of the life elysian,
   Whose portal we call death.

She is not dead—the child of our affection—
   But gone into that school
Where she no longer needs our poor protection,
   And Christ himself doth rule.

In that great cloister's stillness and seclusion,
   By guardian angels led,
Safe from temptation, safe from sin's pollution,
   She lives, whom we call dead.

Day after day, we think what she is doing
   In those bright realms of air;
Year after year, her tender steps pursuing,
   Behold her grown more fair.

Thus do we walk with her, and keep unbroken
   The bond which nature gives,
Thinking that our remembrance, though unspoken,
   May reach her where she lives.

Not as a child shall we again behold her,
   For when with raptures wild,
In our embraces we again enfold her,
   She will not be a child;

But a fair maiden in her Father's mansion,
   Clothed with celestial grace;

And beautiful with all the soul's expansion
　　Shall we behold her face.

And though at times impetuous with emotion
　　And anguish long suppressed,
The swelling heart heaves moaning like the ocean,
　　That cannot be at rest,—

We will be patient, and assuage the feeling
　　We may not wholly stay;
By silence sanctifying, not concealing,
　　The grief that must have way.

"'Twas but a Babe."

I ASKED them why the verdant turf was riven
From its young rooting, and with silent lip,
They pointed to a new-made chasm among
The marble-pillared mansions of the dead.
Who goeth to his rest in yon damp couch?
The tearless crowd past on—"'twas but a babe."
A Babe! And poise ye in the rigid scales
Of calculation, the fond bosom's wealth?
Rating its priceless idols as ye weigh
Such merchandize as moth and rust corrupt,
Or the rude robber steals? Ye mete out grief,
Perchance, when youth, maturity or age,
Sink in the thronging tomb; but when the breath
Grows icy on the lip of innocence,
Repress your measured sympathies, and say,
"*'Twas but a babe!*"
      What know ye of *her* love,
Who patient watcheth, till the stars grow dim,
Over her drooping infant, with an eye
Bright as unchanging Hope, if *his* repose?
What know ye of *her* woe, who sought no joy

More exquisite, than on his placid brow
To trace the glow of health, and drink at dawn
The thrilling lustre of his waking smile?

  Go ask that musing father, why yon grave
So narrow, and so noteless, might not close
Without a tear?

      And though his lip be mute,
Feeling the poverty of speech, to give
Fit answer to thee, still his pallid brow,
And the deep agonizing prayer that loads
Midnight's dark wing to *him*, the God of strength,
Might satisfy thy question.

     Ye who mourn
Whene'er yon vacant cradle, or the robes
That decked the lost one's form, call back a tide
Of alienated joy, can ye not trust
Your treasure to *his* arms, whose changeless care
Passeth a mother's love? Can ye not hope,
When a few hastening years their course have run,
To go to him, though he no more on earth
Returns to you?

      And when glad faith doth catch
Some echo of celestial harmonies,
Archangels' praises, with the high response
Of cherubim, and seraphim, oh think—
Think that your babe is there.

Making a Child's Grave.

N. P. WILLIS.

Room, gentle flowers! my child would pass to heaven'
Ye looked not for her yet with your soft eyes,
O watchful ushers at Death's narrow door!
But lo! while you delay to let her forth,
Angels, beyond, stay for her! One long kiss
From lips all pale with agony, and tears,
Wrung after anguish had dried up with fire
The eyes that wept them, were the cup of life
Held as a welcome to her. Weep, O mother!
But not that from this cup of bitterness
A cherub of the sky has turned away.

One look upon her face ere she depart!
My daughter! it is soon to let thee go!
My daughter! with thy birth has gushed a spring
I knew not of; filling my heart with tears,
And turning with strange tenderness to thee!
A love—O God, it seems so—which must flow
Far as thou fleest, and 'twixt Heaven and me,
Henceforward, be a sweet and yearning chain,
Drawing me after thee! And so farewell!

'Tis a harsh world in which affection knows
No place to treasure up its loved and lost
But the lone grave! Thou, who so late wast sleeping
Warm in the close folds of a mother's heart,
Scarce from her breast a single pulse receiving,
But it was sent thee with some tender thought—
How can I leave thee *here!* Alas for man!
The herb in its humility may fall,
And waste into the bright and genial air,
While we, by hands that ministered in life
Nothing but love to us, are thrust away,
The earth thrown in upon our just cold bosoms,
And the warm sunshine trodden out for ever!
  Yet have I chosen for thy grave, my child,
A bank where I have lain in summer hours,
And thought how little it would seem like death
To sleep amid such loveliness. The brook
Tripping with laughter down the rocky steps
That lead us to thy bed, would still trip on,
Breaking the dread hush of the mourners gone;
The birds are never silent that build here,
Trying to sing down the more vocal waters;
The slope is beautiful with moss and flowers;
And, far below, seen under arching leaves,
Glitters the warm sun on the village spire,
Pointing the living after thee. And this
Seems like a ·comfort, and replacing now
The flowers that have made room for thee, I go

To whisper the same peace to her who lies
Robbed of her child, and lonely. 'Tis the work
Of many a dark hour, and of many a prayer,
To bring the heart back from an infant gone!
Hope must give o'er, and busy fancy blot
Its images from all the silent rooms,
And every sight and sound familiar to her
Undo its sweetest link; and so, at last,
The fountain that, once loosed, must flow for ever,
Will hide and waste in silence. When the smile
Steals to her pallid lip again, and spring
Wakens its buds above thee, we will come,
And, standing by thy music-haunted grave,
Look on each other cheerfully, and say,
A child that we have loved is gone to heaven,
And by this gate of flowers she passed away!

Consolation on the Death of Infant Children.

COMPILED BY A BEREAVED PARENT.*

2 Sam. xii. 23. "I shall go to him." *First,* to him to the grave. *Secondly,* to him to heaven, to a state of blessedness. Godly parents have great reason to hope concerning their children who die in infancy, that it is well with their children in the other world; for *the promise is to us* and *to our seed,* which shall be performed to those that do not put a bar in their own door, as infants do not. This may comfort us when our children are removed from us by death; they are better provided for, both in work and wealth, than they could be in this world. We shall be with them shortly to part no more.—*Matthew Henry's Commentary.*

The child released from sufferings went before to a better world. Our prayers for our children are graciously answered, if some of them die in their tender infancy (for they are well taken care of), and the others live "beloved of the Lord."—*Scott's Commentary.*

Matthew xix. 14. "But Jesus said, Suffer little children, and forbid them not, to come unto me; for of such is the kingdom of heaven." On this text Scott remarks, "Indeed, the expression, 'for of such is the kingdom of heaven,' may also intimate

* Tract No. 233. Published by the Presbyterian Board of Publication.

that *the kingdom of heavenly glory* is greatly constituted of such as die in infancy. Infants are as capable of regeneration as grown persons; and there is ground to conclude that all those who have not lived to commit actual transgressions, though they share in the effects of the first Adam's offence, will also share in the blessings of the second Adam's gracious covenant, without their personal faith and obedience, but not without the regenerating influence of the Spirit of Christ."

Romans v. 14. "Death reigned from Adam to Moses, even over them that had not sinned after the similitude of Adam's transgression."

On this text Scott says,—"There may indeed be a comfortable hope, that as infants die in Adam, without their own personal transgression; so they will be saved in Christ, without their own personal faith in him, as never living to be capable of it; yet that change must be wrought in them by the regenerating Spirit, which would have produced faith, had they lived longer."

"*Dear Sister*,—If our Lord hath taken away your child, your lease of him is expired. And if ye will take a loan of a child from the Lord, give him back again willingly, as his borrowed goods should return to him. Believe that he is not gone away, but sent before; and that the change of the country should make you think, that he is not lost to you, who is found to Christ; and that he is now before you; and that the dead in Christ shall be raised again. As he was lent a while to time, so he is given now to eternity, which will take yourself. And the difference of your shipping, and his, to heaven and Christ's shore, *the land of life,* is only in some few years, which weareth every day shorter, and some short and soon reckoned summers will give you a meeting with him."—*Rutherford's Letter to Agnes Macmath, Oct.* 16, 1640.

"Heaven is greatly made up of little children, sweet buds that have never blown, or which death has plucked from a mother's bosom to lay on his own cold breast, just when they were expanding, flower-like, from the sheath, and opening their engaging beauties in the budding time and spring of life. 'Of such is the kingdom of heaven.' How sweet these words by the cradle of a dying infant! They fall like balm drops on our bleeding heart, when we watch the ebbing of that young life, as wave after wave breaks feebler, and the sinking breath gets lower and lower, till with a gentle sigh, and a passing quiver of the lip, our child now leaves its body, lying like an angel asleep, and ascends to the beatitudes of heaven and the bosom of God. Indeed it may be, that God does with his heavenly garden, as we do with our gardens. He may chiefly stock it from nurseries, and select for transplanting what is yet in its young and tender age—flowers before they have bloomed, and trees ere they begin to bear."—*Dr. Guthrie.*

John Newton says,—" I hope you are both well reconciled to the death of your child. Indeed I cannot be sorry for the death of *infants.* How many storms do they escape! Nor can I doubt, in my private judgment, that they are included in the election of grace. Perhaps those who die in infancy, are the exceeding great multitudes of all people, nations, and languages mentioned in Revelation vii. 9, in distinction from the visible body of professing believers, who were marked on their foreheads, and openly known to be the Lord's."

"Ye have lost a child—nay, she is not lost to you, who is found to Christ; she is not sent away, but only sent before; like unto a star, which going out of our sight, doth not die and vanish, but shineth in another hemisphere; ye see her not, yet she doth shine in another country. If her glass was but a short hour, what she wanteth of time, that she hath gotten of eternity; and ye have to rejoice that ye have now some plenishing up in heaven."—*Rutherford's Letter to Lady Kenmure, January* 15, 1629.

"I have heard also, madam, that your child is removed; but to have or want is best, as he pleaseth. Whether she be with you, or in God's keeping, think it all one; nay think it the better of the two by far, that she is with him."—*Letter to the same.*

"The death of children," says Dr. Lawson, "puts a final period to all that we can do for them; but our grief on this occasion is effectually counterbalanced, by the consciousness that we have earnestly endeavoured to do what lay in our power while they were with us; especially when we have good reason to hope, that our prayers for them have not been rejected, and that Divine mercy led them safe through life and death to a world, from whence they would not for a thousand worlds return. I have lost, for the rest of my time in this world, some children whose faces I always beheld with pleasure; but I hope, young as they were, they were better fitted for leaving this world than I am. We are authorized by Scripture, without expecting a revelation from God respecting their state, to rejoice in the hope that they are sleeping in Jesus, and living with him, and shall be brought with him, in the great day of his appearance."

"I have had six children," said Mr. Elliott, "and I bless God for his free grace, they are all with Christ, or in Christ; and my mind is now at rest concerning them. My desire was that they should have served Christ on earth; but if God will choose to have them serve him in heaven, I have nothing to object to it. His will be done!"

"I was in your condition; I had but two children, and both are dead since I came hither. The supreme and absolute Former of all things giveth not an account of any of his matters. The good Husbandman may pluck his roses and gather in his lilies at midsummer, and, for aught I dare say, in the beginning of the first summer month; and he may transplant young trees out of the lower ground to the higher, where they may have more of the sun, and more free air, at any season of the year. What is that to you or me? The goods are his own. The Creator of time and winds did a merciful injury (if I dare borrow the word) to nature, in landing the passenger so early. They love the sea too well, who complain of a fair wind and a desirable tide, and a speedy coming ashore; especially a coming ashore, in that land, where all the inhabitants have everlasting joy upon their heads. He cannot be too early in heaven."—*Rutherford's Letter to Mrs. Taylor, London*, 1645.

It is a beautiful thought of Archbishop Leighton, in regard to the death of a little nephew, that departed children are but gone to bed a little sooner, as children are wont. "John," said he, "is but gone an hour or two sooner to bed, as children are used to do, and we are undressing to follow. And the more we put off the love of the present world, and all things superfluous beforehand, we shall have the less to do when we lie down."

Your child, though dead, is still, bereaved parents, yours. "God has given me three sons," writes the Rev. Oliver Heywood in his Meditations, "all living, only the youngest lives with God, in his immediate presence, having died in infancy under the covenant."

"Your bairns are now at rest, I speak to you and to your wife, and cause her to read this. They are not lost tò you, that are laid up in Christ's treasury in heaven. At the resurrection, ye shall meet with them; they are sent before, but not sent away. Let not bairns be your idols; for God will be jealous, and take away the idol, because he is greedy of your love wholly."— *Rutherford's Letter to John Gordon, of Cardoness.*

"Take no heavier lift of your children than your Lord alloweth. Give them room beside your heart, but not in the yolk of your heart where Christ should be; for then they are your idols, not your bairns. If your Lord should take any of them home to his house, before the storm come on, take it well. The owner of the orchard may take down two or three apples off his own trees, before midsummer, and ere they get the harvest sun; and it would not be seemly that his servant the gardener should chide him for it. Let our Lord pluck his own fruit at any season he pleaseth; they are not lost to you; they are laid up so well, as that they are coffered in heaven, where our Lord's best jewels lie."—*Rutherford's Letter to the Lady Gaitgirth, Sept.* 7, 1647.

"I sincerely sympathize with you," says Dr. Erskine to a friend who had lost an only son, " in your heavy trial. I have drunk deep of the same cup; *of nine sons,* only one survives. From what I repeatedly felt, I can form an idea what you must feel. I cannot, I dare not say, Weep not. Jesus wept at the grave of Lazarus, and surely he allows you to weep. But oh, let hope and joy mitigate your heaviness. I know not how this shall work for your good, but it is enough that God knows. He that said, ' All things work together for good to them that love God,' excepts not from this promise the sorest trial. You devoted your son to God; you cannot doubt that he accepted the surrender. If he has been hid in the chamber of the grave from the evil of sin and the evil of suffering, let not your eye be evil when God is good. What you chiefly wished for him, and prayed on his behalf, was spiritual and heavenly blessings. If the greatest thing you wished for is accomplished, at the season and in the manner that infinite Wisdom saw best, refuse not to be comforted. You know not what work and what joy have been waiting for him in that other world."

"Should any parent," says Dr. Chalmers, " feel softened by the touching remembrance of a light that twinkled a few short months under his roof, and at the end of its little period expired, we cannot think that we venture too far when we say, that he has only to persevere in the faith and in the following of the gospel, and that very light will again shine upon him in heaven. The blossom which withered here upon its stalk, has been transplanted there to a place of endurance; and it will there gladden that eye which now weeps out the agony of an affection that has been sorely wounded; and in the name of Him, who if on earth would have wept along with them, do we bid all believers to sorrow not, even as others who have no hope, but to take comfort in the thought of that country where there is no sorrow and no separation."

GODLY SUBMISSION.

"There is no way of quieting the mind, and of silencing the heart of a mother, but godly submission. The readiest way for peace and consolation to clay vessels is, that it is a stroke of the Potter and Former of all things; and since the holy Lord hath loosed the grip, when it was fastened sure upon your part, I know that your light, and I hope that your heart also, will yield. It is not safe to be at pulling and drawing with the omnipotent Lord. Let the pull go with him, for he is strong; and say, ' Thy will be done on earth as it is in heaven.' "—*Rutherford's Letter to Mrs. Craig, on the death of her son.*

Rev. i. 17, 18. " Fear not; I am he that liveth and was dead; and behold, I am alive for evermore, Amen; *and have the keys of hell and of death.*"

This consideration should repress, not only the anxieties which we feel in regard to the future, but also the regrets which we are too apt to cherish respecting the *bereavements* with which we have already been visited. It is not less instructive and consoling, when viewed, in reference to the death of relatives and friends, than when it is considered in respect to our own prospect of dissolution. For it teaches us, that the duration of each man's existence here is determined by the Redeemer; that it be-

longs to him to appoint a longer or shorter period to each, as he
will; and in doing so, we have reason to be satisfied, that he
determines according to the dictates of infallible wisdom, although the reasons of his procedure must necessarily be to us,
for the present, inscrutable.   We cannot tell why one is removed
in infancy, another in boyhood, a third in the prime of manly
vigour, and a fourth reserved to the period of old age ; and,
above all, why the most promising in talent and character, and
the most useful in their several stations, are taken away, while
others of inferior worth are often left behind; but suffice it for
us, that this happens not by chance, neither is it the result of
caprice or carelessness, but flows from that unerring wisdom,
whose counsels are formed on a view of all possible relations
and consequences, whether as to the visible or invisible, the
present or the future state of being. The power of death being in the hands of the Redeemer, the duration of human life
is, in every instance, determined by him ; and none, therefore,
ought to entertain the thought, either that death is, in one case,
unduly *premature*, or, in another, unduly *delayed*. None live,
either for a longer or a shorter period than infinite wisdom has
assigned to them ; and as reason teaches that to his appointment we must submit, however unwilling, it being irresistible,
and far beyond our control,—so, as Christians, we should learn
to acquiesce in it cheerfully, as the appointment of one who cannot err. That the determined hour had arrived, is a reflection
that should serve to banish every useless regret; but that this
hour was fixed by One in whose wisdom we confide, and of
whose interest in our welfare we have the strongest assurance, is

a thought which should not only induce resignation, but inspire comfort and peace.

For, when death does seize any of our friends, whether in the ordinary course of disease and decay, or by violence or accident, how consolatory to the mourning relatives is the thought, that it came at the bidding of the Saviour, and that it has not arrived without his sanction and appointment! Otherwise we might be apt to reflect, with unavailing regret, on certain needless exposures that might have been avoided, certain remedies whose virtues might have been tried, certain names high in professional reputation, who might have been consulted; or to dwell, with painful self-reproach, on certain accidents that might have been prevented, and injuries which timely care might have cured. The mind will often busy itself with such reflections after the loss of a near and dear friend; but the very intensity of feeling which is thus called forth, is a sufficient proof that any carelessness or negligence that may have been manifested, was far, very far, from being designed or wilful. And although, where criminal negligence has been shown, no doctrine, however consolatory, can prevent regret, or *should* repress feelings of penitential sorrow; yet, in other cases, where the heart bears witness to its own interest in the beloved object, the doctrine of Christ's absolute command over the keys of death, and the consideration that our friend was summoned away by a deliberate act of his sovereign wisdom, may well assuage the grief which such reflections on the commencement, progress, and treatment of the disease, are wont to awaken in the most sensitive and affectionate minds.—*Comfort in Affliction, by James Buchanan, D.D.*

On the Death of an Infant.

CUNNINGHAM.

Sweet babe, she glanced into our world to see
A sample of our misery,
Then turned away her languid eye
To drop a tear or two, and die.
Sweet babe, she tasted of life's bitter cup,
Refused to drink the potion up!
But turned her little head aside,
Disgusted with the taste, and died.
Sweet babe, she listened for a while to hear
Our mortal griefs, then turned her ear
To angels' harps and songs, and cried
To join their notes celestial, sighed and died.

Sweet babe no more, but seraph now,
Before the throne behold her bow,
To heavenly joys her spirit flies,
Blest in the triumph of the skies,
Adores the grace that brought her there
Without a wish,—without a care,—

That washed her soul in Calvary's stream,
That shortened life's distressing dream.
Short pain,—short grief,—dear babe, was thine,
Now joys eternal and divine.

Yes, thou art fled, and saints a welcome sing,
Thine infant spirit soars on angel's wing:
Our dark affection should have hoped thy stay,
The voice of God has called his child away.
Like Samuel, early in the temple found,
Sweet rose of Sharon, plant of holy ground,
Oh! more than Samuel blest, to thee 'tis given,
The God he served on earth, to serve in heaven.

Look Above.

ANONYMOUS.

O MOURNER! who, with tender love,
  Hast wept beside some infant grave,
Hast thou not sought a Friend above,
  Who died thy little one to save?

Then lift thy weary weeping eye
  Above the waves that round thee swell:
Is not thy darling safe on high?
  Canst thou not whisper, It is well?

Yes, it is well—though never more
  His infant form to earth be given;
He rests where sin and grief are o'er,
  And thou shalt meet thy child in heaven.

The Sympathy of Jesus.

MARGARET JUNKIN.

THE sympathy of Jesus—who
   That ever sobbed one sorrowing moan
On some kind bosom, fondly true,
   Some human bosom like our own,
And felt how much those lips close pressed,
   That hand close clasped could calm our fears,
Can turn to this far tenderer breast,
   Without a gush of thankful tears?

The earthly heart on which we lean
   May have its separate griefs to bear,
Griefs, though unspoken and unseen,
   Yet rankling all the deeper there.
Its faltering strength may scarce sustain
   The torture of its own distress,
And still we add our burdened pain,
   Unconscious how the weight may press.

But He whose human feet have trod
   Earth's hills and valleys—He who knew

No sympathy but that of God,
  Though linked with all that craved it, too—
Knows all our yearning, all our need,
  Yet strong to bear our utmost smart—
He loves to feel the throbbing head
  Close laid against his pitying heart.

To think that on the throne of thrones
  He wears our lowly nature still!
To think that midst the loftiest tones
  That through the eternal mansions thrill,
Earth's humblest pleader he will hear,
  Though only tears his anguish tell;
That sobbing voice falls on his ear
  More sweet than Gabriel's ever fell.

Then, sorrowing spirit, take the grief
  Thou ne'er to mortal couldst disclose,
And he will give thee sure relief,
  Touched with the feeling of thy woes;
And thou shalt understand how sweet,
  How filled with more than human bliss,
How dear—how tender—how complete
  The sympathy of Jesus is!

The Good Shepherd.

MARIA W. LÓWELL.

WHEN on my ear your loss was knelled,
  And tender sympathy upburst,
A little rill from memory swelled,
  Which once had soothed my bitter thirst.

And I was fain to bear to you
  Some portion of its mild relief,
That it might be as healing dew,
  To steal some fever from your grief.

After our child's untroubled breath
  Up to the Father took its way,
And on our home the shade of death,
  Like a long twilight haunting lay;

And friends came round with us to weep,
  Her little spirit's swift remove,
This story of the Alpine sheep
  Was told to us by one we love:

"They in the valley's sheltering care
  Soon crop the meadow's tender prime,

And when the sod grows brown and bare,
   The Shepherd strives to make them climb

"To airy shelves of pasture green,
   That hang along the mountain's side,
Where grass and flowers together lean,
   And down through mists the sunbeams slide.

"But naught can tempt the timid things
   The steep and rugged path to try,
Though sweet the Shepherd calls and sings,
   And seared below the pastures lie,

"Till in his arms the lambs he takes,
   Along the dizzy verge to go;
Then, heedless of the rifts and breaks,
   They follow on o'er rock and snow.

"And in those pastures lifted fair,
   More dewy soft than lowland mead,
The shepherd drops his tender care,
   And sheep and lambs together feed."

This parable, by nature breathed,
   Blew on me as the south wind free
O'er frozen brooks, that float, unsheathed
   From icy thraldom, to the sea.

A blissful vision through the night
   Would all my happy senses sway,

Of the Good Shepherd on the height,
  Or climbing up the stony way,

Holding our little lamb asleep;
  And like the burden of the sea
Sounded that voice along the deep,
  Saying, "Arise and follow me."

The Dying Infant.

LEROY J. HALSEY, D.D.*

THE next example which we select for a few remarks, is the child of David and Bathsheba. It is the fullest narrative of a dying infant in the Bible. The tender bud was smitten, and withered away ere it bloomed. The little light was extinguished, just as it began to shed its cheering beams over an earthly household. But small as it was, it was an event sufficient to send desolation and penitential grief into the most exalted family circle of the land.

The child was sick, and the stern warrior king, whose heart had never yielded in the hour of battle, fasted and wept, and lay all night upon the bare earth, beseeching God to spare it. But when, at the end of seven days, it died, he went into the house of the Lord and worshipped. He comforted his bleeding heart with those precious words of faith and hope which have since cheered so many others in affliction. "Now that he is dead, wherefore should I fast? Can I bring him back again? I shall go to him, but he shall not return to me."

This little one, though born in sin, was taken home to God. The early lost was early saved. Washed in a Saviour's blood,

*From "Life Pictures from the Bible"—a charming book, published by the Presbyterian Board of Publication.

and clothed in a Saviour's righteousness, it was soon introduced into that heavenly kingdom of which he so often spake as the loved abode of little children. It had not sinned after the similitude of Adam's transgression. So that, where sin abounded, grace did much more abound. It had committed no actual sin; and yet it was wholly born in sin. Its death was a judgment and punishment from God. It was smitten of God and died on account of the sins of its parents. It was done publicly before the sun, that all Israel might know that the thing which David had done had displeased the Lord. The king was humbled and chastened, and made a holier man by the stroke. The child was taken from the evil to come. Thus the death and salvation of all who die in infancy. The whole doctrine of the Bible on the subject of the infant dead, is briefly comprehended in this: They died because Adam sinned; they live again because Jesus died.

Nothing more impressively proclaims the fallen condition of our race, and the sad inroads of sin, than an infant's grave. Without the Bible, no mystery would be greater than the suffering and death of infancy. Nature has nothing to account for such a disaster. It is in the very face of all that is natural. Why should the pure and fresh young rosebud be blasted in its opening? Why should the kindly culture and beautiful flower wither even as it blooms? Why should a light just kindled go out so soon; a life just begun so suddenly cease? We might expect the sear leaf of autumn to fall, the aged oak of the forest to decay, the hoary head of the patriarch to be bowed down. But why should the most loved and cherished plant in all the

garden die? Why must this most precious jewel of my heart—
this beautiful boy—and this angel of my household—the loved
and loving daughter—be snatched away?

> "'Twas bright, 'twas heavenly, but 'tis past!
>
> Oh! ever thus from childhood's hour,
>   I've seen my fondest hopes decay;
> I never loved a tree or flower,
>   But 'twas the first to fade away.
> I never nursed a dear gazelle,
>   To glad me with its soft black eye,
> But when it came to know me well,
>   And love me, it was sure to die!"

Surely death never appears so unnatural, and but for the Bible
so mysterious, as when the blooming infant dies. And yet it is
estimated that about half our race die in infancy. Ah! what a
destroyer is death! What desolations hath he wrought in the
earth! What a harvest of tears and of broken hearts has he
been reaping! How many hills and valleys has he planted
thick with little graves! The whole earth has been but a
Bochim—a valley of tears for the infant dead. Tears have
never flowed oftener and more freely than when they have
fallen around the infant's suffering bed and new made grave.

> "Leaves have their time to fall,
>   And flowers to wither at the north wind's breath,
> And stars to set; but all,
>   Thou hast all seasons for thine own, O death!"

But blessed be the name of the Lord, there is consolation in
the Bible, and relief in heaven, for all these tears. There may

be joy in the desolate dwelling even now; for there is hope in this early doom of childhood, the same that sustained the penitent David. "He may not return to me; but I shall go to him." The most precious belief of the church of God is the salvation of the infant dead. Perhaps the greatest of all the triumphs of the cross of Christ will be found at last to be this, that it has saved half our race in a body, by calling them away from the world in infancy. Perhaps the greatest joy that is now felt in heaven, in view of all things done on earth, is caused by this one event, which creates the deepest, widest wave of sorrow here, the infant's death. For if there is joy in the presence of the angels of God over one sinner that repenteth, can we doubt that there is joy there, at the happy release of each little sufferer, as they pass from death's iron gates, one by one, into the heavens, to be for ever blest on the bosom of their God? "Precious in the sight of the Lord is the death of his saints." How beautiful and glorious must be the infant dead!

> "Oh, when a mother meets on high,
>   The babe she lost in infancy,
> Hath she not then, for pains and fears,
>   The day of woe, the watchful night,
> For all her sorrows, all her tears,
>   An over payment of delight?"*

With the word of God in our hands, and the hope of heaven in our hearts, there is no death on earth so blessed, so consolatory, so hopeful as the death of a little child. An infinite gain to the child, it often becomes an instrument of the greatest

---

* R. Southey.

spiritual blessings to the parent. Many a mother will praise God for ever, that the death of her darling babe was made the means of her greater sanctification ; or it may be of her conversion to God. When the good Shepherd would draw his wandering sheep away from danger, and gather them safely into his fold, he has no more effective mode, than to take the little lambs up in his arms. Then the sheep will follow him. So he wins our worthless hearts. He takes our lambs away. He allures to brighter worlds, by removing our brightest objects of affection here. Where our treasure is, there will our hearts be also. He cuts the ties which bind us down, that our affections may be free to aspire upward to things above. How near the gate of heaven seems, when we know that our children have just passed through it ! And how precious the Saviour seems, when we feel that our lambs are in his bosom ! The ties which bound our hearts to earth, will henceforth bind them to heaven. Who would not follow the good Shepherd to that house of many mansions, where he has been gathering these children of our love? Where is the Christian parent, who has the precious, and the unspeakable honour, of a child ascended to God, who has not thereby been made to drink in more of the beauty and power of the gospel? And when the image of that sainted one has been obliterated here, by lapse of time, from all other hearts, how will it still linger, like the fragrance of crushed flowers, around his own ! And though years may pass, and distance intervene, he will still love to breathe forth the tenderest sympathies of the soul in memory of the infant's dying couch and lowly tomb.—

I saw him oft at play,
   As no more I see him now,
With the roses on his cheek,
   And the lily on his brow;
His lisping notes so sweet
   And his laugh so full of joy,
As the sparkle of his eye
   Told the merry-hearted boy.

I stood beside the bed,
   Where the little sufferer lay,
Long struggling with disease
   Till he breathed his life away,
No rose was on his cheek then,
   No sparkle in his eye;
Oh, how it crushed my heart
   For the darling one to die!

In a robe of snowy white,
   We adorned him for the tomb,
And laid upon his breast,
   A sweet rosebud half in bloom;
A smile of beauty lingered
   Upon a face so fair,
It seemed as if an angel
   Were softly slumbering there.

We laid him down to rest,
   In the consecrated ground,
When little ones before him,
   Were sleeping all around;
Amid the summer flowers,
   Beneath the bending skies
We left him in his beauty,
   Till God shall bid him rise.

I saw him once again,
    In the vision of the night,
He seemed a little cherub,
    In his robe of snowy white;
A harp was in his hand,
    A garland on his brow,
For evermore an angel,
    Oh, such I see him now !

To an Infant in Heaven.

THOMAS WARD.

Thou bright and starlike spirit!
   That in my visions wild,
I see, mid heaven's seraphic host,
   Oh! canst thou be my child?

Our hopes of thee were lofty,
   But have we cause to grieve?
Oh! could our fondest, proudest wish
   Another fate conceive?

The little weeper, tearless,
   The sinner snatched from sin;
The babe to more than manhood grown
   Ere childhood did begin.

And I, thy earthly teacher,
   Would blush thy power to see;
Thou art to me a parent now,
   And I a child to thee!

What bliss is born of sorrow;
   'Tis never sent in vain,

The heavenly surgeon maims to save,
He gives no useless pain.

Our God, to call us homeward
His only Son sent down,
And now still more to tempt our hearts,
Has taken up our own.

A Walk in a Churchyard.

RICHARD C. TRENCH.

We walked within the churchyard bounds,
    My little boy and I;
He laughing, running happy rounds,
    I pacing mournfully.

"Nay, child, it is not well," I said,
    "Among the graves to shout;
To laugh and play among the dead,
    And make this noisy rout."

A moment to my side he clung,
    Leaving his merry play,
A moment stilled his joyous tongue,
    Almost as hushed as they:

Then, quite forgetting the command,
    In life's exulting burst
Of early glee, let go my hand,
    Joyous as at the first.

And now I did not check him more,
    For, taught by Nature's face,

I had grown wiser than before,
    Even in that moment's space;

She spread no funeral-pall above
    That patch of churchyard ground,
But the same azure vault of love
    As hung o'er all around.

And white clouds o'er that spot would pass
    As freely as elsewhere;
The sunshine on no other grass
    A richer hue might wear.

And formed from out that very mould,
    In which the dead did lie,
The daisy with its eye of gold,
    Looked up into the sky.

The rook was wheeling over head,
    Nor hastened to be gone—
The small bird did its glad notes shed,
    Perched on a gray head-stone.

And God, I said, would never give
    This light upon the earth,
Nor bid in childhood's heart to live
    These springs of gushing mirth—

If our one wisdom were to mourn,
    And linger with the dead;

To nurse, as wisest, thoughts forlorn
    Of worm and earthy bed.

Oh no! the glory earth puts on,
    The child's unchecked delight,
Both witness to a triumph won,
    If we but read aright:

A triumph won o'er sin and death,
    From these the Saviour saves;
And, like a happy infant, Faith
    Can play among the graves.

29

The Little Pilgrim.

WILLIAM C. RICHARDS.

I saw a little maiden come,
  A-sudden, to that river,
At whose dark brink bold lips close dumb,
  And stout hearts quail and shiver—
  The marge of Death's cold river.

Down to the stream the little maid
  Was led by white-robed angels;
Around her golden harps they played,
  And sung those sweet evangels
  Sung only by the angels.

Five days upon the brink she lay
  Of that appalling river;
And death shot arrows every day,
  From his insatiate quiver,
  At her beside the river.

Oh! but I stood amazed to hear
  Her wan lips sweetly saying,
"Don't pray to keep me, mother dear,

I must not here be staying;"
Such words of wonder, saying:

"Mother, I do not fear to die,
  My sins are all forgiven;
And shining angels hovering nigh,
  Will bear my soul to heaven,
  Through God's dear Lamb forgiven."

And then, from her fond mother's breast.
  She plunged into that river;
Her fluttering pulses sunk to rest,
  Her heart was still for ever,
  Her soul beyond the river.

Now when my children wait to hear,
  Some tender, touching story,
I tell them how, without a fear,
  She died, and went to glory;
  And tears flow with the story.

The Gospel the only Scheme of Pity for Children.

GEORGE W. BETHUNE, D.D.*

A MOST ungrateful wrong would be done to the glorious plan of salvation by free grace through Jesus Christ, if we did not remark how rich, beyond all comparison, are the comforts which it affords in the death of little ones. No other scheme offers us any reasonable hope.

Heathenism, cruel to all, is especially cruel toward infants. The apostle (Rom. i. 31) characterizes the nations who have departed from the true God, as "without natural affection;" and in nothing is this more clearly seen, than their unnatural treatment of their helpless offspring. The Old Testament Scriptures often allude to the custom of sacrificing young children, prevalent among the eastern idolaters. Heathenism, like all superstitions, is a spirit of fear; and the parent offered the life of his child, as the most acceptable proof he could give of devotion to the demon he worshipped. Thus the prophet Micah makes Balaam say to Balak: "Shall I give my first-born for my transgression, the fruit of my body for the sin of my soul?" (Micah vi. 7.) Nor was it confined to the Syrian abominations, but can be traced as accompanying idolatry, more or less, everywhere; in Africa,

* From "Early Lost, Early Saved."

228

Asia, and Europe to the farthest north, throughout Polynesia, and among different races on the American continent.

Infanticide was, and is, yet more prevalent. Even among the most polished nations of antiquity, the exposure of new-born infants, for various reasons, was so common, that an historian of the second century after Christ (Ælian*) praises the Thebans as singular in having a law against it. The rules of several states sternly insisted upon the destruction of such babes as did not promise, from their physical structure, good service to a warlike people. Philosophers in high repute to this day, as masters of various science, embodied the horrid expedient with their political theories, and advocated the murder of unborn infants as a check upon population.† The massacre of the new-born male Israelites by their Egyptian masters, was in perfect accordance with national policy at the time, revolting as it appears to us. Some of the Pacific Islands were nearly depopulated by such inhuman practices, before the arrival of Christian teachers among them. Throughout India, where superstition makes the slaughter of a brute impiety, human offspring are doomed without pity; and the Hindoo woman counts it mercy to save, by immediate assassination, her female child from her mother's misery. The Chinese, wonderful as their civilization is in many respects, scruple not at a wholesale destruction of children they deem superfluous; the crime is never punished; the government connive at it, and the police in some cities assist in it. Moham-

* Various Histories, ii. 7.

† Plato, Republic, v. 6. Aristotle, Politics, vii. 15, 16. Pliny, Natural History, xxxix. 27.

med condemned it as existing among the more ancient Arabs; but the sun-brightened waters of the Bosphorus, and the fruitful Nile, engulf very many victims, whom no law defends from parental cruelty.

No classic philosophy could discover blessing for infants after death; nor was it consistent with any, even the best, of their theories. If, indeed, the spirit of the babe survived, there was no alternative to the belief, that its immortality would be the same state of undeveloped faculties in which it left the world. Hence they say nothing of the infant's future being beyond this life;* or suppose it to be a scarcely conscious existence among the sombre shadows of an eternal twilight.†

Revelation alone defends the life of the little one by making

---

* In the apologue of Alcinus, the most remarkable passage in classic writings respecting futurity, Plato says, what Eros told of infants is not worth relating. Plato, Republic, x.

† The popular sentiment was not more cheering. We have many epitaphs and sad elegies on the death of children, showing the deep sorrow of bereaved parents; but none in the classic anthologies breathe "a lively hope." One of the most touching (from the Greek of Leonidas of Tarentum) is subjoined; and how exquisitely mournful is the desire of the broken-hearted mother, for whom life has no remaining charm, to join her child in "eternal night!"

> Unhappy child! Unhappy I, whose tears
> Rain on the urn that hides thy blighted years!
> Thou'rt early gone, Amyntas—I alone,
> Bereft of thee, through life's long pang must groan:
> Disgusted with each morn's returning light,
> Yearning for refuge in eternal night.
> Sweet spirit, guide thy mother where thou art:
> There only can be still my aching heart.
>
> *(By the Author, from the Anthology.)*

it sacred to God; under the Old Testament in the promise of a Messiah, under the New in the blessing of Christ; and the same grace, which guards its cradle-helplessness from the unnatural hands of enemies here, promises the full redemption of its innocent spirit from the malice of its great enemy hereafter. Bless God, ye affectionate parents, whether your children are in your arms or in a Christ-consecrated grave, that we live not in the regions of the shadow of death, but under the peaceful, holy, hope-giving sunlight of the gospel; which came in the person of a nursling Babe, on the bosom of a humble, pious mother, (whom no popish folly shall keep us from calling, after angelic example and according to prophetic command,) the "blessed" Virgin!

If we in any degree relax our hold on the doctrine of free grace, we lose the strength of this precious comfort. The infant has no promise of salvation, but through the gracious tenderness of Jesus.

Thus, however edifying the commanded Christian rite of baptism is, if we confound it, as many have done, with spiritual regeneration, and make the outward washing the necessary medium of the inward, renewing grace, a babe dying before it can ask the holy washing by its own faith, is rendered dependent for its preparation to enter heaven, upon the fidelity of others; and so. the greater part of our mortal race are, by no fault of their own, shut out of salvation. For this reason the Roman Catholics generally, if not universally, deny heaven to unbaptized infants* (except those slain as martyrs;) and assign to them,

* "Infants, unless they be regenerated by God through the grace of baptism.

on the confines of purgatory, a separate *limbus*, or place of their own, scarcely more lightened by divine love than that the heathen dreamed of. Hence, also, the eagerness of that people to confer baptism upon all whom they can by any means reach. But theirs is at best, as Bishop Hall says, "The hard sentence of a bloody religion;" and part of that system, the policy of which is to claim the prerogative of dispensing heavenly gifts, to make earthly gain of them. It is difficult, nay, impossible, for others, who teach the same doctrine of sacramental regeneration, to avoid the same distressing conclusion;* the supposition of un-covenanted mercy will not avail them, for there is no such mercy written of in the Scriptures; and, if it be necessary to enter heaven, that we be personally and visibly united to an outward church on earth, the infant, dying unbaptized, must have some other destiny than eternal life in the presence of God.

A like difficulty clings about the doctrines of Justification by good works, and of Election because of foreseen good works. Such saving conditions cannot be predicated of dying little ones. They have neither present nor anticipated merit of their own. They must be elected if saved, and saved if elected, only by free sovereign grace.

Nor (as was said in the beginning of this treatise) should our hope for them be based upon their innocence. The Scriptures warrant no such expectation; but, on the contrary, declare the

___

are begotten by their parents, believers or unbelievers, to everlasting misery and perdition."—*Council of Trent.*

* It is the doctrine of the Oxford tracts, that no unbaptized person can enter heaven. See *Pusey on Baptism, and Bridges' Sacramental Instruction.*

whole race of Adam involved by the consequences of his fall, and, as a visible proof of this, death has passed upon all alike. It is in Christ alone, Christ the second Adam, Christ the Almighty Saviour, Christ the only Mediator between God and man, that they can be saved; but in him there is plenteous redemption, and he has claimed them for his kingdom ; nor shall any be able to pluck them out of his hand.

Blessed be thy name, O Lord Jesus Christ, for our knowledge of thy full salvation, free as it is full, which embraces as securely the souls of babes and sucklings, as thine arms did embrace fondly their little forms, when unbelieving men would have kept them from thee! Their hosannas were grateful to thine ear, when thy glory was hidden from the wise and prudent ; how surpassingly sweet must they be to thee now, as thou dost look from thy cross-bought throne upon the countless throng in sinless, immortal beauty, for ever safe from sin, and sorrow, and shame, through thine abounding love!

30

To an Infant in its Grave-clothes.

MRS. L. H. SIGOURNEY.

Go to thy sleep, my child,
  Go to thy dreamless bed,
Gentle and undefiled,
  With blessings on thy head:—
Fresh roses in thy hand,
  Buds on thy pillow laid,
Haste from this fearful land
  Where flowers so quickly fade.

Before thy heart had learned
  In waywardness to stray,
Before thy feet had turned
  The dark and downward way;
Ere sin had seared thy breast,
  Or sorrow woke the tear,
Rise to thy home of rest
  In yon celestial sphere.

Because thy smile was fair,
  Thy lip and eye so bright;

Because thy cradle-care
  Was such a fond delight,
Shall love with weak embrace
  Thy outspread wing detain?
No!—angels,—seek thy place
  Amid the cherub train.

The Death-angel's Mission.

"Go forth," said the heavenly Father,
    To one of his seraph train;
"Go forth on an errand of mercy
    To the world of trouble and pain.

"Loosen the galling fetters
    That bind the weary and worn;
And bear to their glorious mansions
    The souls that for bliss are born.

"And away from earth's noxious vapours,
    Some buds of beauty bring,
To bloom in the heavenly gardens,
    'Neath the smile of perpetual spring."

And the angel with wings resplendent,
    Went out from the heavenly band,
'Midst a chorus of joyful voices,
    Resounding at God's right hand.

In the street of a crowded city,
    An old man beggared and poor,
Hungry, and sick, and sorrowing,
    Sank down by a rich man's door.

Sleep weighed down his heavy eyelids,
  And feebly he drew his breath,
As beside him, with look of compassion,
  Alighted the angel of death.

Then he thought of the years long vanished,
  The lovely, the lost, and the dear,
Till borne on the wings of sweet vision
  He woke in a happier sphere.

There were none on earth to sorrow,
  That the old man's days were o'er,
But myriads bade him welcome,
  As he neared the heavenly shore.

Slowly night's gathering shadows
  Closed round a mother-mild,
Who, tearful and heavy-hearted,
  Watched by her dying child.

Fevered, and restless, and moaning,
  On his little bed he lay,
When the bright-winged angel drew near him,
  And kissed his last breath away.

So gently the chain was severed—
  So gently was stayed the breath—
It soothed the heart of the mourner,
  And she blessed the angel of death.

For she knew the soul of her darling
  Had gone to his Father above,
Clasped in the arms more tender
  Than even her fondest love.

And still on his holy mission
  Did the heaven-sent messenger roam,
Gathering God's wandering children
  To their eternal home.

Those only whose souls were blighted
  And withered by sin and shame,
Saw no light in the path of the angel,
  And knew not from whence he came!

And those only who close their spirits
  In wilful blindness here,
From the light of God's nearer presence
  Need shrink with distrust and fear.

Lucy.

HORATIUS BONAR, D.D.

ALL night long we watched the ebbing life,
  As if its flight to stay;
Till as the dawn was coming up,
  Our last hope passed away.

She was the music of our home,
  A day that knew no night,
The fragrance of our garden bower,
  A thing all smiles and light.

Above the couch we bent and prayed,
  In the half-lighted room;
As the bright hues of infant life
  Sank slowly into gloom.

Each flutter of the pulse we marked,
  Each quiver of the eye;
To the dear lips our ear we laid,
  To catch the last low sigh.

We stroked the little sinking cheeks,
  The forehead pale and fair;

We kissed the small, round, ruby mouth,
    For Lucy still was there.

We fondly smoothed the scattered curls,
    Of her rich golden hair;
We held the gentle palm in ours,
    For Lucy still was there.

At last the fluttering pulse stood still,
    The death-frost through her clay
Stole slowly; and, as morn came up,
    Our sweet flower passed away.

The form remained; but there was now
    No soul our love to share;
No warm responding lip to kiss;
    For Lucy was not there.

Farewell, with weeping hearts we said,
    Child of our love and care!
And then we ceased to kiss those lips,
    For Lucy was not there.

But years are moving quickly past,
    And time will soon be o'er;
Death shall be swallowed up of life
    On the immortal shore.

Then shall we clasp that hand once more,
    And smooth that golden hair;
Then shall we kiss those lips again,
    When Lucy shall be there.

The Child of James Melville.*

MRS. A. STUART MONTEATH.

One time my soul was pierced as with a sword,
  Contending still with men untaught and wild,
When he who to the prophet lent his gourd,
  Gave me the solace of a pleasant child.

A summer gift my precious flower was given;
  A very summer fragrance was its life;
Its clear eyes soothed me as the blue of heaven
  When home I turned, a weary man of strife.

With unformed laughter, musically sweet,
  How soon the waking babe would meet my kiss;
With outstretched arms its care-wrought father greet.
  Oh! in the desert what a spring was this.

A few short months it blossomed near my heart;
  A few short months—else toilsome all and sad;
But that home solace nerved me for my part,
  And of the babe I was exceeding glad.

* Born, July 9, 1586. Died about January, 1588.

Alas! my pretty bud, scarce formed, was dying—
  (The prophet's gourd, it withered in a night!)
And he who gave me all, my heart pulse trying,
  Took gently home the child of my delight.

Not rudely culled—not suddenly it perished,
  But gradual faded from our love away!
As if still, secret dews, its life that cherished,
  Were drop by drop withheld, and day by day!

My blessed Master saved me from repining,
  So tenderly he sued me for his own;
So beautiful he made my babe's declining,
  Its dying blessed me as its birth had done!

And daily to my board at noon and even
  Our fading flower I bade his mother bring,
That we might commune of our rest in heaven,
  Gazing the while on death without its sting.

And of the ransom for that baby paid,
  So very sweet at times our converse seemed,
That the sure truth a gladness made—
  Our little lamb by God's own Lamb redeemed.

There were two milk-white doves my wife had nourished;
  And I too loved, erewhile, at times to stand,
Marking how each the other fondly cherished,
  And fed them from my baby's dimpled hand!

So tame they grew, that, to his cradle flying,
  Full oft they cooed him to his noon-tide rest;
And to the murmurs of his sleep replying,
  Crept gently in, and nestled in his breast.

'Twas a fair sight—the snow-pale infant sleeping,
  So fondly guardianed by those creatures mild;
Watch o'er his closed eyes their bright eyes keeping,
  Wondrous the love betwixt the birds and child!

Still, as he sickened, seemed the doves too divining,
  Forsook their food, and loathed their pretty play;
And on the day he died, with sad note pining,
  One gentle bird would not be frayed away.

His mother found it, when she rose sad-hearted,
  At early dawn, with sense of nearing ill;
And when, at last, the little spirit parted,
  The dove died too, as if of its heart's chill!

The other flew to meet my sad home-riding,
  As with a human sorrow in its coo—
To my dead child and its dead mate then guiding,
  Most pitifully plained, and parted too!

'Twas my first "hansel"* and "propine"† to heaven;
  And as I laid my darling 'neath the sod—
Precious His comforts—once an infant given,
  And offered with two turtle-doves to God!

* Present.   † Earnest, pledge.

The Bereaved Mother.

MRS. H. M. DODGE.

AND I am left! There is a strange delight
In counting o'er one's bitterness, to cull
A flower of comfort from it. I am left
To bear the gathering storms of life, my child,
Still tempest-tost upon its dangerous seas,
While thou art safely moored. Thy little barque
Is anchored in the haven where the winds
Of sorrow never blow. Thy star has risen
In climes of peace and love, to set no more
For ever and for ever. All thy life
Was like a rose-bud—like the gentle breath
Of purest fragrance, wafted on the wing
Of early Zephyr—like the opening ray
Of morning's softest blush. Thy little heart
Had never tasted woe.
    *   *   *   *   Blessed child!
Thy lot on earth was bright, and now thou art
With holy angels. I will cease to mourn!
Oh! had I loved thee less, my foolish heart
Had sighed to keep thee in this changing world—   .

Had fastened thee to life, 'till thou hadst drained
Its very dregs of woe! Never! Oh, never
Could I have knelt and kissed the chastening rod
With such unfeigned submission. Never! never
Could I have looked so calmly on the smile
Thy parting spirit left, had my fond soul
Less dotingly hung o'er thee in thy life—
Less proudly treasured up thy darling name
In the deep recess of my heart. But now
Our very lives were one. There could not be
A deeper, purer tenderness, than heaved
This trembling breast for thee. How could I then
Ask aught for thee but happiness? In life,
When thou wast closely folded in these arms,
And I did feel thy warm breath on my cheek,
Thy smiling eyes fixed tenderly on mine,
My prayers were full of pleadings, agonies
Almost of earnestness, that heaven would bless
Thy opening day with joy and every good
That might be deemed most proper. Oh, are not
These prayers most fully answered? Could my soul
In all its deepest gush of tenderness,
Have asked a holier boon—a blessedness
More durable, more infinite and pure,
More like the nature of a God to give,
Than heaven's own self, with all its blessed ones,
Its high society, its holy love,
Its rapturous songs of gratitude and praise,

Its pure celestial streams, and fruits, and flowers,
And glorious light reflected from the face
Of God's eternal Son? Could I have claimed
A higher boon, my precious babe, for thee?
And then, again, to be exempt from wo
And human suffering, for ever free
From all the toils, and pains, and nameless cares
That gather with our years—and oh! perchance,
At last a hopeless death! Oh! I could weep
With very GRATITUDE that thou art SAVED—
Thy soul FOR EVER SAVED. What though my heart
Should bleed at every pore—still thou art blessed.
There *is* an hour, my precious innocent,
When we shall meet again! Oh! may we meet
To separate no more. Yes! I can smile,
And sing with gratitude, and weep with joy,
Even while my heart is breaking!

The Child is Happier Now.[*]

SAMUEL I. PRIME, D.D.

WE desire our children's happiness; we pray and labour for it; we are willing to make great sacrifices of our comfort to secure it for them. In sickness, we forget our own health and lives for the sake of theirs. We watch them, and toil for them, and would die for them. We more than die for them sometimes.

And if we grieve when their happiness calls them from us, our grief is selfish, it is for ourselves, and not for them, we mourn. But we should not mourn, if we knew what he has gained whom we have lost. Instantly, on being released from the body, the spirit of the infant returns to God who gave it. Endowed with capacities that, if permitted to expand and improve on earth, would in fifty years, perhaps, have made him wiser than Newton, or Plato, or Solomon, it rushes into the mysteries of the Divine mind, and on wings of thought such as angels use in rising into the regions of knowledge that pass all understanding, he begins his flight, and stretches onward, and right onward for ever. He never tires. No weakness, or sickness, no pain to make him pause or falter in his upward way. He bears himself into the presence of the Omniscient, becomes

[*] From "The Smitten Household."

a discip.e in the school of Christ, flies on with Moses, and David, and John, and learns from them the wonderful things of
heaven, the mysteries of the kingdom; and thus, ever advan-
cing, he rises nearer and still nearer to the comprehension of him
who is still infinitely above and beyond his last and loftiest reach.
And what a change is this! Yesterday, an infant in his mother's
arms, or a child amused with a rattle or a straw; to-day a seraph in the midst of seraphim; burning with excessive glory in
the presence of God.

Happiness is the fruit of holiness. Washed in the blood of
the everlasting covenant, and sanctified by the Holy Ghost, he
is now among the holy, as happy as any who are there. Those
faculties of mind, expanded in the atmosphere of heaven, are
employed in the praises of that grace that called him so soon
from Nature's darkness into the light of *eternity;* the gloom of
sin scarce shading the brightness of his rising sun, before the
noon of heaven burst upon him. As if an angel had lost his
way, and for a few days had wandered among the sons of men,
till his companions suddenly discovered him in this wilderness,
and caught him, and bore him off to his native residence among
the blessed; so the child is taken kindly in the morning of its
wanderings, and gathered among the holy and brought home to
his Father's house. How pure his spirit now; how happy he
is now!

> "Apostles, martyrs, prophets, there
> Around my Saviour stand,"

and among them I behold the infant forms of those whose little
graves were wet with the tears of parental love. I hear their

infant voices in the song. Do you see in the midst of that bright and blessed throng the child you mourn? I ask not now if you would call him back again. I fear you would! But I ask you, "*What would tempt him back again?*" Bring out the playthings that he loved on earth, the toys that filled his childish heart with gladness, and pleased him on the nursery floor; the paradise that was ever bright when he smiled within it; hold them up, and ask him to throw away his harp, and leave the side of his new-found friends, and the bosom of his Saviour; and would he come, to be a boy again, to live, and laugh, and love again, to sicken, suffer, die, and *perhaps* be lost? I think he would stay. I think I would shut the door if I saw him coming.

32

A Butterfly at a Child's Grave.

MRS. LYDIA H. SIGOURNEY.

A BUTTERFLY basked on an infant's grave,
  Where a lily had chanced to grow;
Why art thou here with thy gaudy dye,
Where she of the bright and the sparkling eye
  Must sleep in the churchyard low?

Then it lightly soared through the sunny air,
  And spoke from its shining track;
"I was a worm till I won my wings,
  And she whom thou mourn'st, like a seraph sings—
  Wouldst thou call the blest one back?"

Weep not for Her!*

WEEP not for her! Her span was like the sky,
  Whose thousand stars shine beautiful and bright;
Like flowers, that know not what it is to die;
  Like long-linked, shadeless months of polar light;
Like music floating o'er a waveless lake,
While echo answers from the flowery brake:
      Weep not for her!

Weep not for her! She died in early youth,
  Ere hope had lost its rich romantic hues;
When human bosoms seemed the homes of truth,
  And earth still gleamed with beauty's radiant dews.
Her summer prime waned not to days that freeze;
Her wine of life was run not to the lees:
      Weep not for her!

Weep not for her! By fleet or slow decay,
  It never grieved her bosom's core to mark
The playmates of her childhood wear away,
  Her prospects wither, or her hopes grow dark;

* From "Noctes Ambrosianæ."

Translated by her God, with spirit shriven,
She passed, as 'twere in smiles, from earth to heaven!
    Weep not for her!

Weep not for her! It was not hers to feel
  The miseries that corrode amassing years,
'Gainst dreams of baffled bliss the heart to steel,
  To wander sad down age's vale of tears,
As whirl the withered leaves from friendship's tree,
And on earth's wintry world alone to be.
    Weep not for her!

Weep not for her! She is an angel now,
  And treads the sapphire floors of paradise;
All darkness wiped from her refulgent brow,
  Sin, sorrow, suffering, banished from her eyes;
Victorious over death, to her appear
The vista'd joys of heaven's eternal year:
    Weep not for her!

Weep not for her! Her memory is the shrine
  Of pleasant thoughts, soft as the scent of flowers,
Calm as on windless eve the sun's decline,
  Sweet as the song of birds among the bowers,
Rich as the rainbow, with its hues of light,
Pure as the moonshine of an autumn's night;
    Weep not for her!

Weep not for her! There is no cause for woe:
  But rather nerve the spirit, that it walk

Unshrinking o'er the thorny paths below,
　And from earth's low defilements keep thee back;
So, when a few fleet severing years have flown,
She'll meet thee at heaven's gate, and lead thee on!
　　Weep not for her!

Hymn to Night.

GEO. W. BETHUNE, D.D.

YES! bear them to their rest;
The rosy babe tired with the glare of day,
The prattler fallen asleep even in his play;
Clasp them to thy soft breast,
O Night,
Bless them in dreams with a deep-hushed delight!

Yet must they wake again;
Wake soon to all the bitterness of life,
The pang of sorrow, the temptation strife,
Aye, to the conscience-pain.
O night,
Canst thou not take with them a longer flight?

Canst thou not bear them far,
Ev'n now all innocent, before they know
The taint of sin, its consequence of woe,
The world's distracting jar,
O Night,
To some eternal, holier, happier height?

Canst thou not bear them up,
Through star-lit skies, far from this planet dim
And sorrowful, ev'n while they sleep, to Him,
Who drank for us the cup,
O Night,
The cup of wrath for souls in faith contrite?

To him, for them who slept
A babe all lowly on his mother's knee,
And, from that hour to cross-crowned Calvary,
In all our sorrows wept,
O Night,
That on our souls might dawn heaven's cheering light?

Go lay their little heads
Close to that human breast, with love Divine
Deep beating; while his arms immortal twine
Around them as he sheds,
O Night,
On them a brother's grace of God's own boundless might.

Let them, immortal, wake
Among the deathless flowers of Paradise,
Where angels' songs of welcome with surprise
This their last sleep may break,
O Night,
And to celestial joys their kindred souls invite.

There can come no sorrow;
The brow shall know no shade, the eye no tears;
For ever young through heaven's eternal years
In one unfading morrow,
O Night,
Nor sin, nor age, nor pain, their cherub beauty blight.

Would we could sleep as they
So stainless and so calm; at rest with thee,
And only wake in immortality.
Bear us with them away,
O Night,
To that eternal, holier, happier height.

What was thy Life?

RICHARD C. TRENCH.

WHAT was thy life? A pearl cast up a while
  Upon the bank and shoal of time; again,
Even as did the gazers' eyes beguile,
  To be drawn backward by the hungry main.

What was thy life? A fountain of sweet wave,
  Which to the salt sea's margin all too near
Rose sparkling, and a few steps scarcely gave,
  Ere that distained its waters fresh and clear.

What was thy life? A flowering almond tree,
  Which all too soon its blossoms did unfold;
And so must see their lustre presently
  Dimmed, and their beauty nipped by envious cold.

What was thy life? A bright and beauteous flame,
  Wherein, a season, light and joy we found:
But a swift sound of rushing tempest came,
  It past, and sparkless ashes strewed the ground!

What was thy life? A bird in infant's hand
  Held with too slight a grasp, and which, before
He knows no fears, its pinions doth expand,
  And with a sudden impulse heavenward soar.

The Infant in Heaven.

THOMAS CHALMERS, D.D.

OH! the babe little knew what an interest it had created in that home where it was so passing a visitant—nor, when carried to its early grave, what a tide of emotion it would raise among the few acquaintances it left behind it! On it, too, baptism was impressed as a seal: and, as a sign, it was never falsified. There was no positive unbelief in its bosom; no resistance yet put forth to the truth; no love at all for the darkness rather than the light; nor had it yet fallen into that great condemnation which will attach itself to all that perish because of unbelief, that their deeds are evil. It is interesting to know that God instituted circumcision for the infant children of the Jews, and at least suffered baptism for the infant children of those who profess Christianity. Should the child die in infancy, the use of baptism, as a sign, has never been thwarted by it; and may we not be permitted to indulge a hope so pleasing, as that the use of baptism as a seal remains in all its entireness; that He, who sanctioned the affixing of it to a babe, will fulfil upon it the whole expression of this ordinance. And when we couple with this the known disposition of our great Forerunner, the love that he manifested to children on earth, how he suffered them to approach his person, and lavishing endearment and kindness upon them in the streets of Jerusalem, told his disciples that the presence and company of such as these in heaven formed one ingredient of the joy that was set before him; tell us if Christianity does not throw a pleasing radiance around an infant's tomb? And should any parent who hears us, feel softened by the touching remembrance of a light that twinkled a few short months under his roof, and at the end of its little period expired, we cannot think that we venture too far, when we say, that he has only to persevere in the faith, and in the following of the gospel, and that very light will again shine upon him in heaven. The blossom which withered here upon its stalk, has been transplanted there to a place of endurance; and there it will then gladden that eye which now weeps out the agony of an affection that has been sorely wounded; and in the name of Him who, if on earth, would have wept along with them, do we bid all believers present, to sorrow not even as others which have no hope, but to take comfort in the thought of that country where there is no sorrow and no separation.

Little Annie.

J. H. P.

The precious bud had scarce begun to bloom,
    Ere death, relentless, broke its tender stem;
It droop'd its little head, and now the tomb
    Has closed its portals o'er the precious gem.

We sadly gathered round her dying bed,
    With hearts of grief to freely weep and pray,
And many were the bitter tears we shed,
    When little Annie's spirit passed away.

And yet, methinks, it was not meet to weep
    For one to whom a life so brief was given;
The angels closed her little eyes in sleep,
    And gently bore her spirit up to heaven.

The silken curls we parted o'er her brow,
    And clasped the tiny hands upon her breast,
Then in the earth's green bosom laid her low,
    Down sweetly by the village green to rest.

There now the birds of summer blithely sing,
    And gently o'er her weeps the dewy grass,

And village children often fondly bring
  Love's floral off''ring as they chance to pass.

Yes, dearest Annie, thou hast early fled,
  To seek beyond this world a sacred rest,
A sphere above, where all the righteous dead
  In gracious bliss will be for ever blest.

Thy voice of innocence, though hushed on earth,
  Now wakes an echo in the court of heaven;
We felt thou wast an angel from thy birth,
  And feared thy earthly ties would soon be riven.

Sweet child, we miss thy gentle form that late
  Danced gayly round this sad and lonely home,
Where loving little brother mourns thy fate,
  And tearful asks if sister ne'er will come.

Oh, could his boyish vision pierce the veil
  That bounds the region of ethereal space,
No longer would he thus thy loss bewail,
  Since mid the angels he would view thy face.

Lone mother, check thou too the mournful sigh,
  And drop no longer now the silent tear,
Upon the silken curl or treasured toy,
  Or little dress thy darling used to wear.

For while the casket moulders 'neath the sod
  That rises gently o'er yon little grave,

The precious jewel rests secure with God,
  Who only took from earth the gem he gave.

Rest! Annie, rest!—though sacred ties are riven,
  The beauteous flowers around thy pillow bloom;
We'll hope to meet thee at the gate of heaven,
  When we have safely passed death's bitter doom.

My Darling's Shoes.

God bless the little feet that can never go astray,
For the little shoes are empty, in the closet laid away!
Sometimes I take one in my hand, forgetting till I see
It is a little half worn shoe, not large enough for me;
And all at once I feel a sense of bitter loss and pain,
As sharp as when two years ago it cut my heart in twain.

O little feet that wearied not, I wait for them no more,
For I am drifting on the tide, but *they* have reached the
     shore;
And while the blinding tear-drops wet these little shoes so
     old,
And so I lay them down again, but always turn to say—
God bless the little feet that *now so surely* cannot stray.

And while I thus am standing, I almost seem to see
Two little forms beside me, just as they used to be!
Two little faces lifted with their sweet and tender eyes!
Ah me! I might have known that look was born of Para-
     dise.
I reach my arms out fondly, but they clasp the empty air!
There is nothing of my darlings but the shoes they used to
     wear.

O the bitterness of parting cannot be done away
Till I see my darlings walking where their feet can never
    stray;
When I no more am drifted upon the surging tide,
But *with them safely* landed upon the river side;
Be patient, heart! while waiting to see *their* shining way,
For the little feet in the golden street can never go astray.

The Death of a Young Girl.

WILLIAM H. BURLEIGH.

SHE hath gone in the spring-time of life,
　　Ere her sky had been dimmed by a cloud,
While her heart with the rapture of love was yet rife,
　　And the hopes of her youth were unbowed—
From the lovely, who loved her too well;
　　From the heart that had grown to her own;
From the sorrow which late o'er her young spirit fell,
　　Like a dream of the night she hath flown;
And the earth hath received to its bosom its trust—
Ashes to ashes, and dust unto dust.

The spring, in its loveliness dressed,
　　Will return with its music-winged hours,
And, kissed by the breath of the sweet southwest,
　　The buds shall burst out in flowers;
And the flowers her grave-sod above,
　　Though the sleeper beneath recks it not,
Shall thickly be strown by the hand of Love,
　　To cover with beauty the spot—

Meet emblems are they of the pure one and bright,
Who faded and fell with so early a blight.

Ay, the spring will return—but the blossom
    That bloomed in our presence the sweetest,
By the spoiler is borne from the cherishing bosom,
    The loveliest of all and the fleetest!
The music of stream and of bird
    Shall come back when the winter is o'er;
But the voice that was dearest to us shall be heard
    In our desolate chambers no more!
The sunlight of May on the waters shall quiver—
The light of her eye hath departed for ever!

As the bird to its sheltering nest,
    When the storm on the hills is abroad,
So her spirit hath flown from this world of unrest
    To repose on the bosom of GOD!
Where the sorrows of earth never more
    May fling o'er its brightness a stain;
Where in rapture and love it shall ever adore,
    With a gladness unmingled with pain;
And its thirst shall be slacked by the waters which spring,
Like a river of light, from the throne of the KING!

There is weeping on earth for the lost!
    There is bowing in grief to the ground!
But rejoicing and praise mid the sanctified host,
    For a spirit in paradise found!

Though brightness hath passed from the earth,
   Yet a star is new-born in the sky,
And a soul hath gone home to the land of its birth,
   Where are pleasures and fulness of joy!
And a new harp is strung, and a new song is given
To the breezes that float o'er the gardens of heaven.

Words of Consolation.

COTTON MATHER.*

LET not the death of your children cause any inconsolable grief. The loss of children did I say—nay, let me recall so harsh a word. The children we count lost, are not so. The death of our children is not the loss of our children. They are not lost, but given back; they are not lost, but sent before.

Well, this is the calamity which many of you at some time or other have experienced; the death of children is a thing in which the children of Jacob seldom escape a resemblance of their father. Many carry themselves under the trial, as if a death of virtue, yea, as if a death of reason had befallen them; but recollect yourselves, O dejected Christians! and be not like them that mourn without hope this day. Let bereaved parents be still believing parents; the voice of the great God that formed all things is unto them, as in Jer. xxxi. 16: "Refrain thy voice from weeping, and thine eyes from tears, for thy work shall be rewarded, saith the Lord." Let the thoughts which have been set before us compose and settle our minds under this affliction. Let us not say, this thing is against us; but let us say, "the Lord gave, and the Lord hath taken away; blessed be the name of the Lord." It

* From "Right Thoughts in Sad Hours."

is indeed very true, that this affliction is none of the most easy to be borne; the heart of a parent will have peculiar passions working in it, at such a time as this, though there be greater sorrows than those with which we follow a child unto the grave. I bless God it is a more bitter thing to say, "My sin is mighty," or to say, "My soul is guilty," than it is to say, "My child is dead." That moan, "I have pierced my Saviour," is more heart-wounding than to mourn as one mourneth for a first-born. Yet few outward earthly anguishes are equal unto these. The dying of a child is like the tearing of a limb from us. But O! remember that if ever we had any grace in our souls, we have ere this willingly plucked out a right eye, and cut off a right hand, for the sake of God. Why should we not then, at the call of God, readily part with a limb, and leave him room to say, "Now I know that thou fearest me, because thou hast not withheld thy son, thine only son, from Me?" It was from God that we received those dear pledges, our children, and it is to God that we return them. We cannot quarrel with our God, if about those loans he say unto us, Give them up, you have had them long enough! We knew what they were when first we took them into our arms; we knew that they were potsherds, that they were mortals, that the worms which sometimes kill them, or at least will eat them, are but their name-sakes; and that a dead child is a sight no more surprising than a broken pitcher or a blasted flower.

But we did not, we do not know, what they might be, in case they were continued among the living on the earth. We cannot tell whether our sons would prove as plants grown up in their youth, and our daughters as corner-stones polished after the similitude of a palace; or, whether our sons might not, like Isaac's son, do those things that would be "a grief of mind unto us;" and our daughters, like Jephtha's daughter, be of them that trouble us.   Christians, let us be content that our wise and good God should choose our portion for us; he will appoint us none but a goodly heritage.   Our temptation is no more than what is common to men, yea, and to good men.   The greatest part of those human spirits, that are now beholding the face of God in glory, are such as dwelt in the children of pious people, departed in their infancy.   And what have we to say, why we should not undergo it as well as they?   Was the infant whose decease we deplore, one that was very pretty, one that had pretty features, pretty speeches, pretty actions?   Well, at the resurrection of the just we shall see it again.   The Lord Jesus will deal with our dead children as the prophets Elijah and Elisha did by those whom they raised of old; he will bring them to us, recovered from the pale jaws of death; and how amiable, how beautiful, how comely they will then be, no tongue is able to express, or heart to conceive!   Though their beauty consume in the grave, yet it shall be restored, it shall be increased, when they shall put off their bed-clothes in the morning of the day of God.

Again; was the infant now lamented very suddenly snatched away, and perhaps awfully too! not merely by a convulsion, but by scalding, by burning, by drowning, by shooting, by stabbing, or by some unusual harm?   Truly it is often so, that the quicker the death the better.   It is more desirable for our children to feel but a few minutes of pain, than it is for them to lie groaning in those exquisite agonies which would cause us even ourselves to wish that the Lord would take them out of their misery. As for any more grievous and signal circumstance attending our dying children, our best course will be to have it said of us, " They ceased; saying, The will of the Lord be done!" As the love or wrath of God is not certainly declared in, so our grief before him should not be too much augmented by, such things as these. And it is a favour, if so much as one of our children be left alive unto us. Let not the sense of one trouble swallow up the sense of a thousand mercies. The mother from whom a violent death has taken one of her two children, may immediately embrace the other and say, Blessed be God who has left me this.

But once more; is the deceased infant an only child? Are we now ready to sigh—All is gone? Nay, thou hast but a poor all, if this were all. I hope thy only child is not thy only joy. If thou hast ever experienced the new birth, the sense of thy soul is, one Jesus is worth ten children; yea, one Christ is worth ten worlds. What though all thy candles are put out! The sun, the Sun of righteousness is arising to thy soul for ever. An undone man art thou indeed! thou hast thy little glass of water spilt or spoilt, while thou hast a fountain, a living fountain running by thy door! The blessed God calls thee, my child; and that is infinitely better than a name of sons and of daughters.

Finally. Have we any doubts about the eternal salvation of the children which we have buried out of our sight? Indeed AS TO GROWN CHILDREN, there is often too sad cause of suspicion or solicitude; and yet here, the sovereign disposals of

God must be submitted to. Besides, though it may be we could not see such plain marks and signs of grace in our adult children as we could have wished for, nevertheless they *might have the root of the matter in them.* There are many serious, gracious, well-inclined young people, who conceal from everybody the evidences of their repentance, and the instances of their devotion. You cannot tell what the Lord did for the souls of your poor children before he took them out of the world. Perhaps they sought, they found mercy at the last. The child of a good parent is not to be despaired of, though turned off the gallows.

But as to young children, the fear of God will take away all matter of scruple in the owners of them. Parents, can you not sincerely say, that you have chosen God in Christ for the best portion, as of yourselves, so of your children? Answer this: if your children had been spared unto you, would it not have been your care to have them brought up in the nurture and admonition of the Lord? Would you not have used all prayers and pains to have them engaged unto the service of the living God, and unto a just aversion to all the vile idols and vain courses of the world? Then be of good cheer: your children are in a better place, a better state, than you yourselves are yet arrived unto. The faithful God hath promised, I will be their God, as well as thy God. Oh say, This is all my desire, though the Lord suffer not my house to grow. Those dear children are gone from your kind arms, into the kinder arms of Jesus, and this is by far the best of all, to have children this day in heaven. Truly this is an honour which neither you nor I are worthy of.

But so it is: the King of kings hath sent for our children to confer a kingdom on them. They are gone from a dark vale of sin and shame; they are gone into the land of light, and life, and love; there they are with the spirits of just men made perfect; there they serve the Lord day and night in his temple, having all tears wiped from their eyes; and from thence methinks I hear them crying aloud unto us, 'As well as you love us we would not be with you again: weep not for us, but for yourselves, and count not yourselves at home till you come to be, as we are, for ever with the Lord.'

I have done. The fit epitaph of a dead infant (that, that alone is enough to be the solace of a sad parent,) is, 'Of such is the kingdom of heaven.'

35

Is it Well with the Child?

MRS. LYDIA H. SIGOURNEY.

"Is it well with the child? And she answered, It is well."—2 Kings iv. 26.

"Is it well with the child?" And she answered, " 'Tis
    well."
But I gazed on the mother who spake,
For a tremulous tear, as it sprang from its cell,
  Bade a doubt in my bosom awake;
And I marked that the bloom in her features had fled,
  So late in their loveliness rare,
And the hue of the watcher that bends o'er the dead
  Was gathering in pensiveness there.

"Is it well with the child?" And she answered, " 'Tis
    well."
I remember its beauty and grace,
When the tones of its laughter did tunefully swell
  In affection's delighted embrace:
And through their long fringe, as it rose from its sleep,
  Its eyes beamed a rapturous ray,
And I wondered that silence should settle so deep
  O'er the home of a being so gay.

"Is it well with the child?" And she said, " 'Tis well."
    It hath tasted of sickness and pain,
Of the pang, and the groan, and the gasp, it might tell—
    It never will suffer again.
In my dreams, as an angel, it stands by my side,
    In the garments of glory and love;
And I hear its glad lays to the Saviour who died,
    'Mid the choir of the blessed above.

My Angel Brother.

WILLIAM E. SCHENCK, D.D.

ALTHOUGH so many years have since passed, I remember it as if it were but yesterday, when my baby brother came. I was but a "wee bit thing" then, being not quite four years old. It was a bitter cold morning in the month of January, when Jane, my kind and gentle nurse, awaked me with great glee, and told me to dress as fast as I could, for she had something grand to show me. It did not take me long to get ready, when she carried me at once to my dear mother's room.

How well I remember that room. Every piece of furniture and its position, the hickory fire blazing on the hearth, the partially shaded windows encircled by the leafless stems of the trumpet honeysuckle and the tall rose bushes. Even the pattern of the wall-paper is impressed upon my memory. On the further side of the bed stood my father, with a countenance at once grave and happy. On the bed reclined my mother, bolstered up by pillows, and with a face almost as white as the pillows on which she reclined. Before her, on the bed, rested the tiny form of the new-comer to our happy dwelling.

I was obliged to stand on tiptoe to reach the little hand, which I seized with all the ardour of a newly awakened fraternal joy. My mother, in soft and gentle tones, told me how happy I ought to be since God had given me a little brother, and how she hoped that I would always be kind and loving towards him.

Time sped on. The little baby-brother was an object of constant attraction. Every day I watched him, to see how fast he grew, and what signs he gave forth of increasing intelligence. The body and mind rapidly expanded and developed, and already I began to entertain pleasant visions of the time when he would join me in my future plays.

But God's ways are not as our ways. The bleak and icy month of January had passed away, and spring-time had come. The trumpet honeysuckle was covered with its scarlet flowers, and the white and damask roses hung in profusion over the front of the pleasant farm-house. The middle of June had just passed, when the little brother faded from our sight. He was not long sick, and his death came upon us all with a sudden shock.

How sweet he looked as he lay in his open coffin, with a bunch of flowers placed within the pale little hands. Then we followed him to his grave. Across the brook, and out into yonder fields to the old family burial-place. It was a new scene to me, and even in the midst of my childish grief I remember with what curiosity and awe I saw the little coffin lowered into the grave, and the earth thrown in, and the turf neatly placed upon it. Then we returned to the house, and oh! what a sad, sad void there was in that house.

As I have said, many, many years have passed since that

hour. Little feet have pattered around my own hearth-stone, and my own children are on the verge of manhood and womanhood. Yet often does memory revert to the image of that little brother with a tenacious fondness. Occasionally I visit that old family burial-ground in the fields, and look at the white marble stones which stand at the head and foot of that little grave, and think of the intervening years and their many and varied occurrences. Beside that grave are now seen those of our father, our mother, and other dear friends, who have since passed from earth.

Did that little blossom expand only to fade? Was that brief visit to our earth in vain? It cannot, cannot be. I feel humbled as I stand by that little grave to think how, while I have been laboriously toiling here to gather acquisitions of knowledge and picking it up particle by particle, he was ushered at once into celestial light where they " know even as also they are known." During these years, while that tiny form has been mingled with its kindred earth, to what amazing heights of knowledge, wisdom, and goodness too, heights unscaled by the mind of any living man on earth, has he not attained. How much more he knows of the Great God, and of the universe, and of the deep truths of revelation than I do. And while I have been trying to do good, a little here, a little there, feebly, and often unwisely, how has he been honoured to speed on angel wings to obey the Divine behests, not only in heaven and here on earth, but perhaps to other worlds and other systems.

Yet, he is my brother still. Brief though his visit was to earth, he was born in human form, and was linked to me in a relationship which will endure to all eternity. I claim him still as my brother, my angel brother. And if through the rich grace of Jesus Christ our Elder Brother and our Saviour, I shall one day enter Heaven's gates, I fondly look to meet him there, to know him there, and to love him there, throughout a blest eternity.

"Only a Year."

MRS. H. B. STOWE.

One year ago,—a ringing voice,
  A clear blue eye,
And clustering curls of sunny hair,
  Too fair to die.

Only a year,—no voice, no smile,
  No glance of eye,
No clustering curls of golden hair,
  Fair but to die!

One year ago,—what loves, what schemes
  Far into life!
What joyous hopes, what high resolves,
  What generous strife!

The silent picture on the wall,
  The burial stone,
Of all that beauty, life, and joy,
  Remain alone!

One year,—one year,—one little year,—
  And so much gone!
And yet the even flow of life
  Moves calmly on.

The grave grows green, the flowers bloom fair,
  Above that head;
No sorrowing tint of leaf or spray
  Says he is dead.

No pause or hush of merry birds
  That sing above
Tells us how coldly sleeps below
  The form we love.

Where hast thou been this year, beloved?
  What hast thou seen?
What visions fair, what glorious life,
  Where thou hast been?

The veil! the veil! so thin, so strong!
  'Twixt us and thee;
The mystic veil! when shall it fall,
  That we may see?

Not dead, not sleeping, not even gone;
  But present still,
And waiting for the coming hour
  Of God's sweet will.

Lord of the living and the dead,
  Our Saviour dear!
We lay in silence at thy feet
  This sad, sad year!

Can I wish it Back?

PHILIP DODDRIDGE, D.D.

COULD I wish that this young inhabitant of heaven should be degraded to earth again? Or would it thank me for that wish? Would it say, that it was the part of a wise parent, to call it down from a sphere of such exalted services and pleasures, to our low life here upon earth? Let me rather be thankful for the pleasing hope, that though God loves my child too well to permit it to return to me, he will ere long bring me to it. And then that endeared paternal affection, which would have been a cord to tie me to earth, and have added new pangs to my removal from it, will be as a golden chain to draw me upwards, and add one farther charm and joy even to paradise itself. And oh, how great a joy! to view the change, and to compare that dear idea, so fondly laid up, so often reviewed, with the now glorious original, in the improvement of the upper world! To borrow the words of the sacred writer, in a very different sense: "*I said I was desolate and bereaved of children, and who hath brought up these? I was left alone, and these, where have they been?** Was this my desolation? this my sorrow? to part with thee for a few days, *That I might receive thee for ever,*†

---

* Isa. xlix. 21.   † Philem. ver. 15.

and find thee what thou art?" It is for no language but that
of heaven, to describe the sacred joy which such a meeting must
occasion.

In the meantime, Christians, let us keep the lively expectation of it, and let what has befallen us draw our thoughts to
heaven. Perhaps they will sometimes, before we are aware,
sink to the grave, and dwell in the tombs that contain the poor
remains of what was once so dear to us. But let them take
flight from thence to more noble, more delightful scenes. And I
will add, let the hope we have of the happiness of our children
render God still dearer to our souls. We feel a very tender
sense of the kindness which our friends expressed towards them,
and think, indeed very justly, that their affectionate care for
them lays a lasting obligation upon us. What love then, and
what service do we owe to thee, O gracious Father, who hast,
we hope, received them into thine house above, and art now entertaining them there with unknown delight, though our former
methods of commerce with them be cut off! "Lord," should
each of us say in such a case, "I would take what thou art doing to my child as done to myself, and as a specimen and earnest of what shall shortly be done." *It is* therefore *well.*

A Mother's Heart.

RICHARD C. TRENCH.

HERS was a mother's heart,
That poor Egyptian's, when she drew apart
Because she would not see
Her child beloved in its last agony;

When her sad load she laid,
In her despair, beneath the scanty shade
In the wild waste, and stepped
Aside, and long and passionately wept.

Yet higher, more sublime,
How many a mother since that ancient time
Has shown the mighty power
Of love divine, in such another hour!

Oh! higher love to wait
Fast by the sufferer in his worst estate,
Nor from the eyes to hide
One pang, but aye in courage to abide.

And though no angel bring
In that dark hour unto a living spring

Of gladness—as was sent,
Stilling her voice of turbulent lament—

Oh! higher faith to show
Out of what depths of anguish and of woe
The heart is strong to raise
To an all-loving Father hymns of praise.

Death of a Child.

CHARLES WESLEY.

2 Sam. xii. 23,—1 Sam. iii. 18.

WHEREFORE should I make my moan,
  Now the darling child is dead?
He to rest is early gone,
  He to paradise is fled!
I shall go to him, but he
Never shall return to me.

God forbids his longer stay,
  God recalls the precious loan!
He hath taken him away,
  From my bosom to his own.
Surely what he wills is best;
Happy in his will I rest.

Faith cries out, "It is the Lord!
  Let him do what seems him good,
Be thy holy name adored,
  Take the gift a while bestowed;
Take the child no longer mine
Thine he is, for ever thine!"

Realms of the Blest.

ANONYMOUS.

WE speak of the realms of the blest,
Of that country so bright, and so fair,
And oft are its glories confessed,
But what *must it be to be there?*

We speak of its pathways of gold,
Of its walks decked with jewels so rare;
Of its wonders and pleasures untold,—
But what *must it be to be there?*

We speak of its freedom from sin,
From sorrow, temptation, and care,
From trials without and within,
But what *must it be to be there?*

We speak of its service of love,
Of the robes which the glorified wear,
Of the church of the first-born above,—
But what *must it be to be there?*

Say not 'twere a Keener Blow.

T. H. BAYLY.

Oh! say not 'twere a keener blow,
  To lose a child of riper years;
You cannot feel a mother's woe,
  You cannot dry a mother's tears;
The girl who rears a sickly plant,
  Or cherishes a wounded dove,
Will love them most while most they want
  The watchfulness of love!

Time *must* have changed that fair young brow!
  Time *might* have changed that spotless heart!
Years *might* have taught deceit, but now
  In love's confiding dawn we part!
Ere pain or grief had wrought decay,
  My babe is cradled in the tomb;
Like some fair blossom torn away
  Before its perfect bloom.

With thoughts of peril and of storm,
  We see a bark first touch the wave;

But distant seems the whirlwind's form,
   As distant—as an infant's grave!
Though all is calm, that beauteous ship
   Must bear the whirlwind's rudest breath;
Though all is calm, that infant's lip
   Must meet the kiss of death!

37

Extract from a Letter.

ROBERT HALL.

I SINCERELY sympathize with you in the loss of your child; but, my dear friend, do not suffer your spirits to sink. Remember the tenure on which all human enjoyments are held, the wisdom and sovereignty of their great Author, and the gracious promise afforded to true Christians, that " all things shall work together for good to them that love him."

Remember, also, the many blessings with which a kind Providence still indulges you. Ought you not to rejoice, that your affectionate companion in life is spared; and that, though your child is snatched from your embraces, he has escaped from a world of sin and sorrow? The stamp of immortality is placed on his happiness, and he is encircled by the arms of a compassionate Redeemer. Had he been permitted to live, and you had witnessed the loss of his virtue, you might have been reserved to suffer still severer pangs. A most excellent family, in our congregation, are now melancholy spectators of a son dying at nineteen years of age, by inches, a victim to his vices. They have frequently regretted he did not die several years since, when his life was nearly despaired of in a severe fever. " Who knoweth what is good for a man all the days of this, his vain life, which he spends as a shadow?"

Dirge for a Child.

MRS. HEMANS.

No bitter tears for thee be shed,
  Blossom of being! seen and gone!
With flowers alone we strew thy bed,
  O blest departed one!
Whose all of life, a rosy ray,
Blushed into dawn, and passed away.

Yes! thou art fled, ere guilt had power
  To stain thy cherub soul and form,
Closed is the soft ephemeral flower,
  That never felt a storm!
The sun-beam's smile, the zephyr's breath,
All that it knew from birth to death.

Thou wert so like a form of light,
  That Heaven benignly called thee hence
Ere yet the world could breathe one blight
  O'er thy sweet innocence:
And thou, that brighter home to bless,
Art passed with all thy loveliness!

Oh, hadst thou still on earth remained,
　Vision of beauty! fair, as brief!
How soon thy brightness had been stained
　With passion or with grief!
Now not a sullying breath can rise
To dim thy glory in the skies.

We rear no marble o'er thy tomb,
　No sculptured image there shall mourn:
Ah! fitter far the vernal bloom
　Such dwelling to adorn.
Fragrance, and flowers, and dews, must be
The only emblems meet for thee.

Thy grave shall be a blessed shrine,
　Adorned with nature's brightest wreath,
Each glowing season shall combine
　Its incense there to breathe;
And oft upon the midnight air,
Shall viewless harps be murmuring there.

And oh! sometimes in visions blest,
　Sweet spirit! visit our repose,
And bear from thine own world of rest,
　Some balm for human woes!
What form more lovely could be given
Than thine, as messenger of Heaven?

Gone—but not Lost.

MRS. ELLEN STONE.

SWEET bud of Earth's wilderness, rifled and torn!
Fond eyes have wept o'er thee, fond hearts still will mourn;
The spoiler hath come, with his cold withering breath,
And the loved and the cherished lies silent in death.

He felt not the burden and heat of the day!
He hath passed from this earth, and its sorrows, away,
With the dew of the morning yet fresh on his brow:—
Sweet bud of Earth's wilderness, where art thou now?

And oh! do ye question, with tremulous breath,
Why the joy of your household lies silent in death?
Do ye mourn round the place of his perishing dust?
Look onward and upward, with holier trust!

·Who cometh to meet him, with light on her brow?
What angel form greets him, so tenderly now?
'Tis the pure sainted mother, springs onward to bear
The child of her love from this region of care!

She beareth him on to that realm of repose,
Where no cloud ever gathers, no storm ever blows:

For the Saviour calls home to the mansions above,
This frail trembling floweret in mercy and love.

There shall he for ever, unchanged by decay,
Beside the still waters and green pastures stray;
And there shall ye join him, with earth's ransomed host—
Look onward and upward! "he's *gone—but not lost!*"

Epitaph on a Child.[*]

RICHARD HUIE, M.D.

SLEEP on, my babe! thy little bed
  Is cold, indeed, and narrow;
Yet calmly there shall rest thy head,
And neither mortal pain nor dread
  Shall e'er thy feelings harrow!

Thou may'st no more return to me;
  But there's a time, my dearest,
When I shall lay me down by thee,
And when of all my babe shall be
  That sleep around, the nearest!

And sound our sleep shall be, my child,
  Were earth's foundations shaken;
Till He, the pure, the undefiled,
Who once, like thee, an infant smiled,
  The dead to life awaken!

Then, if to Him, with faith sincere,
  My babe at death was given,
The kindred tie that bound us here,
Though rent apart with many a tear,
  Shall be renewed in heaven!

[*] From Sacred Lyrics.

The Loss of Children.

FLAVEL.

Mourner, whatever may be your grief for the death of your children, it might have been still greater for their life. Bitter experience once led a good man to say, "It is better to weep for ten children dead, than for one living." Remember the heart-piercing affliction of David, whose son sought his life. Your love for your children will hardly admit of the thought of such a thing as possible, in your own case. They appeared innocent and amiable; and you fondly believed, that through your care and prayers, they would have become the joy of your hearts. But may not Esau, when a child, have promised as much comfort to his parents as Jacob? Probably he had as many of their prayers and counsels. But as years advanced, he despised their admonitions, and filled their hearts with grief. As a promoter of family religion, who ever received such an encomium from the God of heaven as Abraham? How tenderly did the good man pray for Ishmael! "O that Ishmael might live before thee!" Yet how little comfort did Ishmael afford.

Alas! in these days of degeneracy, parents much more frequently witness the vices of their children than their virtues. And even should your children prove amiable and promising, you might live to be the wretched witness of their sufferings. Some parents have felt unutterable agonies of this kind.

God may have taken the lamented objects of your affection from the evil to come. When extraordinary calamities are coming on the world, he frequently hides some of .his feebler children in the grave. Surely, at such a portentous period, it is happier for such as are prepared, to be lodged in that peaceful mansion, than to be exposed to calamities and distresses here. Thus intimates the prophet Jeremiah, "Weep not for the dead, neither bemoan him ; but weep sore for him that goeth away ; for he shall return no more, nor see his native country." It was in a day when the faith and patience of the saints were peculiarly tried, that the voice from heaven said, " Write, blessed are the dead, which die in the Lord, from henceforth."

38

On the Death of a Child.

CONDER.

When I can trust my all with God,
  In trial's fearful hour,
Bow all resigned beneath his rod,
  And bless his sparing power;
A joy springs up amid distress,
A fountain in the wilderness.

Oh! to be brought to Jesus' feet,
  Though sorrows fix me there,
Is still a privilege; and sweet
  The energies of prayer,
Though sighs and tears its language be,
If Christ be nigh, and smile on me.

An earthly mind, a faithless heart,
  He sees with pitying eye;
He will not let his grace depart;
  But, kind severity!
He takes a hostage of our love
To draw the parent's heart above.

There stands our child before the Lord,
  In royal vesture drest;
A victor ere he drew the sword,
  Ere he had toiled at rest.
No doubts this blessed faith bedim,
We know that Jesus died for him.

Oh blessed be the hand that gave;
  Still blessed when it takes.
Blessed be He who smites to save,
  Who heals the heart he breaks.
Perfect and true are all his ways,
Whom heaven adores, and death obeys.

𝔄 𝔖𝔱𝔬𝔯𝔶.[*]

DURING the absence of Rabbi Meir from his house, his two sons died, both of them of uncommon beauty and enlightened by the law. His wife bore them to her chamber, laid them upon the bed, and spread a white covering over their bodies. When Rabbi Meir returned, his first inquiry was for his sons. His wife reached to him a goblet; he praised the Lord at the going out of the Sabbath, drank, and again asked, "Where are my sons, that they too may drink of the cup of blessing?"

"They will not be far off," she replied, and placed food before him that he might eat. He was in a gladsome and genial mood; and when he had said grace, after the meal, she thus addressed him: "Rabbi, with thy permission, I would fain propose to thee one question."

"Ask it then, my love," replied he.

"A few days ago a person entrusted some jewels to my custody, and now he demands them; should I give them back to him?"

"This is a question," said Rabbi Meir, "which my wife should not have thought it necessary to ask. What! would'st thou hesitate or be reluctant to restore to every one his own?"

"No," she replied, "but yet I thought it best not to restore

* From the Mishna of the Rabbins.

them without acquainting thee therewith." She then led him to their chamber, and stepping to the bed, took the white covering from the dead bodies.

"Ah! my sons, my sons!" loudly lamented their father, "my sons! the light of my eyes, and the light of my understanding. I was your father—but ye were my teachers in the law."

The mother turned away and wept bitterly. At length, she took the husband by the hand and said, "Rabbi, did'st thou not teach me that we must not be reluctant to restore that which was entrusted to our keeping? See, the Lord gave and the Lord hath taken away, and blessed be the name of the Lord!"

"Blessed be the name of the Lord!" echoed the holy man; "and blessed be his glorious name for ever."

The Voice of Spring.

W. J. PABODIE.

I HEAR thy voice, O Spring,
Its flute-like tones are floating through the air,
Winning my soul with their wild ravishing,
    From earth's heart-wearying care.

Divinely sweet thy song;
But yet, methinks, as near the groves I pass,
Low sighs on viewless wings are borne along,
    Tears gem the springing grass.

For where are they, the young,
The loved, the beautiful, who, when thy voice
A year agone, along these valleys rung,
    Did hear thee and rejoice?

Thou seek'st for them in vain:
No more they'll greet thee in thy joyous round;
Calmly they sleep beneath the murmuring main,
    Or moulder in the ground.

Yet peace, my heart, be still!
Look upward to yon azure sky, and know

To heavenlier music now their bosoms thrill,
　Where balmier breezes blow.

For them hath bloomed a Spring,
Whose flowers perennial deck a holier sod,
Whose music is the song that seraphs sing,
　Whose light, the smile of GOD.

Not Lost, but Gone Before.

JAMES MONTGOMERY.

FRIEND after friend departs;
  Who hath not lost a friend?
There is no union here of hearts,
  That finds not here an end:
Were this frail world our final rest,
Living or dying none were blest.

Beyond the flight of time,
  Beyond the reign of death,
There surely is some blessed clime,
  Where life is not a breath;
Nor life's affections transient fire,
Whose sparks fly upwards and expire.

There is a world above,
  Where parting is unknown;
A long eternity of love,
  Formed for the good alone;
And faith beholds the dying here,
Translated to that glorious sphere.

Thus star by star declines,
  'Till all are passed away,
As morning high and higher shines,
  To pure and perfect day;
Nor sink those stars in empty night,
But hide themselves in heaven's own light.

39

Three little Graves.

MRS. LYDIA H. SIGOURNEY.

I sought at twilight's pensive hour
  The path which mourners tread,
Where many a marble stone reveals
  The City of the dead;—
The city of the dead, where all
  From feverish toil repose,
While round their beds, the simple flower,
  In sweet profusion blows.

And there I marked a pleasant spot
  Enclosed with tender care,
Where side by side three infants lay,
  The only tenants there,—
Nor weed, nor bramble raised its head
  To mar the hallowed scene,
And 'twas a mother's tears, methought,
  Which kept that turf so green.

The eldest was a gentle girl,
  She sunk as rose-buds fall,

And then two little brothers came,
  They were their parents' all,—
Their parents' all!—and ah, how oft
  The moan of sickness rose,
Before, within these narrow mounds,
  They found a long repose.

Their cradle sports beside the hearth,
  At winter's eve, are o'er;
Their tuneful tones, so full of mirth,
  Delight the ear no more:—
Yet still the thrilling echo lives,
  And many a lisping word
Is treasured in affection's heart,
  By grieving memory stirred.

Three little graves!—Three little graves!
  Come hither, ye who see
Your blooming babes around you smile,
  A blissful company,—
And of those childless parents think
  With sympathizing pain,
And soothe them with a Saviour's words,
  "Your dead shall rise again."

To Bereaved Parents.

REV. DR. SCHAUFFLER.

IT seems to me, we need infant choirs in heaven, to make up full concert to the angelic symphony. Who will sing like unto them, of the manger, and the swaddling clothes, and of the Lord of all drawing nourishment from the bosom of a mortal mother! True these are themes of infinite interest, and the delight and wonder of angels. But ah! they are too tender for the archangel's powerful trump—too tender for the thundering notes of seraphim and cherubim. We must have infant choirs in heaven. When on some Sabbath-school anniversary the multitude of little children come together, and after hearing some words of tender and affectionate exhortation and advice, they strike up their artless hymn, all the assembly is moved to tears and the single-hearted little ones carry away from the Masters in Israel the palm of eloquence; and the thrill of their tender voices is felt vibrating in the hearts of those who heard them, when the most powerful speeches are long forgotten.

We must have Infant Choirs in Heaven! And is it no privilege to know one of *our* dear ones among them? What an interest does not a father or a mother feel in listening to the

sweet voices of the children when they know their beloved child
is among the happy songsters.   And is it not incomparably more
precious to know them among the songsters in heaven?   And
oh ! with what additional interest, with what quickened anticipa-
tions do I now look beyond the grave!   I think of the moment
when I shall fold my little ones to a father's bosom again and
that *for ever*, and tears of joy and gratitude flow down my cheeks
involuntarily.   Even now while I am writing, the voices of two
of *my children*, is it possible?—yes, of *my* children are singing
praises unto Him who became a poor babe and a man of sorrows
for them and for all men.   O, let them sing then!   I can only
wish to join them soon !

And now, your dear boy has gone to unite with them.   And
while you read this, and it may be weep, he raises his growing
notes of praise and gratitude to the Saviour of all men and learns
in one minute more of God, and Christ, and heaven, than you
would ever have taught him in all your lives.   Oh ! leave them
there—all of them, and let us but become daily more heavenly-
minded, and more ready to join the

> "Angels who stand round the throne,
> And view my Immanuel's face."

And the—

> "Saints who stand nearer than they !!"

All those redeemed by the precious blood of Christ, and called
close around the steps of His Throne to sing the song,—not of
creation and providence only, but of *redeeming love* and *sovereign
grace*.

The Lost One.

MARY HOWITT.

WE meet around the hearth—thou art not there,
  · Over our household joys hath passed a gloom:
Beside the fire we see thy empty chair,
  And miss thy sweet voice in the silent room,—
What hopeless longings after thee arise!
    Even for the touch of thy small hand I pine,
      And for the sound of thy dear little feet—
        Alas! tears dim my eyes,
    Meeting in every place some joy of thine,
      Or when fair children pass me in the street.

Beauty was on thy cheek—and thou didst seem
  A privileged being—chartered from decay;
And thy free spirit, like a mountain stream
  That hath no ebb, kept on its cheerful way:
Thy laugh was like the inspiring breath of spring,
That thrills the heart, and cannot be unfelt;
  The sun, the moon, the green leaves, and the flowers,
    And every living thing,

Were a strong joy to thee—thy spirit dwelt
  Gladly in life, rejoicing in its powers.

Oh! what had death to do with one like thee?
  Thou young and loving one, whose soul did cling,
Even as the ivy clings unto the tree,
  To those who loved thee—thou whose tears would spring,
  Dreading a short day's absence, didst thou go
Alone into the future world unseen,
  Solving each awful, untried mystery,
      The unknown to know,
To be where mortal traveller hath not been—
  Whence welcome tidings cannot come from thee?

My happy boy!—and murmur I, that death
  Over thy young and buoyant frame had power?
In yon bright land, love never perisheth,
  Hope may not mock, nor grief the heart devour:
  The beautiful are round thee—thou dost keep
Within the Eternal Presence, and no more
  Mayst death, or pain, or separation dread:
      Thy bright eyes cannot weep,
Nor they with whom thou art thy loss deplore,
  For ye are of the living—not the dead.

Thou dweller with the Unseen, who hast explored
  The immense unknown—thou to whom Death and Heaven
Are mysteries no more, whose soul is stored
  With knowledge for which men have vainly striven,

Beloved child! oh when shall I lie down
With thee beneath fair trees that cannot fade?
 When from the immortal rivers quench my thirst?
  Life's morning passeth on,
Noon speeds, and cometh the dim evening's shade
And night:—anon is every cloud dispersed,
 And o'er the hills of Heaven the Eternal Day shall burst!

A Father's Lament.

WILLIAM HOWITT.

Two creatures of a pleasant life were mine;
My house they filled with a perpetual joy;
Twin lamps that chased all darkness did they shine—
My fairy girl and merry-hearted boy.
I never dreamed Death would their mirth destroy,
For they were dwelling 'mid life's freshest springs,
And I was busied with a fond employ,
Ranging the future on Hope's fearless wings,
And gathering for them thence how many pleasant things!

In truth, I was a proud and joyful man,
As from the floor unto the very roof
Their murmured bursts of joy and laughter ran,
And jocund shouts which needed no reproof—
All weariness, all gloom was kept aloof,
By their quaint shows and fancies ever new,
Now bending age with staff in its behoof,
Now Island Crusoe and " Man Friday" true,
Now shipmates far at sea with all their jovial crew.

But a dark dream has swept across my brain,
A wild, a dismal dream that will not break—
A rush of fear—an agony of pain—
Pangs and suspense that inly made me quake.—
My boy! my boy! I saw thy sweet eyes take
A strange unearthly lustre, and then fade;
And oh! I deemed my heart must surely break,
As, stooping, I thy pleasant locks surveyed,
And felt that thou must die, and they in dust be laid.

Oh! precious in thy life of happiness!
Daily and hourly valued more and more,
Yet, to the few brief days of thy distress,
How faint all love my spirit knew before!
I turn and turn, and ponder o'er and o'er,
Insatiate, all that sad and dreamy time
Thy words thrill through me—in my fond heart's core
I heard thy sighs, and tears shed for no crime,
And thy most patient love sent from a happier clime.

How dim and dismal is my home!—a sense
Of thee spreads through it like a haunting ill;
For thou—for ever, thou hast vanished thence!
This—this pursues me, pass where'er I will,
And all the traces thou hast left but fill
The hollow of thine absence with more pain;
I toil to keep thy living image still,
But fancy feebly doth her part maintain;
I see, yet see thee not, my child! as I would fain.

In dreams for ever thy dear form I grasp,
In noonday reveries do I rove—then start—
And certainty, as with an iron clasp,
Shuts down once more to misery my heart;
The world from thee as a shorn flower doth part,
Ending its care and knowledge with " Farewell !"
But in my soul a shrined life thou art,
Ordained with memory and strong hope to dwell,
And with all pure desires to sanctify thy cell.

Spring like a spirit is upon the earth—
Forth gush the flowers and fresh leaves of the tree,
And I had planned, with wonder and with mirth—
The bird, the nest, the blossom, and the bee
To fill thy boyish bosom—till its glee
O'erflowed my own with transport! In far years
I felt thy hand in mine, by stream and lea,
Wandering in gladness—But these blinding tears,
Why will they thus gush forth, though richer hope appears?

Far other land thy happy feet have trod,
Far other scenes thy tender soul has known—
The golden city of the eternal God,
The rainbow-splendours of the eternal throne.
Through the pearl gate how lightly hast thou flown!
The streets of lucid gold—the chrysolite
Foundations have received thee—dearest one!
That thought alone can break affliction's might,
Feeling that thou art blest, my heart again is light.

Thanks to the Framer of life's mystery!
Thanks to the Illuminator of the grave!
Vainly on time's obscure and tossing sea
Hope did I seek, and comfort did I crave;
But He who made, neglecteth not to save.
My child!—thou hast allied me to the blest:
I cannot fear what thou didst meekly brave;
I cannot cease to long with thee to rest;
And heaven is doubly heaven with thee, with thee possessed.

My Child.

MRS. S. H. O.

"These were redeemed from among men, being the first fruits unto God, and to the Lamb."—Rev. xiv. 4.

REDEEMED from earth, my gentle child,
  Now thou art of that seraph band,
The pure in heart, the undefiled,
  Who roam the bright immortal land.
By crystal streams, through flowery meads,
Still following where the Saviour leads.

There doth the tender bud expand,
  We watched with many a sigh and tear,
Too fragile for this wintry land,
  Too pure for earth's polluted sphere.
Twelve moons marked thy gentle bloom,
The thirteenth beamed upon thy tomb.

Sweet one! when fondly on my breast,
  I hushed thee to thy soft repose,
And watched the wing of slumber rest
  On violet eye—and cheek of rose—
While gazing on thy trusting eye,
How could I deem that thou would'st die!

That thou would'st die! and from our bower
    Withdraw the sunshine thou hadst shed,
While grief should bid her purple flower,
    Spring up where'er our footsteps tread;
And hopes, and dreams, once green and high,
Like autumn leaves should lowly lie.

When on thy pale, cold brow of snow
    I pressed the last fond kiss of love,
Such love as only mothers know—
    A stream, whose fountain is above,
I felt that life was drear, and wild,
Bereft of thee, my gentle child!

When kneeling by the sacred tomb,
    That held the form so prized, so dear,
A voice dispelled my bosom's gloom
    And whispered soft, she is not here;
Not here, not here, beyond the skies,
Her spirit lives in Paradise.

What rapture thrilled through every vein,
    As faith, with eagle-piercing eye,
Beheld her in that seraph train,
    The infant army of the sky—
By crystal streams, by flowery meads,
Still following where the Saviour leads.

And now, though years have onward sped,
    Through tears and smiles, through light and gloom,

Still memory o'er the lovely dead,
  Bids flowers of fairest verdure bloom—
And wakes her harp all sweet, and low,
Whence soft, delicious numbers flow.

Soft breathing tones, but not of wo,
  Though lonely is the mother's heart;
And time's swift flight is all too slow,
  For loved and cherished friends apart:
Those gentle airs with hope are rife,
And whisper of eternal life.

God is not Dead.

THERE lived in the east of Scotland, a pious clergyman, who had presided for a number of years, over a small but respectable congregation. In the midst of his active career of usefulness, he was suddenly removed by death, leaving behind him a wife and a number of helpless children.

The small stipend allowed him by his congregation, had been barely sufficient to meet the current expenses of his family; and at his death no visible means were left for their support. The death of her husband preyed deeply upon the heart of the poor afflicted widow, while the dark prospect which the future presented, filled her mind with the most gloomy apprehensions. By her lonely fireside she sat—the morning after her sad bereavement—lamenting her forlorn and destitute condition, when her little son, a boy of five years of age, entered the room. Seeing the deep distress of his mother, he stole softly to her side, and placing his little hand in hers, looked wistfully into her face, and said: "Mother, mother, is God dead?" Soft as the gentle whisper of an angel, did the simple accent of the dear boy fall upon the ear of the disconsolate, and almost heart-broken mother. A gleam of heavenly radiance lighted up, for a moment, her pale features. Then snatching up her little boy, and pressing him fondly to her bosom, she exclaimed: "No, no, my son, God is not dead; he lives, and has promised to be a father to the fatherless, a husband to the widow. His promises are sure and steadfast, and upon them I will firmly and implicitly rely." Her tears were dried, and her murmurings for ever hushed.

41

Little Willie's last Words.

C. W. B.

THE Sabbath-day was nearly spent,
  The week that Willie died,
And o'er his pillow still we bent,
  Or kneeling at his side
We watched the waves that came and went
  In life's fast-ebbing tide.

Through all the silent hours—the deep,
  Deep silence of our woe—
We watched, with eyes that could not weep,
  The parting spirit go;
We heard the moanings of his sleep,
  His breathing faint and slow.

But ere his upward flight he took,
  The fevered slumber broke;
His mind the troubled dream forsook;
  Our dying Willie woke;
And with an earnest heavenward look,
  These precious words he spoke:

322

"The blessed Jesus surely died
  To save us from our sin."
He said no more, nor turned aside
  His gaze, that pierced within
Those gates of glory opened wide,
  When soon he entered in.

*　　*　　*　　*　　*　　*

I thank thee, Father! Lord of light,
  That, hidden from the wise,
Thou hast revealed to infant sight
  The secrets of the skies.
Yea, Father! even so, for right
  It seemeth in thine eyes.

I thank and praise, O Saviour Christ!
  Thy mercy rich and free,
That six short cloudless years sufficed
  To bring our child to thee;
Thus early to thine arms enticed,
  Suffered thy face to see.

And when the Holy and the Just,
  Who taketh what he gave,
Shall call me to that sacred dust
  Reposing in the grave,
Be mine as sure and simple trust
  That Jesus died to save.

The little Boy that Died.

I AM all alone in my chamber now,
  And the midnight hour is near;
And the faggot's crack and the clock's dull tick
  Are the only sounds I hear;
And over my soul in its solitude
  Sweet feelings of sadness glide,
For my heart and my eyes are full when I think
  Of the little boy that died.

I went one night to my father's house,
  Went home to the dear ones all,
And softly I opened the garden gate,
  And softly the door of the hall.
My mother came out to meet her son—
  She kissed me and then she sighed,
And her head fell on my neck, and she wept
  For the little boy that died.

I shall miss him when the flowers come,
  In the garden where he played;
I shall miss him more by the fireside,
  When the flowers have all decayed.

I shall see his toys and his empty chair,
    And the horse he used to ride;
And they will speak with a silent speech,
    Of the little boy that died.

We shall go home to our Father's house—
    To our Father's house in the skies,
Where the hope of our souls shall have no blight,
    Our love no broken ties.
We shall roam on the banks of the river of peace,
    And bathe in its blissful tide;
And one of the joys of our heaven shall be
    The little boy that died.

Infant Baptism.

Let us consider the feelings with which parents should retire from the baptismal service.

It is a solemn moment when they take the child away from the altar. They have given it to God; and they bear it away, as the mother of Moses did her own son, to bring it up for another, who, in this case, is God. They have by their vows promised that the will of God concerning their child shall be their will, so that the question of its life or death is left implicitly with him. Though their hearts will bleed if it should be taken away, yet, by the baptismal service, they have engaged to consider the child henceforth as entirely at God's disposal; and whenever they look upon it hereafter, the feeling which they are to have is expressed by these words, *Lent, not given.* If it dies, they will remember its baptism and their vows, and the peace of God, which passeth all understanding, will steal into their breaking hearts. If it lives, it is to be trained up for that God to whom it has been given.

326

Prayer at a Child's Baptism.

Eternal God, in whom we live,
From whom all blessings we receive;
Ourselves and ours we owe to thee,
And thine we would for ever be.

To thee our child this day we bring,
Our willing, grateful offering;
Accept him, Lord, as henceforth thine,
To thee we all our right resign.

Lord, in the covenant of thy grace,
Grant this dear child an humble place;
And with the outward seal now given,
Prepare him for a home in heaven.

The Grave.

THERE is no monument to mark the spot;
  Two feet of grass are all that o'er it wave;
The stranger passes, but he heeds it not;
    It is an infant's grave.

But there are two who know the spot full well,
  And visit it, full oft, at evening tide;
For when the child entombed within it fell,
    Fell all their earthly pride.

The mother as she decks it round with flowers,
  Waters with tears the little new-grown sod;
The father bends his knee, and sadly pours
    His vexed soul to God.

Grieve not, ye sad ones! does the spirit sleep?
  'Tis with the Lord, who took but what he gave,
Angelic spirits nightly vigils keep
    Over your infant's grave.

The Star in the East.

FENELON.

In one of those quiet, secluded valleys of the Alps near the lake's wild margin, embosomed by snow-crowned mountains, lies the little village of Geneva. In its midst stood the moss-covered cottage of Bolien. The departing radiance of a summer's sun played among the leaves of the flowers, and the mountains and tall trees were inverted in the pure waters, now stilled beneath the deep blue sky of heaven. The windows of Bolien's cottage were thrown open, the curtains drawn aside, and there watched the wife of the faithful pastor over her dying child. Now she parted the damp curls from his brow, and then pressed her lips on his little cold fingers, which she held in her hand. Fervently the silent prayer ascended, that the night of sorrow might pass, and the storm of agony be stilled in her bosom; then, as the babe turned restlessly in her lap, in a low tone she sung,

> Sleep, baby, sleep,
> Once more upon my breast,
> Thine aching head shall rest,
> In quiet sleep.
> Sleep, baby, sleep,
> Sweetly thine eye is closing,
> Calmly thou'rt now reposing,

In slumber deep.

Sleep, angel baby, sleep:

Not in thy cradle bed

Shall rest thy little head,

But with the quiet dead,

In dreamless sleep.

As the mother looked on her boy, she saw that his little limbs were stiff with the icy chill of death. A smile was on the cherub face, and the long lashes were closed over the blue eyes. Sweet Babe! no wonder that thy mother's heart is broken when she looks on her only child,—dead! The kind-hearted villagers made a little grave among the trees,—and on the third day, when the morning sun shone upon the Alpine mountains, they took from the mother's bosom her little one, and laid it in the ground; and then they looked along the narrow and wild defile of the mountain for their Pastor, who had been some days absent.

At evening the wife of Bolien sat alone in her cottage. She looked upon the lake. A beautiful light was on its waters. She raised her head. It was the star in the east; and it came and stood over the place where the young child was. Upon her darkened soul it rose as the star of hope—the dawning of that light, which had been for a while withdrawn. "I shall rejoice in Him who was born King of the Jews,—for he hath gathered the sheep in his arms,—and he carries the lambs in his bosom," she exclaimed,—and her feelings were calmed,—her broken spirit found repose.

That night the villagers welcomed their beloved Pastor. No one dared tell him his only son rested beneath the sods of the valley. As he passed from among them, into his own cottage, from which the little light was faintly gleaming, they uttered the heartfelt benediction, "Peace be within this dwelling." The embrace of the Pastor and his wife was close and affectionate, and then the eye of the father glanced on the cradle which stood in its accustomed place "The baby sleeps," he said. "Blessed be God who has preserved you both!" The mother turned to wipe the tears from her eyes, as she replied, "Yes, the baby sleeps,—you cannot wake him." The fearful truth did not enter the mind of Bolien, and he seated himself to partake of some simple refreshment which was set before him. "Your countenance is sad," he exclaimed, as he looked upon the face of his wife. "Methinks your heart should be full of joy. What shall we render to the Lord for all his goodness?" The struggle in the countenance of the afflicted mother was too agonizing to escape the notice of Bolien, and, as he took her hand in his, he exclaimed, "Tell me, I beseech you, what has happened. Christianity I know is not secure, even among the Alpine valleys. It may be, that we are yet to cross the mountains of ice and snow, and seek shelter from those who persecute us for righteousness' sake. Tell me, what has befallen us, that you weep thus?" The eye of the heart-stricken mother glanced towards the cradle of her babe, and there needed no comment. The Pastor fell on his knees, and uttered, "*Our child is dead!*"—then buried his face in his hands, and wept aloud.

An hour passed,—and the Pastor and his wife mingled their tears at the grave of their child. Sweetly did the star in the east shine on that little mound. As Bolien uncovered his head, and gazed upward, he exclaimed, "The Star of Bethlehem shall be our guide to that land which needeth no star to shine upon it; for the glory of God shall lighten it; and the Lamb is the light thereof!"

We must enter into the designs of God, and try to receive the comforts that he bestows. We shall soon find him whom we seem to have lost; we approach him with rapid strides. Yet a little time and we shall shed no more tears. We shall die ourselves. Him whom we love lives, and will never die. This is what we believe; if we believe it rightly, we shall feel in respect to our friends as Jesus Christ wished that his disciples should feel with regard to him when he rose to heaven. "If you loved me," said he, "you would rejoice" in my glory. But we weep for ourselves. For a true friend of God, who has been faithful and humble, we can only rejoice at his happiness, and at the blessing that he has left upon those who belonged to him on earth. Let your grief then be soothed by the hand of him who has afflicted you.

A Mother's Lament.

JAMES MONTGOMERY.

I LOVED thee, daughter of my heart;
  My child, I loved thee dearly;
And though we only met to part,
  —How sweetly! how severely!—
Nor life nor death can sever
My soul from thine for ever.

Thy days, my little one, were few;
  An angel's morning visit,
That came and vanished with the dew;
  'Twas here, 'tis gone, where is it?
Yet did'st thou leave behind thee
A clue for love to find thee.

The eye, the lip, the cheek, the brow,
  The hands stretched forth in gladness,
All life, joy, rapture, beauty now;
  Then dashed with infant sadness;
Till, brightening by transition,
Returned the fairy vision:—

Where are they now?—those smiles, those tears,
  Thy mother's darling treasure?
She sees them still, and still she hears
  Thy tones of pain or pleasure,
To her quick pulse revealing
Unutterable feeling.

Hushed in a moment on her breast,
  Life, at the well-spring drinking;
Then cradled on her lap to rest
  In rosy slumber sinking,
Thy dreams—no thought can guess them;
And mine—no tongue express them.

For then this waking eye could see,
  In many a vain vagary,
The things that never were to be,
  Imaginations airy;
Fond hopes that mothers cherish,
Like still-born babes to perish.

Mine perished on thy early bier;
  No,—changed to forms more glorious,
They flourish in a higher sphere,
  O'er time and death victorious;
Yet would these arms have chained thee,
And long from heaven detained thee.

Sarah! my last, my youngest love,
  The crown of every other!

Though thou art born in heaven above,
   I am thine only mother,
Nor will affection let me
Believe thou canst forget me.

Then,—thou in heaven and I on earth,—
   May this one hope delight us,
That thou wilt hail my second birth,
   When death shall reunite us,
Where worlds no more can sever
Parent and child for ever.

Death of an Infant.

WITH what unknown delight the mother smiled,
  When this frail treasure in her arms she pressed!
Her prayer was heard—she clasped a living child:
  But how the gift transcends the poor request!
A child was all she asked, with many a vow!
Mother—behold the child an angel now!

Now in her father's house she finds a place,
  Or, if to earth she takes a transient flight,
'Tis to fulfil the purpose of his grace:
  To guide thy footsteps to the world of light;—
A ministering spirit sent to thee,
That where she is, there thou may'st also be.

336

Weep On.

WILLIAM COWPER.

WE are forbidden to murmur, but we are not forbidden to *regret;* and whom we loved tenderly while living, we may still pursue with an affectionate remembrance, without having any occasion to charge ourselves with rebellion against the sovereignty that appointed a separation.

Little Mary.

FROM the group of little faces
One is gone.
In the old familiar places,
Sad and lone,
Father, mother, meek-eyed brother,
Sit and moan.

Sit and moan for one departed,
Pure and mild,

Little Mary, gentle-hearted,
    Sainted child—
And as nestling memories thicken,
    Griefs grow wild.

Home, once bright, how cold and dreary!
    Shadows deep
Fall on forms and hearts aweary,
    Eyes that weep—
Thought is in the church-yard seeking
    One asleep.

Still the merry laugh deceiving
    Fills the ear,
Tiny arms yet fondly cleaving
    Dry the tear;
Foot-falls, silvery foot-falls patter
    Far and near.

Ears instinctive, pause to hearken,
    All in vain—
Days drag on and skies shall darken
    O'er with pain,
But the heart will find its lost one
    Ne'er again!

From the treasured fire-side faces
    Here to-day,
From the tender warm embraces,
    Dropped away,

Sleeps she 'mid forgotten sleepers
    In the clay.

Ah! what weary numbers sighing
    To be free,
Little Mary, would be lying
    Low with thee!
Where no care nor eating sorrow
    E'er shall be.

Weep not when ye tell the story
    Of the dead—
'Tis a sunbeam joined the glory
    Overhead!
"For of such sweet babes is heaven,"
    Jesus said.

Appeal to Irreligious Parents.

IRRELIGIOUS, but bereaved parents,—after all, what avails the safety of the departed to you? While hope for your own souls holds aloof so far—while the appeals of mercy are repeated in vain—while conscience tells so fully, and so truly, that the offer of salvation has ever been tendered in vain—what boots the rest? What is it to you that the hope of a glorious resurrection enters the dark and dank habitation of the little one? You meet again : but if there be a single feeling of horror above all others to our present conception, it is that of the ending of a natural and social law, at the judgment seat of God. It is that of a law of affection availing nothing. Your little one became the property of Jesus—not by virtue of any prayer of faith that *you* had uttered—not by a free-will offering that you had made— but by that blood of atonement you have thrust so often from you—by that distinguishing grace whose attractions were too faint for your eye.

Yet you have watched by the bed of the departing spirit of infancy ; and you have caught the last sigh, as the soul winged its passage from earth. And even the loneliness of that sad moment seemed broken by an admonition—" FATHER !"— " MOTHER !"—" COME AWAY !" You heard--you thought—

eternity neared—earth interposed—and you returned to its bosom again.

Impenitent, but bereaved parent!—When a future world, in some hour of reflection, flings its shadow over your path ; and, despite of all your efforts, presses its realities upon your attention, *remember*—that no bond of parental love may abide hereafter, when the frown of an offended God settles the destiny of the lost, and the only relationship that exists, is that of the family of Christ.

If the tender mercies of the Saviour were too little engaging to win your admiration—if the worth of your own soul has not entered into your thoughts of the future—behold what an argument is furnished by an afflictive dispensation ! You loved the departed. To that very affection a most solemn providence of God has appealed. It bids you gaze from earth to heaven. It reminds you of the abode of glorified spirits. It admonishes you to inquire, " am I also ready?" It intimates most earnestly and clearly, that the only true consolation which ever succeeds the stroke of sorrow, must be connected with a reconciliation to God, and an humble hope in the Redeemer's blood. Let these be yours, and your peace will be independent of the precarious tenure of human life. Faith shall scatter the darkness, and explain the mystery, so readily attendant on affliction. You shall look up from the tomb to the late object of your solicitude and care. You shall exclaim with a confidence sure and steadfast,— " though he shall not return to me "—" I SHALL GO TO HIM !"

Grief for the Dead.

O HEARTS that never cease to yearn,
  O brimming tears that ne'er are dried!
The dead, though they depart, return
  As if they had not died!

The living are the only dead;
  The dead live—never more to die;
And often when we mourn them fled
  They never were so nigh.

And though they lie beneath the waves,
  Or sleep within the church-yard dim—
(Ah! through how many different graves
  God's children go to him!)

Yet every grave gives up its dead
  Ere it is overgrown with grass!
Then why should hopeless tears be. shed,
  Or need we cry, alas!

Or why should memory veiled with gloom,
  And like a sorrowing mourner craped,
Sit weeping o'er an empty tomb
  Whose captives have escaped?

'Tis but a mound—and will be mossed
  Whene'er the summer grass appears;—
The loved, though wept, are never lost;
  We only lose our tears.

Nay, Hope may whisper with the dead,
  By bending forward where they are;
But Memory, with a backward tread,
  Communes with them afar!

The joys we lose are but forecast,
  And we shall find them all once more;—
We look behind us for the past,
  But lo! 'tis all before!

Little Lucy and her Song.

A. D. F. RANDOLPH.

I.

A LITTLE child, six summers old,
  So thoughtful and so fair,
There seemed about her pleasant ways
  A more than childish air,
Was sitting on a summer eve
  Beneath a spreading tree,
Intent upon an ancient book,
  Which lay upon her knee.

She turned each page with careful hand,
  And strained her sight to see,
Until the drowsy shadows slept
  Upon the grassy lea;
Then closed the book, and upwards looked,
  And straight began to sing
A simple verse of hopeful love—
  This very childish thing:
" While here below, how sweet to know
  His wondrous love and story,

And then, through grace, to see His face,
 And live with him in glory!"

II.

That little child, one dreary night
 Of winter wind and storm,
Was tossing on a weary couch
 Her weak and wasted form,
And in her pain, and in its pause,
 But clasped her hands in prayer—
(Strange that we had no thoughts of heaven
 While hers were only there)—

Until she said: "O mother dear,
 How sad you seem to be!
Have you forgotten that He said,
 'Let children come to me?'
Dear mother, bring the blessed Book,
 Come, mother, let us sing,"
And then again, with faltering tongue,
 She sang that childish thing:
"While here below, how sweet to know
 His wondrous love and story,
And then, through grace, to see His face,
 And live with him in glory!"

III.

Underneath a spreading tree
 A narrow mound is seen,

Which first was covered by the snow,
    Then blossomed into green;
Here first I heard that childish voice
    That sings on earth no more;
In heaven it hath a richer tone,
    And sweeter than before:
For those who know his love below—
    So runs the wondrous story—
In heaven, through grace, shall see His face,
    And dwell with him in glory!

The Child's Wish.

I THINK when I read that sweet story of old,
  When Jesus was here among men,
How he called little children as lambs to his fold,
  I should like to have been with them then.

I wish that his hands had been placed on my head,
  That his arm had been thrown around me,
And that I might have seen his kind look when he said,
  "Let the little ones come unto me."

Yet still to his footstool in prayer I may go,
  And ask for a share in his love;
And if I thus earnestly seek him below,
  I shall see him and hear him above.

In that beautiful place he is gone to prepare,
  For all who are washed and forgiven;
And many dear children are gathering there,
  "For of such is the kingdom of heaven."

I long for the joys of that glorious time,
  The sweetest, and brightest, and best,
When the dear little children of every clime,
  Shall crowd to his arms and be blest.

The Boy and his Angel.

CAROLINE M. SAWYER.

"O MOTHER, I've been with an angel to-day!
I was out alone in the forest at play,
Chasing after the butterflies, watching the bees,
And hearing the woodpecker tapping the trees;
So I played, and I played, till, so weary I grew,
I sat down to rest in the shade of a yew;
While the birds sang so sweetly high up in its top,
I held my breath, mother, for fear they would stop!
Thus a long while I sat, gazing up to the sky,
And watching the clouds that went hurrying by,
When I heard a voice calling just over my head,
That sounded as if 'Come, O brother!' it said,
And there, right up over the top of the tree,
O mother, an angel was beckoning to me!

"And, 'Brother! once more, come, O brother!' he cried,
And flew on light pinions close down by my side!
And, mother, oh, never was being so bright,
As the one which then beamed on my wondering sight!
His face was as fair as the delicate shell;
His hair down his shoulders in long ringlets fell;

While his eyes resting on me, so melting with love,
Were as soft and as mild as the eyes of a dove!
And somehow, dear mother, I felt not afraid,
As his hand on my brow he caressingly laid,
And murmured so softly and gently to me,
'Come, brother, the angels are waiting for thee!'

"And then on my forehead he tenderly pressed
Such kisses—O mother, they thrilled through my breast
As swiftly as lightning leaps down from on high
When the chariot of God rolls along the black sky!
While his breath, floating round me, was soft as the breeze
That played in my tresses, and rustled the trees:
At last on my head a deep blessing he poured,
Then plumed his bright pinions, and upward he soared:
And up, up he went, through the blue sky so far,
He seemed to float there like a glittering star;
Yet still my eyes followed his radiant flight,
Till, lost in the azure, he passed from my sight!
Then, oh, how I feared, as I caught the last gleam
Of his vanishing form, it was only a dream!
When soft voices murmured once more from the tree,
'Come, brother, the angels are waiting for thee!'"

Oh! pale grew that mother, and heavy her heart,
For she knew her fair boy from this world must depart;
That his bright locks must fade in the dust of the tomb
Ere the Autumn winds withered the Summer's rich bloom!

Oh, how his young footsteps she watched, day by day,
As his delicate form wasted slowly away,
Till the soft light of heaven seemed shed o'er his face,
And he crept up to die in her loving embrace!
"Oh, clasp me, dear mother, close, close to your breast,
On that gentle pillow again let me rest!
Let me once more gaze up to that dear loving eye,
And then, oh, methinks, I can willingly die!
Now kiss me, dear mother! oh quickly! for see!
The bright blessed angels are waiting for me."

Oh, wild was the anguish that swept through her breast
As the long, frantic kiss on pale lips she pressed,
And felt the vain search of his soft pleading eye,
As it strove to meet hers, ere the fair boy could die!
"I see you not, mother, for darkness and night
Are hiding your dear loving face from my sight—
But I hear your low sobbings—dear mother, good-bye!
The angels are ready to bear me on high!
I will wait for you there—but, oh, tarry not long,
Lest grief at your absence should sadden my song!"
He ceased, and his hands meekly clasped on his breast,
While his sweet face sank down on its pillow of rest;
Then, closing his eyes, now all rayless and dim,
Went up with the angels that waited for him.

It is Well with the Child.

It is well!—nor would we our babe recall,
And soothing and sweet are the tears that fall;—
But a few brief pangs on his mother's breast,
And we laid him down in his holy rest;
Ere the world its snares around him threw,—
Or its sins and its cares he ever knew.

It is well! since the Saviour's word is given,
That of such as our child is the host of heaven!
No struggle for him,—no doubts or fears,
His young cheek spared repentant tears.
It is well! and we "bear" and adore "the rod,"
For the wielding hand was the hand of God.

The Sting of Death.

MOURN not o'er early graves—for those
   Removed whilst only buds are shown,
For God, who sowed and watered, knows
   The time to gather in his own.

Weep Not.

NOT for the babe that sleepeth here
   My tears bestow, my sorrows give,—
Pass on, and weep with grief sincere
   For those who innocence outlive.